He'd met Scott's wife only once...

It was back when he was at Nellis years ago. But a man didn't forget a woman like that.

Her hair had been longer then. With her pictures plastered on the wall of their barracks, every guy in their first squadron was envious of Scott—or Spade, as they called him.

Nate closed his eyes.

Spade...whose career had escalated too fast, who'd died in the prime of life....

The pregnant woman in the elevator couldn't possibly have been his widow—could she? When he'd crashed and died six months ago, Nate knew his friend's only regret was that he and his wife had never been able to have children.

Was this woman, this pregnant woman, really his friend's wife? If so, that could mean only one thing: she'd betrayed her husband.

Dear Reader,

Family relationships can bring us the greatest happiness and the greatest sorrow. One thing is certain. They're always complicated, complex and intriguing.

In this novel, *Another Man's Wife*, and the sequel, *Home to Copper Mountain* (coming from Superromance in May 2003), I've focused on the lives of two extraordinary brothers, Nate and Rick Hawkins, whose worlds are forever changed when tragedy strikes their remarkably close family.

As both men strive to put the pain behind them and make sense of their lives, we see them run the gamut of loss, anger, bitterness, guilt, confusion, self-doubt, struggle and growth—especially when they encounter the strong women whose love is able to heal their tortured souls.

I hope you enjoy their stories! And please check out my Web site, www.rebeccawinters-author.com.

Rebecca Winters

Books by Rebecca Winters

HARLEQUIN SUPERROMANCE

Don't miss any of our special offers. Write to us at the following address for information on our newest releases.

Harlequin Reader Service
U.S.: 3010 Walden Ave., P.O. Box 1325, Buffalo, NY 14269
Canadian: P.O. Box 609, Fort Erie, Ont. L2A 5X3

Another Man's Wife

Rebecca Winters

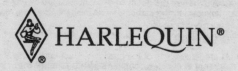

HARLEQUIN®

TORONTO • NEW YORK • LONDON
AMSTERDAM • PARIS • SYDNEY • HAMBURG
STOCKHOLM • ATHENS • TOKYO • MILAN • MADRID
PRAGUE • WARSAW • BUDAPEST • AUCKLAND

ISBN 0-373-71112-3

ANOTHER MAN'S WIFE

Copyright © 2003 by Rebecca Winters.

Visit us at www.eHarlequin.com

Printed in U.S.A.

Another Man's Wife

CHAPTER ONE

Major Nate Hawkins got ready to climb out of the military transport at Peterson Air Force Base in Colorado, aware that the moment his foot touched the tarmac, he'd be a civilian again.

Though he'd planned to stay in the Air Force until retirement, his mother's unexpected death during an avalanche six months ago had brought huge changes to the Hawkins family. It seemed life had other plans for him.

He reminded himself that he could've been like Spade, who'd bought it during that damn air demonstration in Italy at the same time Nate had been burying his mother.

Nate knew he should be grateful to be alive....

The transport door opened. He filed out behind a couple of crewmen. After leaving the milder temperatures back in Holland, the frigid March air came as a shock. You'd never know spring was officially here.

He grimaced to think that his mother wouldn't be home when he got there, and a sense of grief, of bleakness, settled over him. If this was how his father felt now that she was gone, then Nate understood why his parents' ski business was in danger of going under.

"Hey, Nate! This way!"

His brother's voice broke through the heavy shroud of oppression that had enveloped him during the long flight.

"Rick!" Thank God for that constant in his life.

A warm feeling displaced the sadness, and he rushed past people to reach his brother. Only a year apart in age, both men were six feet two, an inch taller than their father. They'd inherited his powerful athletic build, but it was Rick with the gray eyes who looked most like their dad.

Nate, on the other hand, had dark-blond hair and resembled their deceased mother, a statuesque, blue-eyed blonde from Are, Sweden. According to her, when the boys were toddlers people had often mistaken them for twins because Rick's hair hadn't turned brown yet.

They gave each other a fierce hug. "It's good to see you, man."

"You don't know the half of it," Rick muttered.

Nate took a second look at his younger brother. Since tragedy had struck their family, the happy-go-lucky attitude—which had earned him the name "lucky" on the ski slopes and the racetrack—was still missing.

That didn't surprise Nate, but the set of Rick's features did.

"I take it you've already seen Dad." Their plan had been to walk into the house together and surprise him.

"You could say that," came Rick's cryptic comment.

"Have you told him what we've done?"

"Not yet."

Something else was wrong, something besides the fact that being home again was a painful reminder of their mother's death.

"Is Dad waiting in the car?"

"No."

"You're not going to tell me anything else?"

Rick's lips formed an unpleasant twist. "You don't want to know yet. Come on. Let's get out of here, so we can be private."

On that mysterious note, Nate followed his brother through freshly fallen snow to the four-wheel-drive Blazer bearing the Eagles' Nest Ski and Bike Shop logo on the side. He tossed his duffel in the back seat and walked around to the front passenger door.

Nate had to admit he was relieved that Rick had come alone. Nate wasn't ready to be united with his father yet. The deep lines of grief carved in the older man's sunbronzed face before they'd closed the casket still kept him awake nights.

For the two hours it would take to reach Copper Mountain, he and Rick could discuss how they were going to proceed from here.

Their mother had been their father's soul mate, his joie de vivre. Since the funeral, the fear that he might never recover had haunted both brothers.

It hadn't helped that after her burial, the demands of Nate's career had forced him to leave his desolate father. Having just returned from another long deployment with NATO forces, he'd been told to report to Edwards Air Force Base in California to get checked out in the MATV jet.

A couple of the guys had flown there in their Vipers to act as bandits. For several weeks, they did tactical fighting before he was sent to Holland. When he was on the ground there, he'd concentrated on his studies of Dutch for the exchange pilot program. Throughout that period there'd been little time to devote to his father's mental state.

Rick had left the day after Nate for Phoenix, Arizona, the U.S. headquarters for Mayada auto manufacturing, based in Kyoto, Japan. On the professional Formula I racing circuit for the Japanese, he'd accumulated an impressive number of wins around the world.

The heavy demands on his time meant he'd found it as difficult as Nate to keep in close touch with their dad.

Through sporadic, unsatisfactory phone calls to him and to each other, it became clear to both of them that their father wasn't doing well. Without the woman who'd been his life's partner in every conceivable way, he'd changed dramatically from the man he'd once been. Even the business they'd run together had started to fail.

Before her death, their father had always displayed an indomitable will, or so Nate had thought. There were Olympic medals and world championship medals for alpine skiing events hanging on the wall in the den. They provided evidence of their parents' remarkable talents and shared zest for life.

To Nate's chagrin, her untimely passing had sent their father into a sharp decline. The fear that he might remain in a permanent state of mourning had alarmed Nate enough to cut short his flying career and come home.

On his own, Rick had made the same decision. No one could bring their mother back, but they could try to bring a little happiness to their father's life. Not only that, Rick had chosen to give up his racing career in order to help salvage their parents' business, with its inevitable highs and lows.

Nate rubbed his face. He badly needed a shave. Rick looked like he could use one, too.

"Okay." He nudged his brother's shoulder. "Let's have it." They'd left Colorado Springs and were headed for Copper Mountain on Highway 9. The road was one continuous ribbon of black ice, but Nate never worried when Rick was at the wheel. "I'm assuming Natalie didn't take the news well. How soon will she be joining you?"

"I'm afraid I didn't invite her along."

He turned in his brother's direction. "Why not? I thought you two were destined for something serious."

"So did I at first. There's a strong attraction between us, but—"

"But it never did feel right," Nate finished the thought.

"No. What about you and Kari?"

"She'd never be happy in the U.S. It just wouldn't have worked for us."

"It's the 'feel right' part neither of us has found yet," Rick muttered.

Nate glanced at him, nodding. "We're quite a pair, you know that?"

He expected some sort of response from his brother, but nothing was forthcoming. "Rick? You've kept me in suspense long enough."

His brother's solemn gaze swerved to him. "It's Dad. When was the last time you talked to him?"

"Two weeks ago, before our wing was deployed on a mission. We didn't return until yesterday."

"What was he like on the phone?"

"Preoccupied more than anything."

"At least you talked to him. After my race last Wednesday, I called him from England. There was no answer so I called the ski shop. Jim said he'd gone to Denver and wouldn't be back for the rest of the week."

"What's in Denver?"

"I asked him the same question. He claimed to have no idea. I sensed he was being evasive about something."

Jim Springmeyer had worked for their parents ten years. "That means he was covering for him. Not a good sign," Nate said. "In Dad's frame of mind—"

Rick broke in. "Since I couldn't reach you, I decided to fly home from London early. I thought I'd give him a surprise."

Nate's patience had run out. *"And?"*

A strange sound escaped Rick. "I'm afraid I'm the one who got the surprise. You could say I received the shock of my life." His voice was unsteady.

"You're not about to tell me he's turned to drinking—" The facetious comment wasn't meant to be taken seriously. It disturbed him that he couldn't get his brother to lighten up a little more.

Rick shook his head. "Sorry. You're not even close."

Nate's chest tightened. "Just spit it out!"

"When I walked through the house, I found *our father* in the kitchen. He wasn't alone...."

Nate noticed his brother's strong grip on the steering wheel. His knuckles had gone white from the pressure.

"Rick—"

"He had this woman in a clinch by the sink."

A clinch? *What?*

Nate blinked.

"They were so far gone, they never saw or heard me. I don't know how I did it, but I managed to tiptoe back to the living room before calling out to Dad that I was home."

The picture those words conjured up plunged Nate into a different realm of pain than he'd ever experienced before. The kind only a parent can inflict on his child.

"This soon after Mother?" he whispered.

"It gets worse. After dad brought her into the living room and introduced us, he announced that they're engaged to be married. They'd gone to Denver to pick out her ring."

Nate felt like he'd gone into an inverted dive and had waited too late to pull out of it.

"Dad said he was glad I'd decided to come home for a surprise visit because that saved him having to phone me with the news."

"If this woman is someone Mom and Dad knew before the accident, I don't wa—"

"Noooo. She's a Texan who came to Colorado a month ago because of a friend's wedding reception. Apparently she's never been on a pair of skis. While she was shopping for sunglasses in the ski shop, Dad challenged her to get out on the slopes and try it. He gave her a few lessons, and things went from there.''

At fifty-three, their father was still an attractive man—and he could still outski the best skiers in the area. As early as sixteen he'd been on the U.S. ski team. By the time he'd met their mother five years later, he'd garnered many wins. They were married soon after, and within a year she was pregnant with Nate. People commented on their devotion to each other.

She'd been gone such a short while, it simply hadn't occurred to Nate that his father would be interested in another woman. Not this soon anyway. The idea of his marrying again...

"Are you still with me?"

"Yes," Nate murmured, utterly staggered by the news. "Is she divorced, widowed, what?"

"Ms. Pamela Jarrett has never been married. She lives and works on a ranch outside Austin, Texas."

"What I'm hearing doesn't make any sense."

"It does to Dad. Hell, Nate—she's only eleven years older than I am."

With a little calculating, Nate realized she was fourteen years younger than their mother had been when she'd died.

"Dad looked so different from the man we saw at the funeral, it's like another person's inhabited his body. It made me feel...weird. You know?"

Nate understood exactly what his brother was trying to say. They'd been so busy establishing their own careers, neither of them had settled down to marriage for the first time. Yet their father was already jumping into a second marriage with a younger woman he'd barely met.

"Does Ms. Jarrett know Dad doesn't have any money except what's tied up in the business?" Nate's flare of anger couldn't be held back. He was stunned to think his father could replace his mother with another woman this quickly.

"I asked him that in private. He told me not to worry about it. She lives on her own piece of the Jarrett ranch."

His head jerked toward his brother. "What the *hell* could he be thinking?"

"It's gone beyond thinking. Our father has the hots for her." Rick sounded as embittered as Nate felt.

The hots. It was a term younger guys used all the time. But when it was applied to their own father, a man Nate had loved and revered all his life, it sounded crude, distasteful.

"If it'd been anywhere but our home…"

Rick seemed to be reading his mind. "That's what we get for planning to surprise him," Nate told him.

"Sorry, man, but I never thought the day would come when I wouldn't feel free to walk into the house where we were born and raised."

"You forget we grew up and went away. Isn't there an old saying that you can never go home again?" Nate was still trying to process these painful new facts. "What's she like?"

"As different from Mom as you can get."

His eyes closed tightly. *What had happened to love everlasting?* "Go on. I'd rather hear it all now and get it over with."

"Pamela's a petite brunette. She's got that Texan drawl." He shrugged. "She's nice enough I suppose."

Anja Soderhelm Hawkins had been a tall, beautiful, athletic blonde. Sometimes when their dad had teased him or Rick because they hadn't found the right women to marry yet, he'd comment that their mother was probably a difficult act to follow. They'd have to look long and hard to find anyone as perfect.

Interesting how it had only taken him six months to find perfection again.

Texans flocked to Colorado in the winter. When Nate and Rick were growing up, they'd always found a Texan accent amusing, especially on the women who seemed to stuff more words into one minute than any other female they'd encountered. Since neither of their parents were verbose people, Nate couldn't imagine his dad with a fast-talking Texan.

"Dad's thinking of moving to the ranch with her, and leaving the house and business to us."

Nate hadn't seen that blow coming. His eyes smarted with tears, and he realized that home as he'd known it no longer existed. It made the moment surreal.

He darted Rick a searching glance. "How are you handling it?"

"I'm not."

"Well, that makes two of us."

"Dad's got to be out of his mind!"

"Have they set a date?" Though it nearly killed him, Nate had to ask.

"While they were in Denver, they talked about getting married in Las Vegas. That is, as soon as you and I give the okay. When I told him you were arriving tonight, Dad looked kind of relieved.''

Nate could think of nothing to say.

''Dad said he would've told us about Pamela sooner,'' Rick went on, ''but he's been putting it off, since he knew our feelings must be pretty raw because of Mom.''

''He's right about that. Good grief—she has to have some kind of hold over him. We left him alone too long after Mom died. I wouldn't be surprised if he's had a nervous breakdown and this woman's taking advantage of his vulnerability.''

After a few moments' silence, Rick eventually spoke. ''As I see it, there's only one reason Dad would want to act this fast.''

Nate's thought had been the same. ''No matter what, we're not going to let him run off to Nevada because he's afraid she might already be pregnant,'' he said. ''None of our family's friends or acquaintances would understand. Dad will have to arrange to be married here.''

''Just not at our house,'' Rick whispered. This time there were tears in his voice.

''No,'' Nate concurred. Not at the home where their close-knit family had once known happiness. ''There's always Vale or Breckenridge.''

Rick cleared his throat. ''You know something? Seeing them in the kitchen where he and Mo—''

''Don't say it.'' Nate couldn't imagine what that must've been like for Rick.

His brother pounded his fist against the steering wheel. ''I saw Dad's car out in front. I had no idea what I was walking in on when I let myself into the house.''

''Neither of us could have foreseen this.''

''I don't know about you, but suddenly I feel… old.''

''I know what you mean.''

''LAUREL? Phone's for you.''

Laurel Pierce was lying on the couch in the den with her legs propped up. She put down the baby magazine she'd been reading. ''I hope it's Mom.'' She mouthed the words as her sister walked into the room and passed her the cordless.

Julie shook her head. ''Scott's mom,'' she mouthed back.

Laurel groaned.

''You can't keep ignoring her. Just talk to her for a minute and get it over with,'' her sister whispered.

Julie was right, of course. For the last half year, Laurel had asked her sister to screen her calls and make excuses when she couldn't face talking to certain people on the phone. It had become a habit and it wasn't fair to Julie.

She put the phone to her ear. ''Hi, Reba.''

''Laurel, dear. Finally! I've made several attempts to call you, but it seems like you're never there. We haven't heard from you in over a week!''

''I know. I'm sorry. It's been busy around here with the kids coming and going to music classes and ski lessons. Didn't Mom tell you everything was fine at my last appointment with the obstetrician?''

''Yes, but it's not the same as hearing the details from you,'' Reba said in a hurt voice. ''Have you changed your mind about not wanting to know if you're having a boy or girl?''

''No. I'd rather be surprised.''

''That's too bad. It limits the choice of colors for baby gifts. We're planning a big shower for you, but we can't mail the invitations without a date. How soon are you leaving Denver to come home?''

Guilt weighed Laurel down. How many times had she heard that question over the last few months? She flashed her sister a look of distress.

Philadelphia was the city where she'd been born and raised, where she'd gone to high school and met Scott. But being married to an Air Force man for ten years had taken her to so many places around the globe, no *one* spot felt like home anymore—Philadelphia least of all, now that Scott was dead.

More than eleven months had passed since the last time she'd curled up in his arms. Little had she known that after he'd left the next morning for a long deployment with NATO forces, those arms would never hold her again....

Thank heaven she'd been able to get through to him before the air show and tell him the implant had worked. They were expecting.

The joy in his voice was her final remembrance of him before word came that he'd crashed. If she could be thankful for one thing, it was that he went to his death knowing she was pregnant with his baby.

She hadn't wanted to adopt until they'd tried every other option, including fertility drugs. In vitro fertilization had been their last resort. The doctors had made several attempts to fertilize her eggs using his frozen sperm; finally an embryo had been implanted and the procedure was successful.

It helped her more than anyone could know that their final communication over the phone had brought them closer than they'd been in a long time. They'd expressed their love and had talked about a future that included this unborn child. The three of them would be a family, and Scott would become a father, as he'd always wanted.

She had military friends who'd lost husbands or wives during difficult periods in their marriages. Some still grieved because their last words to each other had been said in anger.

When all was said and done, Laurel felt very blessed. Although the demands of Scott's career had taken him away a lot, the times they'd spent together she would cherish forever. It was true that if she'd had a child, the periods when he was gone wouldn't have felt so long and lonely. But all of that was in the past now.

"Laurel?"

"Yes?"

"Why didn't you answer my question? You only have four weeks left. Scotty arrived ten days early."

I know. I know it all.

"That doesn't leave much room for a party, dear."

The time had come to drop her bombshell. Her gaze clung to Julie's for moral support.

"You're right, Reba, but my doctor says it's too late to fly anywhere now."

Her sister broke into a smile and gave her a thumbs-up. Before her mother-in-law could react, Laurel decided to get it all said. It was long past time.

"Realistically speaking, I won't be able to travel anywhere until after my delivery. Why don't we plan on a shower once I've had my six week checkup in May? I'll fly out with the baby and take turns staying with you and Mom."

"But that's months away! I don't understand you, Laurel. You've changed since the funeral. Have you stopped loving us?"

She closed her eyes tightly. "Of course not, Reba. I'll always love you and Wendell. You're my baby's grandparents."

"But you don't want to be around us." Underlying her mother-in-law's accusation, Laurel felt her pain.

She put her feet to the floor and sat up. "It isn't that. But I've had to face the fact that Scott's never coming back."

Those words needed to be said. She'd heard other pilots' widows say them after the healing process had begun. Now she was able to say them herself.

"I've found that being away from reminders of him has made this period easier to bear. Being with Julie and her family in new surroundings—knowing my baby is almost here—everything's helped me get over the worst of my grief."

It was true. Six months ago she hadn't thought it possible.

Julie's eyes turned suspiciously bright.

"What about our family's pain? Did you ever consider how much *we've* needed you?"

"Yes." She swallowed hard. "The only thing that's helped me in that regard was knowing you and

Wendell still have each other and your other children and grandchildren for comfort.''

"So you're cutting us out of your life. Is that it?''

"You know that's not true! I told you I'll come for a visit in May.''

"And then what?''

That was a good question, one for which Laurel had no answer.

"I don't know yet.'' She eyed her sister once more. "In the meantime, I'm in the happiest place I could be while I wait for this baby.''

It was Julie and her husband, Brent, who'd understood Laurel's need for space—and for different surroundings—while she grieved.

Of her three married sisters, Julie, the oldest, was the one with whom Laurel had always felt a special bond. Over the years they'd kept in almost constant touch through phone calls, e-mails and the occasional visit when she and Scott were stationed in Okinawa and in Spain.

To her undying gratitude, they'd told her they were taking her back to Colorado with them where Brent worked for a nationwide telecommunications company. Their two-story colonial house in Aurora had more than enough room for her and their boys.

Coming on the heels of Scott's funeral, their offer had rescued Laurel from the Pierces, whose well-meaning attention was suffocating her. She didn't think she would have survived otherwise.

"Please try to understand, Reba. Please be happy that you're going to be grandparents again very soon. Scott would want it this way.''

"Our son would be shocked to know his wife has purposely stayed away from us."

It was no use. Laurel couldn't make her understand that it was too soon to be around his family with all the attendant memories.

"I'm sorry you feel hurt. That's not my intent."

She heard Reba gearing up for the next volley. "When you're a mother, maybe then *you'll* begin to understand. I think it might be better if we don't talk for a few days."

"I'll call you soon. I promise."

"I don't think you realize how much you've changed, Laurel. You're not the same girl our son fell in love with." There was a click.

I'm not a teenager anymore, Reba.

Laurel had married Scott as soon as she'd graduated from high school. Her plans to become an elementary school teacher had to be put on hold to accommodate his career. She'd been a very young bride, too young to recognize what life in the military really meant. Scott never gave it a thought. Being a top gun provided him with the continual thrills and excitement he craved.

He'd been the youngest of five children, all of whom were now married and living in or near Philadelphia. With hindsight, Laurel could see that his parents had never gotten over losing him to the Air Force.

It was a case of arrested development on their part, she decided. They were the proud parents of an outstanding son who'd left home too soon. They were stuck in the past.

Laurel couldn't help them with that.

It was the reason she didn't want to live around them on a permanent basis. Nothing was going to restore Scott to life. She refused to let her child become the focus of their unassuaged longing to have their son back.

Primarily because of that, she hadn't let the ultrasound technician tell her the sex of her baby.

Secretly she was praying for a girl. A sweet little girl who wouldn't be the embodiment of the son they'd doted on before Scott left home.

Scotty, their thrill-seeking, daredevil son. Scotty, who'd taken Laurel's heart on a roller-coaster ride around the world before it all came to a screeching halt decades sooner than they'd expected.

"Laurel?" her sister said. "Are you all right?"

Suddenly back in the present, she turned off the phone and stood up. "No," she said in a quiet voice. "It was awful. I hated hurting her."

"But you *had* to do it." Julie hugged her as best she could, considering Laurel's pregnancy. "I'm proud of you."

"I'm pretty proud of myself. When I first met Scott's mother, I couldn't imagine ever talking to her the way I just did. I love his parents a lot, but they have this way of taking over, you know?"

Her sister winked. "That's probably why Scott went into the Air Force."

"You mean to get away from them?" Soon after she'd married Scott, the same thought had crossed Laurel's mind, but she would never have voiced it aloud.

"Maybe. If you've noticed, the rest of their children haven't been as courageous."

"That's because they didn't inherit Scott's genes."

"Nope. He came into this world with attitude."

In spades.

That was probably why the guys in his squadron had nicknamed him Spade. When he walked into a room, he energized it. According to his parents he'd always been that way. They would never overcome their loss.

She bit her lip. "Julie—I know I've been a burden to you and Brent. Maybe—"

"Oh, no, you don't!" her sister cut in before she could walk out of the room. "Reba's made you feel guilty again. I'm not listening to any of this," she called over her shoulder.

Laurel had to hurry to catch up with her. She followed her through the door to the kitchen. Brent was just coming in the back door from doing errands. Julie ran to give her attractive, sandy-haired husband an enthusiastic kiss

"Now that you're here, will you please tell my sister she's not a burden? A few minutes ago her mother-in-law laid an enormous guilt trip on her. That was after Laurel told her she wouldn't be returning to Philadelphia until May for a visit."

"Well, what do you know? You did it!" Brent grinned. "You want me to phone and tell her you're the best baby-sitter we ever had? Julie and I get a honeymoon weekend whenever we want. And—" he made an expansive gesture "—because of you, Julie's been able to take a part-time job so we can build our dream home that much sooner. I'd say *we've* been taking advantage of *you.*''

Without hesitation Laurel crossed the room and hugged both of them. "I love you guys. You'll never know how much."

"We love you, too," he said. "In fact, I'd like to show our appreciation for all the help you've given us. Since I have to drive up to Breckenridge to pick up the kids, why don't we all go?"

"I'd love it!" Laurel blurted. After the difficult session with her mother-in-law, she needed something to wipe that depressing conversation from her mind.

Julie frowned. "I don't know. Three hours up and back in the car might be a little much for you at this stage."

"Not if we spend the night to break it up," Brent reasoned.

"That's a terrific idea! Now we don't even have to fix dinner." Julie smiled and nudged her sister.

"The boys are going to be as excited as I am," Laurel responded, smiling too. What a nice way to end their week at ski camp."

"Good. I'll call the Rustler Lodge and make reservations for a suite."

"It's Saturday, my love. With Snowfest on, I'll bet there won't be any rooms available."

"Oh, yes, there will, my love. Harry Wilke's daughter runs the desk."

"You're kidding! Isn't he your regional supervisor?"

"That's right. Getting that last account put me on

his good side. He told me she'd do us a favor anytime.''

Brent grabbed the phone directory from the drawer
and reached for the cordless Julie had brought back
to the kitchen.

"Come on, Laurel. Let's get packed. We'll have
to throw in some extra clothes for Mike and Joey.''

"*I'll* do it,'' she offered as they hurried through
the house to the stairs. Since her arrival, one of her
self-appointed jobs besides chief cook on the days
Julie went to work was to do the wash and fold
clothes. She knew exactly where to find everything
the boys would want.

It didn't take long for the three of them to get
ready.

When Laurel walked through the back door to the
garage with Julie, Brent was putting their skis on the
rack. He glanced up, then whistled.

"Hey, people are going to be jealous when they
see me with two beautiful raven-haired women.''

Laurel burst into laughter. "Thanks for making
this ten-ton-Tessie feel so good. I was just telling
your wife how terrific she looks in the red sweater
you bought her for Christmas.''

"I appreciate it,'' Julie said, "but my husband's
right. In that black sweater coat, you look wonderful.''

"Thanks, Julie.''

Laurel was still smiling as he packed their overnight bags and snow gear in the trunk. Soon he'd
reversed the car out of the garage and they were off.

Laurel hadn't left the house all day. It felt liber-
ating—exciting—to be going on a brief vacation. She

was looking forward to the drive and to seeing the boys. At eight and ten years of age, they were still delightful. Laurel adored her nephews.

Two hours later, she had to ask Brent to pull in to the nearest gas station at Copper Mountain. "Sorry, guys. I was hoping we wouldn't have to make a rest room stop, but I'm afraid we do."

"No problem."

After a few minutes, they were on the road again. Within another half hour they'd reached the Rustler Lodge in Breckenridge. Brent drove up to the waiting area in front of the entrance, then turned to his wife.

"Tell you what. I'll grab a couple of bags and take Laurel inside so she can stretch. Then I'll come back and we'll find the boys over at the lift. We've timed this just right. It ought to be closing in about ten minutes."

"Sounds perfect."

"Let's go register." Brent got out of the car and collected some of the luggage, then walked her into the lodge.

Before long, one of the people at the desk had checked them in. Brent handed Laurel a key card and kept the other for himself. They strolled down the hall to the elevator.

They had to hurry to reach the next one going up; there was just enough room for the two of them to slip inside before the door closed. At the dinner hour, it was filled with people wearing everything from ski outfits to formal evening dress.

"It's all settled, Brent. The kids will sleep with me tonight. The girl in reception said there was a sofa with a hide-a-bed in my room."

"You're sure you don't mind?" Brent sounded so thrilled at the thought of being alone with his wife, she couldn't wait to tell her sister.

"How can you even ask me that?" She kissed his chin rather than his cheek because it was as far as she could reach with her baby protruding. He gave her an affectionate hug before the door opened to the third floor.

"This is where we get off. After you."

CHAPTER TWO

DURING THE SHORT RIDE to the third floor, Nate's eyes had been drawn to the chin-length, wavy black hair on the woman dressed in the black sweater. She was standing at the front of the crowded elevator.

He had to cock his head to the side, the better to examine its glistening quality brought out by the ceiling light. In Europe he'd only seen hair with that high a gloss on a few Italian and Spanish women.

When she turned to kiss her companion, Nate caught sight of her attractive profile, the contrast of sooty black lashes against ivory skin. In that moment he had the strongest impression he'd seen her before.

As the man put his arm around her and ushered her into the hall, Nate saw that she was pregnant. Then she was gone.

The elevator continued on to the dining room atop the Rustler Lodge. The door opened and everyone exited. Everyone except Nate...

He was supposed to be joining the private wedding party of twenty for dinner. A live band was playing, and all the elements were in place to make it a festive occasion.

After driving the newlyweds from the little white chapel a few streets over, he'd parked the car while

Rick accompanied their father and the second Mrs. Hawkins into the lodge.

Though he and his brother had tried their hardest to be accepting of their father's marriage, they were simply going through the motions.

But for the moment all thoughts of the day's events left his mind because he suddenly remembered where he'd seen that lovely face before.

Though he'd only met Spade's wife once, back when she was at Nellis years ago, a man didn't forget a beautiful woman like that.

Her hair had been long then. With her pictures plastered on the wall of their barracks—along with other family photos—every guy in their first squadron was envious of Spade's luck. Only two of the fourteen were married at the time.

Nate closed his eyes.

Spade...the hotshot of the group who'd been noticed by the brass right away and was transferred too soon to suit Nate. Spade...whose career had escalated too fast, who'd died in the prime of life...

The expectant mother in the elevator couldn't possibly have been his widow. When he'd crashed and died six months ago, Nate knew his friend's only regret was that he and his wife had never been able to have children.

The news of his death didn't reach Nate until after he'd flown back to Edwards Air Force base following his mother's funeral. By then it had been too late to attend the services for him in Philadelphia.

Nate had tried to reach his wife by phone, but a family member explained that she wasn't up to talking yet. Nate understood; she would have been inconsolable. There was no greater guy than Spade.

Needing to communicate that sentiment to her, Nate had expressed his feelings in a letter, which he mailed to her family's address.

As for anything else, all he'd been able to do was send money to Duce, another buddy, who'd arranged for flowers on behalf of all the guys in their old squadron.

A month later, Nate received a printed thank-you card. At the bottom was a handwritten postscript telling him she would always cherish his tribute to her husband.

Seeing the woman in the elevator who bore such an uncanny resemblance to her reminded Nate that he still had unfinished business. Tomorrow he'd phone Spade's widow in Philadelphia and see how she was doing.

He imagined she was still going through hell. Theirs had been a love affair that had begun in high school and would have lasted a lifetime. Spade had been crazy about her.

After graduating from the Air Force Academy, pilots earned the right to have their names and call signs painted on their first F-16s. Their group gave Spade a hard time with his. *016 Laurel, my first and only love.*

"Excuse me."

Nate had been so preoccupied with his memories, he didn't realize the elevator had descended to the foyer once more, and he was blocking the exit.

"Sorry," he murmured and stepped out into the

hall to make room. But when he would have moved back inside, something stopped him.

As long as he was on the ground floor, it wouldn't hurt to go over to the front desk and make a simple inquiry.

The pert redhead in reception flashed him a warm smile. "What can I do for you?"

"I'd like to ring Mrs. Scott Pierce on the house phone, but I don't know her extension."

"Pierce?" She scanned the screen of her computer. "No."

She checked it several different ways. "Sorry. There's no one registered under that name. Is there anything else I can do?"

"That's all right. Thank you."

Nate turned away. His first instincts had been right; the woman in the elevator was a look-alike. No doubt the man Nate had seen her kiss was her husband. They were going to have a baby soon.

Spade's widow would have remained in Philadelphia, where she had the kind of support from two loving families her husband would have wanted for her.

Nate felt a need to expend some energy and opened the door to the stairs. He took them two at a time. But when he reached the third floor, his legs refused to move any farther.

Despite all his logic, he sensed something was wrong. It was exactly the way he'd felt the last time he'd been in action, when he couldn't raise an immediate response from his wingman during a sortie.

What if, by some stretch of the imagination, that woman *had* been Laurel Pierce?

Nate recalled the man in the elevator who'd pulled her close to him with such familiarity.

Her lover? If so, the two of them would have checked into the lodge under his name.

Spade had only been gone six months... Before that, he and Nate had been flying with NATO forces, so he couldn't possibly have been with his wife at the time of conception.

Following those thoughts to their inevitable conclusion, Nate felt the bile rise in his throat. It was like the night Rick had told him their father was getting married again—and yet it wasn't.

Because the baby couldn't possibly be Spade's.

He curled his fingers around the railing, unaware he was cutting off his circulation.

According to the investigators on the scene, his jet had crashed due to mechanical failure. But what if their report was wrong?

Spade had been the true pride of the Air Force. The best of the best. They'd wanted to show him off in that air show before he flew to England for a long-awaited reunion with his wife.

What if one of the guys had tipped him off that she'd been having an affair? What if he hadn't been able to handle her betrayal?

You thought you knew someone inside out. But did anyone know how a man would react if he learned that the wife he worshipped had been sleeping with someone else?

Nate felt a spasm of pain at the thought that his friend might have been suffering such agony he'd actually become suicidal.

Horrified by his own gruesome speculation, he realized there was nothing he could do about it, even if she was enjoying a full-fledged affair with the guy in the elevator.

Perhaps they were married now.

Maybe he was her second husband.

Why not? It had been six months. Apparently it was the season for throwing off the old.

To hell with enduring love.

He sprinted the rest of the way to the restaurant. When he approached the table in the corner by the picture windows, Rick sent him a ''what's up?'' glance.

The wedding party, consisting of their dad's closest friends, had already reached the main course. Jim and his wife sat to one side of Rick, Nina Farr and her husband on the other. Those two couples were the people running the day-to-day business. They nodded to Nate.

His father gazed at him anxiously. Nate could see the pleading in his eyes. Nate couldn't stand it that their lives had come down to this—a furtive look that begged forgiveness.

Nate didn't have to forgive his father. In fact, forgiveness didn't enter into it.

This was life.

This was the real stuff of which life was made. Apparently, the last thirty years had merely been a prelude.

He found his chair opposite Rick and sat down. ''I'm sorry to be so long, everybody. I got stuck in the elevator.''

It was as good a lie as any. In a way, it wasn't

really even a lie. The elevator had become his prison for those few minutes of bitter reflection.

Pam's expressive brown eyes were compassionate. "That happened to me once at Nieman Marcus. There was a claustrophobic woman who became hysterical. It was a dreadful experience, so I know how you feel."

She spoke the truth. It *had* been dreadful. He wanted to put it behind him. He wanted to put Pam at ease.

Nate had come to the same conclusion as Rick. Pam was a nice person. So far he hadn't been able to find anything wrong with her. Like the rest of them, she'd been trying hard.

He smiled at her. "How about a dance? That is, if Dad says it's all right."

His request caught his father off guard. Once he'd cleared his throat, he nodded, then said, "I'll tell the waitress to bring your dinner."

Nate couldn't possibly eat right now, but all he said was, "Thanks." Getting to his feet, he went around to Pam's chair to help her up from the table.

She *was* a little thing. He felt as if he was twirling a pixie around the floor. It shouldn't have surprised him that she was a good dancer. Nothing ought to surprise him anymore.

"I love your father," she declared in a quiet voice. "Only time will tell if he learns to love me." Nate almost missed a step. "I hear that my family's already laid bets on how soon he leaves me. That's the reason I didn't ask any of them to the wedding."

Without stopping for breath she said, "If I were in your shoes, I couldn't have accepted what's happened with the kind of grace you and Rick have shown. It's another testimonial to the exceptional parents you've had.

"Maybe you don't want to hear this, but I feel strongly that you need to know the truth about something. On your father's insistence, we haven't slept together yet. In fact, I've never stayed overnight at your house. I realize you don't need me to tell you he's a very special man, but I had to say it anyway."

Nate's memory of Texas women had been right. She could pack more words into a few minutes than any other woman he'd ever met. In this case he was glad.

"Thank you," he whispered.

On impulse he gave her a hug. The first one he'd felt like giving her. She relaxed in his arms as they continued around the dance floor.

LAUREL HAD STARTED to put another piece of prime rib in her mouth when she saw him.

He was out of uniform, but it had to be Nate Hawkins.

Scott had introduced them years ago in Nevada. He was the one who'd written her such a touching letter. With so many people to thank after the funeral, she'd sent only printed notes expressing her gratitude. He had deserved much more.

Over the years she'd collected hundreds of photos and several dozen videos immortalizing her husband's career in the Air Force. They were packed away in storage. The attractive man on the dance floor was in most of the early pictures.

Scott had said his best buddy in their first squadron

was originally from Colorado. She didn't think she could be mistaken.

Putting down her fork, she leaned toward her brother-in-law. "Brent? Would you do me a favor and dance with me quick?"

"I thought you didn't want to dance because your stomach was too big," said Joey, their youngest.

"Joey!" his mother admonished him.

"You mean right this second?" Brent was in the process of devouring his sirloin steak.

"Yes. Otherwise it might be too late."

Julie gave her a quizzical look.

Brent must have sensed it was important. He wiped his mouth with his napkin, then got up to assist her.

"See that dark-blond man across the floor dancing with the short brunette? I think I know him. Just get me over there so I won't look too conspicuous."

His gaze traveled to her prominent mound. "I'll try," he said with a grin.

Brent wasn't the greatest dancer, but all she needed was a prop to get her to her destination.

The closer they drew, the more she became convinced this was the man who'd flown with her husband at the beginning of their careers, and later during their deployment with the NATO forces. He was the man Scott had admired more than any other.

His back was still toward her, but even his formal midnight-blue suit couldn't disguise his solid build which had been noticeable in all those old pictures.

When she'd met him, he'd reminded her of an Olympic cross-country skier who could do a 50 K race, like the men from Norway or Sweden with their tall, splendid bodies in the peak of physical condition.

She'd never confided those thoughts to Scott who'd stood five eleven and worked out whenever possible to try and emulate his friend's appearance. There were some things you didn't tell your husband.

Laurel was in touching distance of him now. She let go of Brent and put a hand on the man's arm.

"Hawk? It *is* you, isn't it?"

Now it was the other couple who'd stopped dancing.

Like a person who'd just been shot, the man dropped his hands. The woman excused herself before he turned slowly in Laurel's direction.

It had been nine years since they'd met. Time and experience had refined the rugged good looks she remembered, but the cold blue eyes staring back at her weren't familiar.

One strong hand closed over his other arm at the wrist. Not a word came out of him. The negative tension he emanated was so palpable she felt unsure of herself and searched for Brent's hand, gripping it for support.

"You probably don't remember me. It's been too many years. I'm—"

"I know who you are," he broke in before she could say her name or introduce him to Brent. "If you'll excuse me, I'm attending a wedding party."

As he strode away from her, she could've sworn he muttered "Have a nice life."

Brent was there to cradle her so she wouldn't fall. She buried her face against his shoulder for a moment to hide her pain, then pulled away in embarrassment.

"W-would you help me to the elevator, please?"

Ruddy color had filled his cheeks. "That bastard! Who the hell does he think he is to treat you like that?"

"It doesn't matter. Just dance me over to the entrance. Don't say anything to Julie or the kids."

The next few minutes were a blur as he took her all the way to the room. When he would've stayed to comfort her, she had to push him out the door to make him leave.

"I'm so sorry to have dragged you from dinner. Go back upstairs and enjoy the rest of the evening with your family. I'm going to take a shower and get into bed. By the time you're all back, I'll be fully recovered."

"Laurel—"

"I feel like a fool and I don't want to talk about it. You're a good man. My sister's the luckiest woman I know. Now go."

"All right, but we won't be long."

The second he'd gone, she crept over to the bed and lay on her side.

No one had ever treated her as cruelly as Hawk had done a few minutes ago.

She felt as if he'd lifted her from the ground and thrashed her against a wall.

Hot tears gushed from her eyes. It had been months since she'd cried like this.

What did Scott or I ever do to you, Hawk?
What?

RICK WALKED into the house ahead of Nate. He flipped on the living room lights, and they stared at each other. "It's just you and me."

Nate tugged at his tie before he threw it and his suit jacket over the back of a chair. He missed. Everything fell in a heap on the floor. Not bothering to pick them up, he unfastened the top button of his shirt. It popped off.

Rick's eyes followed his out-of-control movements. "Want to start by telling me what you and our father's new bride were talking about on the dance floor? Or shall we cut to the chase? Explain why you looked so ill after you came back to the table."

His brother deserved explanations if anyone did, but for the life of him he couldn't find the words.

Lord. Her eyes.

Could a woman who looked that hurt be guilty of the crime he'd accused her of in his heart?

"I couldn't eat dinner, either, but I feel like a beer," Rick said. "Do you want one?"

"Yes. Thanks."

While his brother went to the kitchen, Nate studied the various family pictures their mother had placed around the room. He had his favorites. Like gravity, they pulled him in for a closer look.

"Do you remember the ad on TV?" Rick handed him an ice-cold lager. "The one that said, 'it's eleven o'clock. Parents, do you know where your children are?'"

Nate nodded.

"It's like the roles have been reversed. Children,

it's eleven o'clock. Do you know where your parents are?''

Their eyes met again.

"We don't have to worry that Pam could be expecting a baby," Nate began. "Dad chose not to sleep with her until after they'd said their marriage vows."

Rick did a double take. "She came right out and told you that?"

"She did." Nate chugged down half the contents of his can. "There's more."

In a few minutes he'd told Rick the essence of their conversation on the dance floor.

His brother let out a long whistle. "What if her family's right?"

"I've been asking myself the same question."

"A few minutes ago I was thinking there's no more reason for us to be here. Jim hasn't said anything, but I suspect he'd buy Dad out, given the opportunity."

"With a good loan from the bank, he could probably do it," Nate agreed. "The house could be rented."

Rick sat down on the couch. "I can see we're on the same wavelength, as usual. But after what Pam told you, maybe there's a chance Dad doesn't know his own mind yet...."

"That's the kicker." Nate had the strongest suspicion it would break Pamela's heart. "Under the circumstances, there's no point in both of us staying here."

His brother's head reared up. "I was just going to tell you the same thing! What I've been doing for a living is selfish and has little redeeming value. In contrast, my brother protects our country's freedom and puts his life on the line every time he goes up in the air. Nothing's more noble than that.''

"We need people to race cars, too. It brings in advertising, which in turn keeps the world economy going.''

"You're so full of it, you almost convince me.'' Rick heaved a sigh. "But it's a moot point now. When I broke the racing contract with my sponsor, they made it clear I've burned my bridges.'' He took a moment to drink some of his beer. "Let's agree to table this discussion until next week, after they're back from Hawaii.

"Maybe home will feel good to Dad. They might not leave for her ranch right away, if at all. He may need us yet.''

"I suppose anything's possible.''

Rick leaned forward, hands clasped between his legs. "What else has been tearing you up for the last couple of hours?''

"It has to do with Spade.''

"I've lost a close buddy on the track. I don't think it's something you ever forget. What made tonight so difficult?''

"His wife was out on the dance floor. Correction. His merry widow.''

His brother frowned at him. "How about a translation?''

"His very pregnant widow.''

"That still doesn't help me.''

"Not only could Spade never give Laurel a child, we were flying with the NATO forces when the conception would've taken place. It's been less than seven months since the crash. I've got eyes in my head. She's close to her delivery date. Plus, earlier tonight, I saw her kissing another man in the elevator.''

"Ouch."

"I don't give a damn about her. But what if Spade called her before his accident and found out she'd been playing around....''

Rick got to his feet. "You can't assume she had anything to do with the reason he crashed.''

"Why can't I?" Nate challenged.

"Because pilots like you and Spade are chosen for extraordinary qualities. You're not as weak as the rest of us, especially when you're at the controls. Our country's security depends on you."

"No pilot or racing pro is a superman, Rick. Every man has his breaking point. We all hope we'll never have to be tested to that degree. It hurts to think Spade's wife might've been the one ultimately responsible for his death. He really loved her.''

After a long silence, his brother said, ''Did you talk to her?''

"It was unavoidable. She approached me.''

"And?"

"In so many words I told her to go to hell.''

Rick shot him a troubled glance. "That doesn't sound like the brother I know.''

"I'm *not* the brother you knew.''

"Neither of us knows who we are right now. It's too soon. Emotions are still too fragile.''

"Since when did you turn into the philosopher?''

"Don't ask.''

Nate wasn't about to. He already knew the answer. "If you want to sleep in, I'll drive Dad and Mom to the airport."

The second the word slipped out, they both froze.

"I made the same mistake earlier in front of Dad," Rick confessed. "It'll probably happen a lot until everything sinks in."

"Let's hope you're wrong."

"Whether I sleep tonight or not, I plan to go to the airport with you in the morning. Pam seems grateful for the smallest crumb."

"So does Dad," Nate said.

Rick's cell phone rang, disturbing the quiet. He plucked it from the coffee table and glanced at his call display.

"*Damn.* It's Natalie."

"That doesn't sound like the brother *I* know."

Rick raised his head. Their eyes met in brotherly understanding. "Touché."

"I'll leave you alone. If something comes up, call me on my cell."

"Where are you going?"

"After I change clothes, I thought I'd drive over to the ski shop and take a look around. Since Dad missed the buying trip this year, I'm curious to see how low the inventory is."

"Hang on and I'll join you. This call won't take long."

Nate grabbed his jacket and tie from the floor, then bounded up the front stairs to his old bedroom. Once he'd dressed in jeans and a well-worn sweatshirt, he made his way to the foyer.

Rick was still on the phone.

A disturbing restlessness drove Nate to the den. He turned on the light. Ever since childhood, the framed Olympic medals hanging over the mantelpiece were always the first thing that drew his gaze.

Only once had they been removed from this wall. He'd begged his parents to let him bring the medals to school for "Show and Tell." Initially they'd refused—out of modesty, he now understood—but they'd given in when they saw how much it meant to him. His teacher and eight-year-old classmates had been duly impressed.

His mother had taken the silver for the women's downhill. In those same Olympic games, his father had won gold in the giant slalom. That was where they'd met.

Like some of the paired ice-skaters who were husband and wife, his parents' passion for the sport had led to the grand passion of their existence. Each other. They'd married soon after and decided to live the rest of their lives at ten thousand feet in Colorado's Rocky Mountains.

Life had been idyllic for Nate and Rick. The family that prayed together, that worked and played together, stayed together. How many times had Nate heard that maxim from the pulpit? He'd always believed it.

The trick was to find one's soul mate first.

In just one week Nate had decided there was no such thing. Judging by Rick's savage expression as they met in the hall, he'd reached the same conclusion.

CHAPTER THREE

LAUREL WAVED the family off. "See you at twelve." She'd driven them over to the lift so they could ski as many runs as possible before noon. Brent wanted to get an early start back to Denver to avoid the worst of the traffic.

By tacit agreement, any reference to last night's unfortunate incident was avoided. When the family returned to the suite from dinner, Laurel had put on fresh makeup, and she greeted them with a smile. She insisted the boys sleep in her room. Brent and Julie had no choice but to go along with her wishes.

Today was a new day, and she intended to enjoy it. First on the agenda, she'd have a leisurely breakfast in the coffee shop. Afterward she'd drive into town to do a little shopping. Maybe she'd see something cute for a baby girl in one of the stores at the Bell Tower mall.

If she was having a boy, Julie had saved enough baby and toddler clothes to fill every need. Brent had already set up their old crib in Laurel's room. She was as prepared as she could possibly be.

She pulled into the lodge parking lot and got out of the car. During the night a storm front had moved in, bringing lower temperatures and the threat of more snow. Her breath curled in the air.

Glad of Brent's old black-and-white parka, which covered most of her, she made her way toward the lodge, hoping no one noticed that she walked like a fat penguin these days.

A line of cars idled outside the entrance. Sunday mornings tended to be the busiest time, with the majority of guests departing. As she walked between two of the vehicles where people were loading their bags, she got the distinct impression she was being watched.

The feeling grew so strong she glanced to her right and caught a glint of blue. The wintry blue of eyes that had condemned her last night. It was Hawk at the controls of a four-wheel-drive Blazer.

There was a logo on the side. Eagles' Nest Ski and Bike Shop, Copper Mountain. Was it a loan from a friend for the occasion?

Her timing couldn't have been worse. He'd told her he was with a wedding party. Maybe it had been his own. If so, good luck to his little brunette bride. Any woman foolish enough to marry a man carrying around that much rage—that much cruelty—would need it.

Laurel picked up her pace and walked through the huge glass doors of the lodge. When she reached the coffee shop, it looked filled to capacity. Making a snap decision, she headed back to the suite. It would be easier to order breakfast from there, then visit the mall.

But once inside the room, she discovered she was too angry to eat, let alone shop. She removed her parka and sank down on the bed.

During the night she'd relived the hurtful experience on the dance floor over and over again. No matter how many times she'd tried to analyze it, she couldn't understand why it had happened. There was no way to reconcile his behavior with what she knew about Hawk.

If he and Scott had suffered a falling-out, she had no idea when it would have occurred. Once her husband had been transferred from Nellis, their careers had taken them to different parts of the world, although they'd always stayed in touch.

Twice there'd been periods where they both served with NATO forces for many months at a time. The most recent had been right before Scott had returned to perform in the air show that had cost him his life. Her husband would have told her if there'd been trouble between them.

Now that she'd recovered from the initial shock of their meeting, she was more curious than devastated by his rudeness. From everything she knew about him, he'd acted out of character last night.

Scott might be gone, but for her own peace of mind she intended to solve the mystery. If some wrong *had* been done, if Scottie had somehow offended the man he used to idolize, Laurel wanted to know. Perhaps it was too late to make amends, but she could try.

If memory served her right, after seeing action, Hawk had been sent to Edwards Air Force base, then Holland. Duce had mentioned something about his testing jets with the Dutch Air Force. No telling if he was still stationed there.

The fact that he'd come to Colorado for a wedding

meant he was only here on leave. If she didn't act fast, she could miss him before he returned to active duty.

Grabbing the phone directory from the nightstand, she looked up the Eagles' Nest Ski and Bike Shop. If she couldn't obtain any information there, she'd try to locate his family.

The local operator could make a search of every Hawkins listed in Colorado, starting with this area of the state.

She picked up the phone, pressed nine for an outside line, then used her phone card to call the number she'd found. There were two rings before the message came on.

"You've reached Eagles' Nest Ski and Bike Shop. We're open Monday through Saturday, seven to seven. Sundays, seven to one. Come and check out our ski rentals for the whole family. If you wish further assistance, please stay on the line."

Laurel waited.

"Rental shop. This is Nina."

"Hello. Excuse me for bothering you, but I'm trying to locate someone I saw driving one of your vehicles this morning. His name is Major Nathan Hawkins."

"You've reached his father's place of business."

"Oh, good! May I speak to his father please?"

"I'm sorry. Clint's out of town."

"I see. Do you know how I could reach his son?"

"He'll probably be here on Monday. If you'd like to leave a phone number, I'll make sure he gets it."

It didn't sound as if Hawk had been the bridegroom, after all. Not if he hadn't gone away on a honeymoon.

"I'm afraid he won't be able to contact me. At least I know where to call now. Thank you very much for your help."

Laurel hung up before the other woman could ask for a name. If Hawk did show up and discovered that someone was looking for him, he might *think* it was Laurel, but he wouldn't have proof.

She checked the telephone directory once more. Hawkins. Ah, there it was. Clint Hawkins in Copper Mountain.

Laurel wrote down the address and phone number. It was her insurance in case Hawk didn't want to be found.

Now that she knew he wasn't leaving Colorado for at least another day, she could relax. In a much better frame of mind, she rang for room service and stretched out on the bed to watch TV until it was time to pick up the family.

WITH SECURITY SO TIGHT at the Denver airport, there was no opportunity to do anything more than deposit the newlyweds at the curb. Nate reached over the seat to squeeze Pam's arm and wish her a happy trip.

While Rick helped them with their bags, Nate lowered the car window to say goodbye to his father, who'd come around to the driver's side. He'd always been a strong man. This morning his grip on Nate's shoulder was almost bruising.

"Thank you, son. I love you."

"I love you, too," he whispered.

"When we get back, I want to sit down with you and Rick. We'll talk about everything."

He nodded. "Sounds good."

A minute later Rick climbed into the front seat. Nate took advantage of a break in the traffic and headed away from the terminal.

"I don't think Pam said more than a dozen words on the way down from Breckenridge."

"She did while Dad was paying the bill."

Nate turned his head toward his brother. "Problems already?"

"I don't know what to think. She said she'd been waiting for the right moment to explain why she was at our house the morning I surprised them. Apparently Dad had just picked her up at the Copper Mountain Inn where she'd been staying all month.

"To quote her, 'Your father and I did a lot of soul-searching on the previous night. The love he felt for your mother poured out of him. All I could do was listen. When he asked me to come to your house for breakfast, I told him I was terrified he was going to say our engagement was a mistake.'"

Rick took a deep breath. "She told me that after they'd eaten and she was helping him with the dishes, he admitted that getting married could be a mistake. But apparently he said it might be an even bigger one if they didn't find out what there could be between them."

"That's interesting," Nate murmured, "and we know Dad's traditional enough to insist on marriage, but we still don't know what *she's* all about."

"Nope, and Dad isn't the type to tell us something personal about her until he's ready."

Nate was about to say their father might never be ready, but his cell phone rang. Curious, he pulled it from his pocket and checked the caller ID. "It's the ski shop."

"Already?"

"You heard Dad earlier. We're in charge now." He clicked on. "This is Nate. What's up?"

"Hi, Nate."

"Nina?"

"I wouldn't be bothering you if I didn't think this might be important."

"Go ahead."

"A woman phoned the shop a few minutes ago looking for a Major Hawkins. She said she'd seen you driving the Blazer and wanted to talk to you, but she didn't leave a name or number."

Laurel Pierce had her nerve, he'd say that much.

"For security reasons I didn't give out any phone numbers. However, I did tell her you'd probably be in the shop sometime tomorrow. In case it was someone from the military, I thought you should know."

"Thanks, Nina. You did exactly the right thing. I'll see you tomorrow."

He clicked off the phone, then gave his brother a speaking glance. "Spade's wife is looking for me."

"After the way you treated her, you're not really surprised, are you?"

"I thought you were on my side."

"Always."

"She knows I know her secret. It appears the woman has no shame."

"I agree it looks that way," Rick murmured.

"It *is* that way."

"What are you going to do about it?"

"Nothing. If she has the temerity to show up at

the ski shop, it'll be a wasted trip for her. I didn't tell you I saw her this morning while you were inside getting Dad.''

''Did she try to talk to you again?''

''No, but then I didn't encourage it.''

Rick eyed him for a moment before turning his head away.

Nate saw his brother rummage in his pocket for something.

''Here. I picked these up in the lodge.'' Rick handed him a candy bar. ''What do you say we go home and take a couple of runs on Eagles' Nest for old times' sake?''

''You're on.'' An afternoon tearing the mountain apart wasn't like taking to the sky, but it would do. Anything to put off thinking for a little while.

Within an hour they'd returned to Copper Mountain. After they'd donned their old ski outfits and Laplander hats, they went to the laundry room off the kitchen, where their mom had made a place for the family to store their skis and poles.

Her favorite pair of G-41 Vokyls were still there, as if waiting for her to grab them for a quick run. Nate noticed his brother staring at them for a moment before he reached for his own.

One of these days they would stop reacting to reminders of her and the avalanche that had come out of nowhere to sweep her and two friends to their deaths.

A series of storms had hit in early September. Carrying their skis, the three women had hiked up in the back country to get the first fresh tracks of the year. Normally fall wasn't avalanche season. Colorado

Search and Rescue speculated that they'd dropped down from a cornice, which had started a massive slide.

It shouldn't have happened.

Spade's crash shouldn't have happened, either.

Nate's mouth thinned. He collected his skis and poles. "Ready?" he called to his brother.

"As I'll ever be. Let's go."

He followed Rick through the house to the front door. A wind had come up while they were inside, and it had started to snow. They'd be lucky to get in one run before it grew into a blizzard and the lift shut down.

As he stopped to lock the front door, he heard another car pull into the driveway. He turned in time to see a figure get out of the front passenger side. A pregnant figure in black.

Nate froze in his tracks.

She hurried toward Rick who was putting his skis on the rack of their Blazer. If they exchanged any conversation, it was brief. She darted back to the waiting car before Nate could make it down the front steps of the house.

By the time he caught up with his brother, the driver had backed up and headed off.

Rick's speculative glance swiveled to Nate. "This is for you." He extended a white envelope. "At first she must've thought I was you because she said, 'for Scott's sake please don't tear this up before you read it.'"

"That woman doesn't know when to quit!"

He'd had about all he could take for one weekend. It was a little late to be using her dead husband's name to get to Nate. Not that he could figure out why she'd even *want* to.

"I'll hold on to it for now." Rick stashed it in a pocket of his parka while Nate put his skis on the rack. "If we don't step on it, we won't be able to ski at all."

"LAUREL? Are you all right?" Julie called from the back of the car where she was sitting with the boys. Both she and Brent had insisted Laurel ride in front to give her a little extra leg room.

"I'm fine now that I've delivered my letter. Thanks for stopping."

She'd realized too late that she'd approached Hawk's brother instead of him. Scott had mentioned he had a sibling. They bore a strong resemblance to each other, except that he had gray eyes and they were questioning rather than damning.

It wasn't until she'd gotten back in the car that she saw another tall figure on the pathway, carrying a pair of skis. That was when her heart jumped.

In truth she was glad it had turned out the way it did. Most likely Hawk would have flung the letter back in her face. This way, at least, there was a chance that his brother might pass it on.

After talking to the salesperson at the ski shop earlier, Laurel knew the woman would tell Hawk about the phone call and he'd disappear in order to avoid her.

The only thing Laurel could think to do was make a surprise visit to his parents' house. She'd hoped no one would be there so she could stick her letter to the front door with some tape.

"Was that the man who made you cry?"

So much for the kids not knowing what was going on.

"No, Joey. It was his brother."

"How do you know?"

"Because they look alike, the way you and Mike do."

"I don't look like Joey," Mike muttered.

"Yes, you do," their mother insisted. "And you both look like your dad."

"If you have a boy, it'll look like Uncle Scott, huh, Aunt Laurel?"

"Not necessarily, Joey." This was from Brent, who hadn't chosen to interfere until now.

"It might be a girl."

"We want a boy cousin, Mom."

Brent grinned. "You should've put in your order sooner, Mike. I'm afraid it was decided eight months ago."

"Who decided it?"

"The father does, Joey."

"Then Uncle Scott would've picked a boy!"

"Your dad didn't mean the father really decides. Remember in that book we all read together? When the sperm and the egg unite to make a baby, there's something in the man's sperm that'll make it a boy or a girl."

"But what if we don't want our sperm to make a girl?" Joey blurted.

Laurel bit her lip to keep from laughing. Like Julie, she felt it was important to teach children the truth using correct terms. However she could see that honesty didn't necessarily answer all the questions.

"That's why God's in charge," his mother explained.

"You always say that."

"That's because it's true, Mike," their father said.

"I guess He didn't want our family to have girls, then."

"Oh, I don't know."

Before Laurel had time to react to Julie's mysterious comment, Brent had already pulled over to the side of the highway. He turned in the seat to stare at his wife.

"Did you just say what I think you said?" Laurel heard incredulity and excitement in his voice.

Julie's low chuckle gave her away. "I was going to wait until tonight to tell you."

"Tell Dad *what,* Mom?" Mike asked.

Laurel couldn't resist interjecting. "It sounds like you're going to be getting a new little brother or sister later on in the year."

How wonderful, wonderful.

Her sister's pregnancy had just settled something that had been a big question in Laurel's mind. After her own baby was born, she'd love to buy a small house in Aurora, so they could all still be close and she could help her sister when the time came for her delivery. They could raise their children together.

But only if Brent felt right about it. He'd put up with her for months now. Maybe he was counting the days until she left their house and Denver for good. No one could have been as terrific to her as he'd been since Scott's death. To expect more might be assuming too much.

During the rest of the drive home, Laurel remained

silent. For the moment she was content to put her head back and listen to the happy flow of conversation from her favorite people.

Every once in a while, she'd sneak a glance at Brent. She wondered if Scott had beamed like that after he'd heard the news about his baby.

Their child was almost here. It moved constantly in the womb, preventing her from finding a comfortable position. Since her seventh month she hadn't had a good night's sleep. Yet she reveled in every stage of her pregnancy because she no longer felt alone.

NATE HAD BEEN SKIING in the Alps many times with different friends, but none of them could keep up. Only Rick exceeded him in speed and technique. If his brother hadn't learned to love car-racing at such an early age, he could have trained for the Olympics, too. He was that good. But then, he was good at everything, just like their parents.

This afternoon, his brother had given him a real workout on Eagles' Nest.

"That's our pizza," Rick said when the doorbell rang. "I'll get it."

Following an afternoon of hard skiing, pizza normally sounded good to Nate, but not today. He pulled on his sweats and went to get a couple of Cokes from the fridge.

When he saw a rumpled envelope with the name Hawk written on it stuck to the door with a magnet, he forgot why he'd come into the kitchen.

Hell.

He yanked the refrigerator door open to get the

drinks. When he slammed it shut, he did it so hard the magnet and letter fell to the floor.

Much as he wanted to leave it there, he realized he was behaving like an immature child. How could a thirty-year-old man—a man who'd experienced everything he had, including the deaths of family let one insignificant woman's actions rule his emotions like this?

As if operating in slow motion, he put the cans on the counter, then reached for the letter and magnet. After attaching the souvenir magnet to the door again, he turned the envelope over and opened it. She'd confined her remarks to one page.

Dear Hawk,
I should probably address you as Major Hawkins, but Scott always called you Hawk. That's the way I've thought of you over the years.

My husband admired you greatly. If he did something to ruin your relationship, he wasn't aware of it or he would have told me.

Since last night I've been thinking hard about the way you treated me on the dance floor. No matter how many times I've gone over it in my mind, I can't imagine why you were so cruel, unless you wanted me to know Scott had committed some unpardonable offense.

He's gone now, so he can't ask your forgiveness or make amends. I would do both if I knew what was wrong.

It hurts to think that someone Scott loved like a brother still harbors so much bitterness toward him. Whatever it was must have been very serious to wipe out nine years of friendship.

To be frank, I'm still asking myself how you could've written such a beautiful letter at Scott's death, only to show me a completely different side of you last night.

I'm assuming that when your leave is over, you'll be returning to Holland. The last I heard about you, Duce said you were stationed at Leeuwarden, where you were testing the MLU jet with some other pilots from Norway and Belgium.

If ever the day comes when your anger subsides enough to tell me what went wrong, you can reach me by phone in Denver where I live.

He saw the phone number she'd written.

I guess I'm human enough to want life to be perfect. But as I found out years ago, life takes you down roads you hadn't planned on traveling.

Wherever your road takes you, Hawk, I wish you luck. I mean that sincerely. Scott's career in the Air Force wouldn't have provided the same thrill for him if you hadn't been a big part of it from the very beginning.

Fly high and watch your tail.

Laurel.

Nate stood there in shock.

If he'd expected anything, it would've been defensiveness on her part or an attempt to hide her culpability. Instead, nothing he'd read, either in her words or between the lines, suggested she felt an ounce of guilt.

His eyes closed. Laurel Pierce was a beautiful woman. Even in the last stage of pregnancy she looked as stunning as ever.

Had she always been this amoral?

Scott had married her out of high school. Two years younger than he was, she'd been plucked from her home at an early age. Perhaps it was the long separations from Scott while they were stationed overseas that had made her vulnerable to other men's attention. One of them had given her a child....

As Nate's father had once told him, being a hot-shot pilot came at a price. If he was determined to have a career in the Air Force, he needed to keep that in mind if he wanted a family too.

At the time Nate had half listened to the warning. Not until now did he grasp the full essence of what his father had been trying to tell him. Though Scott hadn't let it show, there'd obviously been trouble in the Pierce marriage.

"The pizza's getting cold."

His gaze flicked to his brother who'd just entered the kitchen.

"You took so long getting the drinks, I figured you'd decided to read her letter. What did she have to say?"

Nate held it out. "Go ahead. Then you'll know I was right the first time."

Rick took it from him.

Not waiting for a reaction, Nate picked up the drinks and headed for the living room, where Rick had set up a game of chess. Their father had taught them well, and only Rick could beat him.

Without their dad around, maybe Nate could out-maneuver his brother for a change. He was in the mood for a challenge.

Halfway through a can of pop, Rick joined him. He was still holding the damn letter.

"Let's get started," Nate muttered.

His brother didn't sit down at the card table. "If she's as guilty as you think she is, it took guts for her to write that letter after you rebuffed her not once, but twice."

Rick was beginning to sound like their mother. When there was a problem, she always resorted to logic to make her sons see reason.

"I'm not sure the woman knows the difference between right and wrong."

"Wouldn't you like to find out?" His brother was goading him like no one else could—and still get away with it.

"Don't say anything else, Rick. We're not little kids anymore."

"That's true," he retorted. "Little kids make wild judgments without the necessary knowledge to back them up. Spade's wife must really be hurting if she dared face you a third time. It isn't like you to enjoy someone else's pain."

"She's going to have another guy's baby. That's all the knowledge I need. Spade was my friend!" He could feel the veins standing out in his neck.

"But your friendship doesn't include the woman he loved? Is that what you're implying?"

"I didn't know her."

"You knew her through her husband's eyes. She knew you the same way. In many respects that's even more intimate," he said as he placed the letter on the end table. "If she has anything to confess, it would make sense that you're the one she'd turn to, given half a chance."

Nate folded his arms. "Do you want to play chess or not?"

"Are you in the mood to be beaten?"

"Winning too many races has made you cocky."

Rick straddled the chair and sat down. "Flying too many combat missions has made you ruthless."

He hadn't seen that coming. Not from his brother. Nate averted his eyes, wondering if any part of what Rick had just said was true.

The next week was going to be endless for both of them. Until their father returned from his honeymoon, they couldn't make any definite plans for the future.

"It's your move, big brother."

They both knew Rick wasn't talking about chess.

An hour later Nate still couldn't concentrate on the game. The two of them looked at each other in resignation before agreeing to call it a night.

Rick pushed himself away from the card table. "See you in the morning."

Nate nodded to his brother, who left the living room first. His gaze followed Rick before it shifted to the letter. Without disturbing the chess pieces, he got up and plucked it from the end table to read again. One particular paragraph leaped out at him.

My husband admired you greatly. If he did some-

thing to ruin your relationship, he wasn't aware of it or he would have told me.

Her words had kindled his anger the first time around. On second reading, he'd reached flash point.

How dare she pretend Scott had anything to do with Nate's reaction to her last evening!

His chest heaved as he turned out the lights and dashed up the stairs to his bedroom. When he started to get undressed, he realized he still held her letter. To his surprise, he'd crumpled it completely without being aware of it.

As he tossed it into the wastebasket, he knew exactly what Spade would have done if their positions had been reversed and he'd seen Nate's supposedly barren widow pregnant with a child that couldn't possibly be Nate's.

Spade had been a man of action. You knew where you stood with him. That was where he'd gotten his nickname—the fact that he always called a spade a spade.

Grinding his teeth, Nate walked over to the wastebasket. Slowly he smoothed out the paper to find a certain phone number.

CHAPTER FOUR

THROUGHOUT HER PREGNANCY Laurel hadn't developed cravings for any particular foods. However she'd always loved peanut butter and plum jam sandwiches. For the last few months she'd enjoyed one every night before going to bed. Tonight was no exception.

While she was putting the bread and jars back in the fridge, the phone rang. She ignored it. At nine-thirty it was probably a business call for Brent, who was in the family room with Julie and the kids watching TV.

A couple of seconds later, her brother-in-law appeared in the kitchen doorway. He wore a grim expression.

"What's wrong?"

"It's Nate Hawkins."

Her pulse rate doubled. She stared at Brent. "That's good news. I wasn't sure he'd get back to me at all."

"He hurt you a lot. You're sure this is what you want?"

"Absolutely. The sooner I get to the bottom of things, the sooner I can put the whole experience away. I'll answer it in here." She reached for the cordless phone.

"I'll go back to the study and hang up."

"Thanks, Brent."

He still hadn't made a move to leave. His protective instincts were out in full measure, and Laurel loved him for being so good to her.

"It'll be fine," she assured him.

"I don't want him to upset you and send you into early labor."

She smiled. "If I didn't have a strong constitution, I'd probably have had the baby on Saturday night. Don't worry. Anything he has to say to me now couldn't have the same shock value. Trust me."

"It looks like I'm going to have to. Holler if you need help."

Laurel nodded, then clicked the "on" button. She put the phone to her ear. "Hello, Hawk? I appreciate your calling me."

"Any thanks should go to my brother." She winced. "I know it's late so I won't keep you. If you really want to talk, it would be better accomplished in person."

Clipped and to the point. His hostile attitude was so far removed from the tone of the letter he'd sent her six months ago, she had trouble believing this was the same man.

Over the years, there'd only been a few times when he'd phoned Scott at their base residence and she'd happened to answer the phone first. On those occasions he'd been friendly and polite.

She leaned against the counter, more puzzled than ever. "I was hoping you'd agree to meet me. I live in Aurora. There's a Fordham's Pancake House just off the exit for Aurora at Washington Avenue."

"I know the spot."

"Good." Her hand tightened on the receiver. "Depending on your schedule, I could meet you there anytime Tuesday or Thursday of this next week." Thursday she had an appointment with her OB, but she would change it if she had to. "That is, if you haven't used up all your leave."

Those were the days Julie didn't work. Laurel could borrow her car to drive the short distance to the restaurant. Under the circumstances, she was certain Hawk would prefer meeting her on neutral ground. Laurel felt the same way. She had no desire to involve her family in any further unpleasantness.

"Tuesday's fine," he said without hesitation. "Shall we say 10:00 a.m.?"

It was evident he wanted to get this over with as soon as possible, too.

"I'll be there. Thank you for getting back to me so quickly."

"Make no mistake. I'm doing this for Spade."

The line went dead.

For Spade? She translated that to mean he wouldn't have given her the time of day otherwise.

A perplexed Laurel put the phone back on the charger. Without conscious thought she reached for her sandwich, wondering what kind of grievance he could possibly have against *her*.

Julie soon appeared in the kitchen, watching her anxiously.

Laurel answered her unspoken question. "It appears that Hawk thinks that I'm the one who's done something unpardonable, not Scott. We're meeting on Tuesday at Fordham's where he'll deliver a few home truths. Ten in the morning, no less.''

"He didn't give you a clue what's wrong?"

"No. It reminds me of the story Nana Hayes used to tell us all the time."

"You mean about Dr. Childers, the university professor who failed her because she thought Nana told the board of regents Dr. Childers smoked?"

"That's the one. Nana had to go to college another semester and take the same English literature class over with a different professor. She couldn't graduate with her class and was denied the right to graduate magna cum laude."

"It's hard to believe she wasn't even allowed to meet with Dr. Childers so she could deny the charge to her face. There should have been a board of inquiry."

"I agree, but sixty-five years ago professional women weren't supposed to smoke, and the students didn't have the same rights they enjoy today. Nana never got over being accused and punished for something she didn't do."

"I guess Dr. Childers never lived it down, either," Julie surmised.

"For some reason Hawk's made me feel the same way. Like I've done a terrible thing and there's no chance of forgiveness."

"That's absurd, Laurel."

"Well, I guess I'll find out on Tuesday." She finished the other half of her sandwich, then drank the glass of milk she'd poured. "Let's hope our meeting has a positive result. I wouldn't want to go through the rest of my life with this haunting me."

"He's really gotten to you, hasn't he."

"Yes. Even *I'm* surprised." She put the milk carton back in the refrigerator. "I suppose it's because he and Scott were so close. It makes me wonder how many things my husband shared with Hawk that I don't know about—things Scott didn't like about me."

Julie shook her head. "Scott adored you, Laurel."

"I know he loved me, but we both had our flaws. Some of mine were glaring. Maybe he complained to Hawk once too often."

"Name one."

"After the way I cried because we still hadn't conceived after our first three years of marriage, he couldn't understand why I refused to start the adoption process. Maybe deep inside he felt cheated of a family and confided his frustration to Hawk."

"But Scott knew the fertility specialist hadn't given up on the idea of the two of you having your own baby. As it turns out, you *are* going to have Scott's child!"

"Even so, it might've created too much pressure to bear over the years. If Hawk picked up on that, he could resent me for it."

"What goes on between a husband and wife is no one else's business!" Julie said staunchly.

"Try telling that to two buddies in combat who depend on each other for their very lives, knowing they might not make it back." She washed her empty glass. "I would imagine Hawk considers me a very selfish woman."

"He has no right to judge."

She flashed her sister a frank glance. "I'm afraid

Scott gave him the right. They had their own private brotherhood. Every Air Force wife knows that."

Julie's features softened with compassion. "Did Scott exclude you sometimes?"

"Not purposely. But there were occasions when he had to talk something over with Hawk. It wasn't enough to tell me."

"I didn't know that."

"It's okay. It goes with the territory when you're married to a hotshot. If my not wanting to adopt until we were a 100 percent sure we couldn't have our own children hurt him more deeply than he let on, then I suppose he made it Hawk's business."

Julie moved closer. "If he's holding a grudge against you for something your husband told him in confidence, then he isn't the terrific guy Scott thought he was."

"Thanks for saying that. I happen to agree with you. Fortunately for me, I'll be able to face my accuser as early as Tuesday morning, unlike our poor Nana…" She pasted on a smile. "We've come a long way, baby."

Julie gave her an encouraging hug before they left the kitchen together.

THE FORDHAM PANCAKE HOUSE chain covered Colorado to Oklahoma. Before going overseas, Nate had eaten at several of them. No matter the day or hour, they were always crowded.

He'd arrived at nine-thirty under an overcast sky to give the head waitress his name and get in line so he'd be assured a table.

Earlier he and Rick had grabbed a breakfast of

toast and coffee at the house. After dropping his brother off at the ski shop with the promise that he'd be back by noon, Nate left for Denver.

Since Laurel Pierce was so determined to hear an explanation of his treatment of her, he would oblige. It would take about one minute. Once he'd satisfied her curiosity, he'd pay for her meal and leave her to enjoy it by herself.

Unless of course she chose not to show up alone...

It was possible that the man who'd answered the phone would be with her. Fine; what he had to say could be said to both of them. In fact, Nate would derive great pleasure from confronting the two parties involved in Spade's betrayal.

When Nate's name was called, he followed the waiter to a table that was being cleared. It happened to be near the window, where he had a view of the parking lot. From this vantage point he'd spot her the moment she arrived.

While he waited for her to make an appearance, he ordered coffee and scanned the front page of the *Denver Post* he'd purchased on his way inside.

Normally he wouldn't have paid any attention to the people seated around him. But when he heard a couple of truckers comment on the good-looking woman coming toward them, he thought they meant one of the waitresses. Distracted, he looked up from the article he'd been reading.

By now it seemed that most of the males within his vision were also watching the progress of the stunning woman with black hair and long legs walking toward Nate. She'd come alone.

During the few moments he'd been reading, Laurel Pierce had entered the restaurant.

She was dressed in the same long-sleeved black sweater he'd seen her wearing on the elevator. Actually, it was a stylish short sweater coat with a matching skirt.

This time he got a glimpse of the deep-purple top she'd worn with her outfit. The black belt made of the same sweater material tied above her belly, subtly revealing her voluptuous shape.

An unexpected rush of adrenaline sent a wave of heat through him, driving him to his feet.

"I'm sorry if I'm a few minutes late." She sounded a little breathless as she sat down in the chair he held out for her. A sweet lemon fragrance caught him off guard, putting his senses on full alert.

"I was early."

Disturbed because he couldn't stop his body's involuntary reaction to her presence, he signaled the waiter before sitting down.

More surprises awaited Nate when she met his gaze head-on. He saw no guilt or evasion there. Instead, the blue eyes gazing into his seemed to implore him.

For what? Forgiveness? Understanding? He'd already been down that road with his father. Forgiveness had nothing to do with it. Only shock and pain.

The waiter chose that moment to come to the table. After Nate passed on ordering anything except a refill of coffee she said, "I'll have a small orange juice and a cinnamon Danish."

When their server walked off, she sat back in the chair. Nate noticed she wore no rings.

"Well, Hawk. This is your opportunity to tell me why you've developed such a strong aversion to me. It must've been building for years to have such a negative effect on you.

"Now that I know Scott has nothing to do with it, I'm ready for whatever blame you want to assign. That way if we should ever meet again in this lifetime, I'll understand when you walk past me as if I don't exist."

That would be an impossibility. He could never feel indifferent to Spade's widow. There was too much history. She'd done something too painful to forget. She was too attractive....

"I'd hoped to avoid this," he began.

She frowned. "If that was true, you wouldn't have interrupted me midsentence on the dance floor. Now that we're alone, so to speak," she said with quiet irony, "why don't you get this off your chest? I can handle it. I'm a big girl now, no pun intended."

Forthrightness seemed to be an integral part of her personality. It was too bad constancy to her spouse hadn't been part of the mix. His gaze lowered to her unborn child, the baby that should have been Spade's.

"Did your husband know about your pregnancy before he died?"

"Yes," she answered without hesitation. After a pause she cocked her head. "What's the matter? Could it be that when you saw me in Breckenridge, you felt left out because it was a piece of news he hadn't shared with you?"

Nate grimaced. "What are you insinuating?"

"Why are you so angry?" Her calm demeanor

shook him. "Let's not pretend that Scott didn't confide in you about...almost everything."

"Is that how you saw our relationship?"

"It was a fact of life I came to grips with early in our marriage. Fifteen thousand miles apart, and he'd steal from our bed to talk to you in the middle of the night. You were his mentor and confidante, as well as his hero."

Mentor? Hero?

This meeting wasn't going the way he'd imagined.

"Tell me, Major. Did you ever see the film *Ben Hur?*" He blinked, nodding briefly. "Scott once compared you to the anchor horse in the chariot race, the strong one that steadied the others and helped them keep their heads as they roared around the Circus Maximus."

Nate wanted her to stop. He didn't want to hear anymore. *Just get this over with, Hawkins.*

"When did you tell him you were pregnant?"

She leaned forward with a puzzled expression on her face. "You mean you want chapter-and-verse-when?"

Perspiration broke out on his body. "Yes."

"Approximately an hour before his jet malfunctioned," she said dry-eyed. "I have no doubt that if he'd survived, *you* would've been the first person he phoned with the news once the demonstration was over."

His hands formed fists on his thighs. She'd just confirmed his growing suspicion that the crash had been due to pilot error.

Her eyes glittered with a strange light. "You're directing all your pent-up anger at the wrong person.

We both know Scott didn't have to fly that day, but he never could resist the opportunity to show the brass how to get the job done right.'' He heard a distinct tremor in her voice.

''When you two meet again in the next life, you have my permission to tell him how you feel about it. But I'm warning you now, you'll have to stand in line!''

Before he knew what had happened, she'd pushed herself away from the table and walked off without looking back. Nate leaped from his chair and threw a twenty on the table, then dashed after her.

She moved fast for a woman so close to her delivery date. He didn't catch up with her until they'd exited the outer doors of the restaurant. A cold gust of air bringing the snow with it blew around the corner of the building, disheveling her hair.

''Laurel! Stop for a moment!''

Her steps slowed. She turned, revealing a face devoid of animation. ''I thought I could handle this meeting. I was wrong.''

The wind whipped against her body, outlining her pregnant shape. She made a brazen picture, standing there with the fur trim of her sweater brushing her cheeks. Almost as if she was mocking him—daring him to speak his mind before she disappeared.

''I must admit I wondered where you found the nerve to face me when we both know Spade wasn't the father. If you left him to figure that out once he got up in the air, then *you'll* have some explaining to do when the two of you meet in the next life.''

He zipped up his leather bomber jacket to insulate

himself against the wind and snow. "That's it. That's all I had to say."

Turning his back on her, he walked toward the Blazer, which was parked at the end of the first row of cars. He released the lock to open the door, but a detaining hand on his arm prevented him from climbing in. When he turned around, he discovered that Laurel had followed him.

Here it comes, tear-filled eyes and all.

"I know you truly believe what you've just accused me of, and I can understand why. But you'd be a 100 percent wrong."

What was she leading up to? He'd let her have one last shot for the hell of it, then he'd take off.

"I thought Scott shared every secret with you. Obviously he kept this one from you, probably because he was afraid to admit something he considered a flaw, especially to someone he admired as much as he did you.

"The truth is, before he went into combat the last time, he had his sperm frozen for in vitro fertilization."

In vitro?

"He didn't have much faith in the procedure, but he was willing to try it for my sake. You know Scott. He wanted to get me pregnant without the help of modern technology." She grimaced wryly. "Never mind that he flew planes that were the very latest in modern technology."

Nate gave her a sympathetic smile, well aware of the irony in Scott's attitude.

"While he was gone, I went into the hospital for

an implant. A couple of months later the doctor confirmed I was pregnant.''

At the unexpected revelation, a tremor rocked Nate's body.

''The second I left his office, I phoned Scott while he was suiting up for that air show. When he heard the news, do you know what he said as soon as he'd stopped whooping for joy as only he could? 'If we have a boy, we're naming him Hawk.' That came as no surprise to me, of course. The rest is history.''

By now Nate couldn't breathe, let alone move. His boots seemed to take root in the snow-swept pavement.

She raised herself on tiptoe to press a kiss against his jaw. The warmth of it stole through his system, melting the chunks of ice already breaking up around his heart.

''Thank you for being so fiercely loyal to him. No wonder he loved you. But I have to tell you I couldn't handle the whole squadron giving me the Hawk treatment. Once was enough.'' She laughed gently as she wiped her eyes.

''I'm sorry, Laurel,'' he said in a tortured whisper. Her explanation had plunged him into a new world of pain.

Thrilled as he was that Spade had known he was going to be a father, Nate would never be able to forgive himself for his cruel treatment of her.

''It's all right now that I understand.''

He didn't deserve her generosity of spirit. He squeezed his eyelids together as if to blot out his shame, the very word he'd used in discussing her with his brother.

She knows I know her secret. It appears the woman has no shame.

I agree it looks that way.

It is that way.

A groan of self-condemnation escaped his throat before he opened his eyes again. She was smiling at him, drawing his attention to the shape of her mouth. He forced himself to look away.

"I can see I'll have to send out birth announcements to all his buddies with the explanation that thanks to modern medical technology, Scott really is the father. The guys will read between the lines and figure it out." He managed an answering smile as he glanced at her again. "They're not hotshots for nothing."

She brushed a hand over her face to wipe off the snow descending on them. Huge flakes covered her black hair, creating an illusion of lace. It brought back memories of the lace mantilla—handmade by nuns—that he'd bought for his mother in Alencon, France, several years earlier.

"Since Scott isn't here to do it, I promise to send you an announcement with a picture after the baby arrives. I'll mail it care of your father's store in Copper Mountain."

Catching the edges of her sweater to her throat, she said, "Now if you'll forgive me, I need to get home before this becomes a whiteout. Goodbye, Hawk."

The second she started to turn away, he grasped her arms to prevent her from leaving.

"I'm not letting you drive anywhere in this. Where's your car?"

"At the other end."

"What make is it?"

"A blue Cavalier."

"I'll find it. Give me your keys."

"You don't have to do this. I'm perfectly capable."

"Don't argue with me. Please."

"All right." She rummaged in her purse and handed him her key ring.

"Stay right where you are," he warned.

"Yes, *sir!*"

With her humorous comeback ringing in his ears, he raced down the line of cars until he found hers. He backed it out and drove it to where the Blazer was parked.

When he saw her walk around to the driver's door, he got out and headed her back to the passenger side.

"What are you doing?"

"I'm driving you home, of course."

"But how will you get back here?"

"A taxi. In you go." He waited until she'd swung her legs inside before shutting the door. Despite her pregnancy, she managed the maneuver with grace. Snow had built up on the windshield. He turned on the engine and the wipers, then asked for directions. As soon as she told him, they drove out of the parking lot.

Once they'd joined the mainstream of traffic, he reached for his cell phone. The information operator gave him the number of a taxi company, and he called for a cab to meet him at the address Laurel had given him.

"It's lucky we weren't inside the restaurant long. Your heater's already putting out warm air."

"It feels good in here."

He cast her a furtive glance. In profile her straight nose gave her face strength and character. Nate had seen very few women in his life he considered true beauties in the classic sense. Laurel was one of them.

It wasn't simply her physical features. It was the way she moved, the way she held herself. Even in the last stage of pregnancy, or maybe because of it, she radiated an inner confidence he hadn't noticed when he'd first met her ten years ago.

She would've been only nineteen back then. Since that time she'd matured. Approaching motherhood had made her even more appealing, if that was possible. Spade had been cheated out of this image of her.

He cleared his throat. "How soon are you due?"

"Three and a half weeks. But as my mother-in-law reminded me the other day, Scotty came ten days early, so you never know."

That was a piece of information Nate hadn't heard before. He grinned. "Sounds like Spade."

"Doesn't it?"

He turned left on Lima Street as she'd instructed. This was an older neighborhood, filled with solid family homes and well-kept yards.

"It's three houses ahead on the right."

Nate slowed down and pulled into the driveway of a two-story colonial. They'd arrived at their destination sooner than he'd anticipated. Sooner than he would've liked...

To him, it felt good to talk about Spade, but he

didn't know if Laurel felt the same way. She'd been quiet on the short drive from the restaurant. After what he'd put her through in the last few days, she had every right to hope she'd seen the last of him.

He came to a stop and shut off the wipers but kept the motor running so she'd stay warm.

"Laurel—before I leave, I need to apologize. There are no words to describe how I feel for my appalling behavior toward you.

"The truth is, I saw you in the elevator with someone before dinner. You kissed him. I assumed he was the other man—the baby's father. Later, when the two of you approached me on the dance floor, I'm afraid I lost it."

She turned her head in his direction. "There's nothing to forgive. If your position and Scott's had been reversed, I'm sure his behavior would've been much worse. He'd have taken one look and knocked my poor brother-in-law unconscious without even asking any questions."

Her brother-in-law.

The sandy-haired man had to be from her side of the family, not Spade's. "Still, I didn't—"

"You're to be congratulated for your restraint," She broke in, her voice amused.

Nate shifted in the seat. "Don't give me any credit. My brother Rick could tell you how close I came to doing real damage."

Her chuckle was as attractive as the rest of her. "It was an honest mistake. Scott would love it if he knew how you rushed to his def—"

Nate never heard the rest of her sentence because someone had wiped the snow from his window and was tapping on the glass. He pressed the button to lower it.

"Oh!" a woman cried in surprise when she saw him at the wheel. She bore a strong resemblance to the woman seated next to him.

"It's all right!" Laurel said. "Major Hawkins brought me home so I wouldn't have to drive back in this storm. Nate? I know that's your real name. Do you prefer Hawk or Nate?"

"Nate's fine."

"I'll try to remember. Anyway, Nate, this is my older sister, Julie Marsden. It was her husband, Brent, you saw at the lodge with me."

They both said hello at the same time, but her sister looked anxious.

"Forgive me for interrupting, but there's a taxi right behind you. I thought maybe your labor had started and you needed help."

Laurel shook her head. "Not yet."

"I called for a cab to run me back to the restaurant," Nate explained.

At this point he had no choice but to put his words into action. It was the last thing he wanted to do. After shutting the window, he turned off the engine and got out of the car.

Once he'd signaled the taxi driver to wait for him, he went around to Laurel's side to help her out. It had already snowed three inches and wouldn't be stopping anytime soon. She and her sister needed to get inside the house. He needed to leave.

She grasped his forearm. "Thank you for taking the trouble to drive me home. I appreciate it more than you know."

"I'm grateful to you, too," her sister added. "When the snow started, I worried about the roads icing up."

The taxi driver laid on the horn and Laurel looked up at Nate. "He sounds like he's in a hurry. I guess you'd better go. Goodbye and thanks again."

"Laurel—" he began. There was a lot more he wanted to say, but he'd run out of time. He nodded to her instead before getting into the cab. He gave the driver the address of the restaurant—then had to fight with himself to look straight ahead and not back at her as he wanted to.

Her eyes had seemed strangely haunted just now. In the next few minutes, he imagined, she'd be sobbing her heart out.

Their conversation had forced her to remember the dreadful day she'd received the news that her husband had died. Talking with Nate had been too great a reminder of Spade and everything she'd lost.

Nate's memories were different. Although she'd been Spade's wife, she didn't remind him of Spade, except indirectly. And during their marriage, Nate hadn't really seen them interact as a couple.

Laurel Pierce was a strong, vital force in her own right. A person who'd taken on new stature with her ability to face death, the implacable enemy, and then forgiven Nate's cruelty with a completeness of heart. A brave woman who was preparing to bring a child into the world alone.

He grimaced at the thought that after wanting to be a father for such a long time, Spade wouldn't be there to experience it.

CHAPTER FIVE

LAUREL HURRIED into the living room. She peeked through the front curtain in time to see the cab disappear from view. It left her with a disturbing emptiness....

"I assume there's been a reconciliation? Otherwise he wouldn't have insisted on bringing you home. Want to talk about it, or would you rather be alone for a while?"

She whirled around to face her sister. Julie could read her moods better than anyone. However, this was one time Laurel didn't know where to start when it came to sorting out her feelings.

Julie must have picked up on her ambivalence. She simply said, "Why don't you at least get out of that wet sweater coat."

"I must look like a drowned rat," Laurel murmured as she walked into the hall to hang it up in the closet.

Her sister followed. "All drowned rats should look so good. By the way, I had no idea the legendary Hawk was that attractive. His nickname doesn't suit him."

"Not physically anyway." Laurel shut the door. He didn't want her to call him Hawk. She could understand. Those nicknames were reserved for the men within their own private fraternity.

"Funny," Julie murmured. "All these years I'd been picturing someone dark and wiry with an aquiline nose."

Laurel averted her eyes. "He's hardly that."

"Hardly," her sister mocked. "He must be something in full dress uniform."

"Don't you know all men are supposed to look better in them?"

"Well, let's agree Major Hawkins doesn't need one to make a serious impact. Don't tell Brent I said that."

"Don't worry. When I first met Hawk—I mean Nate—I was careful to keep my observations to myself around Scott."

"Wise girl. It might give a husband a complex."

"I think a lot of the guys hit the gym more often because of him."

"Scott included?"

Their eyes met before Laurel nodded.

"Tell me what happened this morning."

"You won't believe it. Now that I've had a chance to think about it, I realize I should've figured it out days ago."

"Figured out what? Don't keep me in suspense!"

"The short version is, he thought I was pregnant with Brent's child."

"*What?*"

"That's only part of it. If you want to hear the long version, we'll have to go into the study where I can put my feet up. I'm starting to swell."

"I should have suggested it, but your news made me forget everything else. Come on."

They walked through the hall to the den. Laurel stacked some cushions to prop up her feet. After removing her shoes she lay on the couch with a sigh.

"It's a good thing I'm about ready to deliver." She rolled her eyes toward her sister. "You'll be needing this couch before long."

"Not for a while. At least I haven't had any morning sickness this time around."

"Lucky you."

"All right," Julie murmured. "Tell me what went on."

Laurel turned on her side toward her sister, who sat in the chair opposite her, the one Brent claimed whenever there were sports on TV.

"It's very touching really." Without warning, tears stung her eyes. "As soon as Nate realized his mistake, he apologized. I heard the sorrow in his voice. It was something I'll never forget."

She felt her sister's speculative glance. "Considering he was so horrible to you, that's quite a turnaround."

"I won't deny how much it hurt, but he had his reasons. In the first place, he didn't know Scott and I were trying to get pregnant through in vitro fertilization. Secondly, he did the math and knew I hadn't been with Scott for almost a year.

"Ever since he saw me on Saturday night, he's been worried that I was unfaithful to my husband."

"Ooh."

Laurel sat up. "That's not the worst. He thought that when I told Scott we were having a baby, Scott was devastated because he knew it wasn't his child and…his plane crashed.''

"Good heavens!" her sister cried.

"Nate didn't say that in so many words, but I read between the lines. As I told you, he and Scott were so close, I assumed he knew everything personal about our lives.

"Obviously we've both made some false assumptions, but everything he thought or did was out of loyalty to Scott. You can't blame a man for that.''

"No," her sister concurred.

"If Nate hadn't agreed to meet me today, he would've gone on assuming I'd done the worst thing you could do to a spouse who was about to climb into the cockpit. And I wouldn't have known anything about it.

"Imagine if some of the other guys were to see me right now. They'd think the same thing—that I'd betrayed Scott!''

She buried her face in her hands until she could regain control of her emotions.

"Don't worry, Laurel. I'm sure Nate will inform everyone who matters of the true situation.''

She finally lifted her head, smoothing the tears from her cheeks. "I told him I'd send out birth announcements making it clear that Scott was the father.''

"That's a good idea," Julie said quietly.

"You know, when Scott died I hurt so much in the beginning I couldn't even talk about it. Many friends called Mom and Dad's house, including Nate, but I asked the family to tell them I couldn't come to the phone.''

"That was only natural. If anything happened to Brent, I can't even imagine how I'd cope."

"Still, if I'd been a stronger person, I would have talked to them and shared the news that I was pregnant with my husband's baby. Then none of this would've happened. Not until this morning did I realize how much Scott's buddies needed a chance to mourn with me."

"I'm sure they understood, but I wonder why Nate didn't attend the funeral."

"In his letter he said something unavoidable had come up, which made it impossible for him to be there."

"It must have been fairly serious for him, of all people, not to attend."

"I agree." Laurel wondered about that, as well as other times when Nate had disappointed Scott by not being available to join them somewhere.

"Well, now that everything's been resolved, you and Nate had a chance to talk about someone you both loved, and that's a good thing."

Laurel nodded. "I didn't want him to go. In fact, I had the impression he would've liked to stay longer, but the taxi was waiting. Something tells me Nate's leave has come to an end, which is why he agreed to meet with me today. Thank God he did!"

"You were smart to deliver that letter in person. It led to the best possible outcome.…"

"Apparently I have his brother to thank for that."

"What do you mean?"

"Nate more or less said he wouldn't have phoned me if it hadn't been for his brother's urging. I wish I could thank him."

"Why can't you? Just pick up the phone. When he understands how important his intervention was, he'll be glad he played such a vital role."

"I don't know. If it was confidential…"

"Then phone him right now, before Nate returns to Copper Mountain. He'll know whether or not to tell Nate you called."

"That's true." Laurel sniffed. "I've got the phone numbers for the store and the house in my purse."

"Good. Bring them into the kitchen." Julie got to her feet. "You can call while I fix lunch. I'm starving. I'm afraid I'm going to put on more weight than usual with this baby."

"I was constantly hungry at first, too." Laurel followed her through the house. "It'll be just my luck if his brother's not home."

"If you do reach him and all goes well, find out if Nate's going to be in Colorado a while longer. You could invite them both to dinner. If they have wives or girlfriends, invite them too."

"I didn't see a ring on Nate's finger, but you never know. I'm through making assumptions about anything."

"It's a lesson to all of us. Well, if he can make it, you'll be able to have the visit you were deprived of at the funeral. In fact, it wouldn't hurt for my husband to see another side to Scott's friend."

"Brent was so angry that night," Laurel said.

"That's why I decided to wait to tell him about the baby. The major has no idea how close my husband came to popping him one, even though he would've ended up on the floor."

Few men would be a match for Nate Hawkins.

"Thank goodness it didn't come to that." Laurel hugged her sister. "You're too good to me, you know that? If Nate and his brother can come, I'll prepare dinner."

"How about we do it together?"

RICK HAD BEEN going over the books in his dad's office when he heard the phone ring. Nina or Jim usually answered so he kept on working. In another minute Jim poked his head inside the door. "Phone's for you."

"I should've gotten it. Thanks."

Only a handful of people knew Rick was in Colorado. If they'd tried to reach him, they would have used his cell number. It couldn't be his father or brother, or Jim would've said something. Natalie knew better than to phone him again.

He picked up the receiver. "This is Rick."

"Oh, good!" said a female voice. To his relief it didn't sound like Natalie. "I'm glad I found you. This is Laurel Pierce."

Rick's gaze flicked to his watch. It was twelve-thirty. Nate was supposed to have met her at ten. She wouldn't be calling unless the storm had prevented Nate from arriving at the restaurant. Maybe he was stuck in a snowdrift on the mountain road without his cell phone.

"Mrs. Pierce. What can I do for you?"

"I realize you're at work so I'll make this short. I'm calling to thank you for giving Nate my letter. This morning he indicated that if you hadn't encouraged him to get in touch with me, our meeting would never have taken place."

So they did make contact. "I had very little to do with it."

"He told me otherwise," she said with tangible warmth. "Because of you, we were able to clear up a serious misunderstanding. You don't have any idea how grateful I am to you."

Rick sat forward in the swivel chair. "I'm glad there was a satisfactory resolution to your problem." He meant it. He'd never seen his brother manifest such forbidding behavior before.

"You can't imagine what it meant to me." There was an unmistakable tremor in her voice. It led him to believe she'd really suffered. So had Nate. "I have one more favor to ask."

"What is it?" he asked, intrigued.

"If you're free, I'd like to invite you and Nate to dinner this week or next. That is if his leave isn't up yet."

She didn't know he'd retired? "That sounds very nice."

"I hope it means you can come. You see, the storm got so bad Nate insisted on driving me home in my car. But the taxi he called for came the second we reached the driveway. As a result, we didn't get a chance to finish talking."

Nate had insisted on driving her home? What was going on with his brother?

"I'll tell you what. As soon as I see Nate, I'll ask him to call you."

"That would be wonderful. Oh, and this invitation includes your wives or girlfriends."

His eyes widened in surprise. How was it she still

knew so little after meeting with Nate? But all he said was, "I'll pass that along, Mrs. Pierce."

"Thank you. Now I'd better let you go. I hope to talk to you again shortly."

"Me, too."

No sooner had he hung up the phone than the subject of their conversation walked into the office covered in snow. His arms were loaded with food and drinks. That in itself suggested a major change in his mood.

"I thought you just had breakfast with Laurel Pierce," he said.

"Neither of us could eat. Now I'm famished."

That was obvious as his brother emptied everything onto the desk. Rick counted four double cheeseburgers, two orders of chicken strips, two large fries and two cheesecakes.

Incredible, considering Nate hadn't exhibited an appetite since they'd flown in last week.

Her surprising phone call had given Rick some idea of what had happened. At this point he could sit back and patiently watch as his brother consumed two-thirds of their lunch without talking.

Nate finally lifted his head and their eyes met. "What?"

"I was about to ask you the same question," Rick said as he munched on a fry. "But I can wait till you're through eating. If you're still hungry, go ahead and have my cheesecake, too."

"You don't want it?"

"Evidently not as much as you do."

"Thanks."

His lips twitched when his brother immediately helped himself to a second dessert.

"How was the weather in Denver?"

"Typical. Two or three inches. It'll melt the minute the sun comes out." He finished the cheesecake in a couple of bites.

"That's odd. I heard it was so bad, a certain pregnant woman had to be driven home from a certain pancake house."

Nate's head shot up. "You've talked to Laurel?"

Rick had been right; his brother had undergone a complete transformation since he'd left Copper Mountain that morning.

"I just got off the phone with her."

"Is she all right?" Nate's voice was urgent.

"She's fine."

"Thank God." He took a deep breath. "She seemed okay when I dropped her off, but after the hell I've put her through, it wouldn't surprise me if she went into early labor. I couldn't take that."

No…I don't think you could.

"We've been invited to dinner," Rick murmured, watching carefully for his brother's first reaction.

"When?"

"It's up to you. I told her you'd call as soon as you got back from Denver." He pushed away from the desk and stood up. "I'll go find Nina so she can take her lunch break."

His words were wasted on Nate, who'd already unfolded the badly crumpled letter to find Laurel Pierce's phone number. Rick paused at the door.

"She mentioned we could bring our wives or girlfriends. Better make it Saturday night. That way we'll have time to hustle up a couple of women.''

Without waiting for a reply Rick hustled out of the office.

Five minutes later Nate joined him in the rental shop. Instead of pitching in to help him put returned skis back in place, he prowled around like a hungry wolf.

''What's up?''

''The line's busy,''

''Don't jump to conclusions.''

''What's that supposed to mean?''

''Just what I said. Her baby will come when nature intends. So, who's the father?''

''Spade,'' Nate whispered.

For everyone involved, Rick had to admit he was happy about that piece of news. ''By what miracle?''

During the lull between customers, Nate treated him to the full explanation.

''That's pretty miraculous, all right.''

His brother nodded. ''Under the circumstances, I don't know why she's even speaking to me.''

''Neither do I,'' Rick said, baiting him, ''but for some reason she wants to see you again.''

''Talking to me has brought back memories of Spade.''

''I'm sure that's part of it.''

Nate darted him a puzzled glance. ''What do you mean?''

He was so quick to respond, Rick suspected Nate had feelings he didn't even recognize yet.

Like Nate, Rick had perfect vision. He'd only seen

Laurel Pierce for a moment when she'd thrust that letter at him. The woman was a genuine knockout.

"Nothing," he murmured. "What did you think I meant?"

After an extended pause, Nate's eyes slid away. "I'm going back to the office to try her number again."

"You do that," Rick said to his retreating frame.

LAUREL WAS UPSTAIRS making the boys' beds when the phone rang. Dropping Joey's pillow, she hurried into her bedroom to answer it. However, when she picked up the receiver, she discovered her sister had already picked up the kitchen extension.

Nate was on the line asking for her. Excited that he'd gotten back to her this fast, she said, "I'm here, Julie."

"Oh—good. I'll hang up."

As soon as she heard the click, she said, "Nate?"

"Hello, Laurel. My brother told me you called."

It was so wonderful to hear warmth instead of anger in his tone, she felt a wave of happiness wash over her.

"Did he tell you I want both of you to come to dinner?"

"You're sure it wouldn't be an imposition?"

"I wouldn't have asked if it was. Naturally, the invitation includes partners."

"Rick and I are still single. Since we only flew to Colorado for a family visit, we'd be coming alone."

That meant Nate would be leaving soon... Thank goodness Julie had encouraged her to make the call today.

"I didn't realize that. When I reached your brother at the ski shop, I assumed he worked there. How soon do you have to report back to the base?"

There was an odd silence before he said, "I don't."

"What do you mean?"

"Let's just say everything's uncertain at the moment."

"You mean about returning to Leeuwarden? Has your assignment changed since then?"

"It's a long story. Because of a family crisis, I resigned my commission in the Air Force, but it may have been premature."

Resigned? The legendary Hawk? She sank down on the side of her bed.

"Depending on the outcome, I may go back in. Right now, all plans are on hold."

A top gun like Scott—or Nate—might lose his life for the Air Force, but he didn't leave it of his own free will. Whatever had happened in Nate's family must be extremely serious for him to even consider giving up a career that had defined his life....

She wished she knew him better. There was so much he wasn't saying. Maybe in time he'd feel comfortable enough to tell her what was wrong.

"You must be climbing the walls with boredom," she teased, hoping to add a little levity to the unexpected turn in their conversation. "You probably need a distraction. We'd better get you over to the house quick!" His deep chuckle informed her she was right. "How about tomorrow evening?"

"That's fine."

Good.

''The reason it has to be soon is that you never know when this baby is going to make its entrance.''

When she saw the doctor on Thursday, he might tell her she'd dilated another centimeter and he'd curtail her activities until the big event. She wasn't about to take a chance on that happening. Who knew when she'd see Nate again otherwise?

''For the moment, and I'm stressing that last word, all is quiet on the Western Front,'' she whispered.

He broke into uninhibited male laughter, the kind that resonated clear through her body. When it subsided, he said, ''Tomorrow night it is. What time?''

''Six? Is that too early?''

''No, no. We'll be there. I'm looking forward to meeting your family under more…favorable circumstances.''

She smiled into the phone. ''You'll like Mike and Joey. Just be prepared for a thousand questions, and remember my nephews are down on girls.''

''How old are they?''

''Eight and ten.''

''Sounds normal for their age. Which boy is which?''

''Joey's the younger. He plans to be a test pilot for the Air Force.''

''What about Mike?'' She thought she could hear him smiling back.

''He's gotten past that stage. At the moment he wants to be a pro golfer.''

''Where did that come from?''

''Brent. He might've turned pro if he hadn't met Julie.''

''Now you tell me.''

"Tell you what?"

"I came close to being decked by a lethal weapon on the dance floor."

It was her turn to laugh. "I guess he could do some damage with that golf arm if he wanted to."

"He would've had every right." Another pause. "I'm sorry about the other night, Laurel. All of it." She could still hear his pain.

"Will you stop?" Her hand tightened on the receiver. "I know how sorry you are, but I honestly haven't given it another thought. You're beating yourself up for no reason."

"You're a remarkable person."

I could say the same thing about you.

"I'm a woman on the brink of becoming a mom. It puts everything else in perspective."

"And no wonder... Are you frightened?"

He demonstrated a surprising sweetness she hadn't noticed in many men.

"I think every pregnant woman experiences some fear. The thought of being responsible for another human being is quite daunting."

"Yes, it would be."

"However, now that I've reached my ninth month, I have to admit all I can think about is getting this show on the road. A ride in an F-16 might just do the trick, but since you don't have a plane to call your own right now..."

"There's no back seat in an F-16, but if there was one, I'd be so panicked I'm afraid I'd go into a dive I couldn't control."

"We'd make a pair, all right," she said before

joining in his laughter. "I guess I'll just have to stay weighted to the ground until the blessed event."

"Are you having a boy or a girl?"

"I've decided to find out when he or she is born."

"That's worked for centuries."

"Both families are upset with me. The parents, I mean."

"It's your baby."

"Exactly. Thank you for backing me up. Anyway, I'm looking forward to seeing you and your brother tomorrow night."

"We'll be there. Thank you, Laurel."

"You're welcome. Bye."

Pleased with the arrangements, she hung up the receiver and walked back to the boys' room. Julie had finished making the beds. She looked up.

"I heard a lot of laughter coming from your room. Do you know how good it sounded?"

"It felt good. He and his brother are coming at six tomorrow night."

"Are they bringing anyone?"

"No. I didn't think Nate was married yet, and he confirmed it. His brother's single, too. According to Scott, there were several women who wanted to become Mrs. Hawkins, but it didn't happen.

"Julie, help me plan a menu! I want it to be special."

"When it comes down to it, most men love plain old roast beef with mashed potatoes and gravy."

"You're right. I think beef tenderloin and your homemade rolls."

"And Mom's gelato for dessert," they said simultaneously.

Laurel realized she hadn't laughed this much in more than a year.

CHAPTER SIX

"WELCOME TO BUNDLES OF JOY. Can I help you gentlemen?"

"I'm looking for a baby gift. Something in white or yellow since I don't know if it's a boy or a girl."

"Were you thinking along the lines of clothing? Or a blanket to wrap the baby in?"

"I'm not sure."

"Give me a moment and I'll gather some things to show you."

"Thank you."

"Hey, Nate," Rick called to him. "Look at this." Nate wandered over to his brother. "A baby monitor. It tells the parents what their child is doing from another room."

"How would you ever get any sleep?"

"That's what I'm trying to figure out."

Nate had been a lot of places around the globe. He'd done a lot of unusual things in his life. But he'd never shopped in a store devoted to babies. Judging by Rick's reaction as he moved from one display to another in wonder, this was a new experience for him, too.

"Here we are." The clerk caught his attention

again. They both went back to the counter, where she held up a little white fleece sleeper outfit with feet.

"Are you sure you're not showing us doll clothes?" Rick teased the woman.

She laughed. "I can assure you this was made for an average-size newborn. It's soft, lightweight and washable. See these mitts? They're sewn in to fit over the baby's hands so their nails won't scratch their faces.

"To go with it is this lovely pale-yellow chenille blanket with fringe. It too is washable and makes a wonderful wrap because it aligns itself to the baby's body."

The picture of Laurel Pierce's pregnant figure outlined in the wind refused to leave Nate's mind.

"You'll notice the yellow stitchery on the embroidered portion of the sleeper matches it."

Nate plunged his hand into the cotton fabric. The softness sold him.

"I'll take both." He reached for his wallet and pulled out a credit card. "Will you wrap them as a gift?"

"Of course. We have some little courtesy cards right here. Go ahead and pick something you like."

There had to be several dozen. He thumbed through the selection until he came to one that stood out. "For your highflyer."

Reaching for a pen on the counter, he made a minor insertion above the "For" and the "your." Now it read, "For the son or daughter of your highflyer. God keep you both in His care. Nate."

"Here we are." The clerk had entwined a baby rattle in the ribbon.

"That's perfect." He handed her the enclosed card. "Would you tape this to the package please?"

"I'd be happy to." After the woman had attached the card, she put the package in a sack and they left the shop. When they reached the car park Nate checked his watch.

"We're going to have to step on it. We've only got a half hour to get across Denver and we'll be fighting five o'clock traffic all the way."

"Relax. I'll get us there on time."

"I'm holding you to that."

"I do believe you're nervous. How did you ever end up as a pilot?"

"How about concentrating on your driving?"

"She's forgiven you, man."

"I don't see why," Nate lamented.

"Because she's an understanding woman."

"She's courageous, too."

"Yeah. She had guts to confront you in the state you were in."

Nate grimaced. "That goes without saying, but I'm talking about the baby."

"Women have them every day."

"Not in her circumstances."

"She appears to be managing fine. Otherwise how do you explain the way she was enjoying herself on the dance floor the other night—before she saw you, I mean?"

Any reminder of that painful encounter increased Nate's guilt. "It's all a big cover-up. She and Scott had something special."

"Maybe so, but it's been close to a year since she

was with her husband. It looks like she's chosen to go on living.''

"How the hell do you do that when you've been madly in love?''

"I don't know, and I pray I never have to find out," Rick muttered. "I suppose we could ask Dad when he gets back from his honeymoon.''

That was another painful subject they hadn't touched on since the newlyweds had been dropped off at the airport.

"Sorry, Nate. I didn't mean to bring that up. But the situation isn't the same. Dad's not having a baby.''

"At least not that we know about.''

"Jeez.''

"WHAT DO YOU THINK?'' Laurel asked as she walked in the kitchen to get the Caesar salads from the refrigerator. "It was either the beige-on-black print or the green two-piece.''

Her sister looked up from the gravy she was stirring. "Pregnant or not, you know that's my favorite outfit on you. Black's your best color. Mike had just entered the kitchen, and Julie turned to him. "Aunt Laurel has the salads made. Will you please put them on the dining room table?''

"Joey has to help, too.''

"He's already filling the glasses with ice. As for you, young man, all you're supposed to say is 'Yes, Mother.'''

"Sorry. Yes, Mother.''

"Be sure to place them above and a little to the left of the left fork.''

"I know where they go from the last time we had a party."

"Just making sure," she teased.

Laurel watched him take two plates into the other room with the greatest of care.

"You're such a wonderful mother, Julie."

Her sister scoffed. "You heard Mike just now."

"But you don't let him get away with anything. You're constantly teaching, yet you do it with kindness and love. I'm getting nervous. I'm afraid I'll never be the kind of mom you are."

"After observing all the mistakes I've made, you'll be much better."

"I've been with your family far too long," Laurel said. "When you and Brent invited me to stay with you for a while, I'm sure you never dreamed I'd still be here."

She waited until Mike had returned for more salads. When he'd left the kitchen she said, "Julie, if I asked you a question, do you think you could be honest with me? Even if you thought it would hurt me?"

"If you're going to ask whether it's all right if you settle in Denver after the baby's born, Brent and I already discussed it months ago. In fact Brent was the one to bring it up. You know his Realtor friend, Jed?"

"Yes?"

"Brent asked him to keep an eye out for a condo you might like. Someplace close to us. Does that answer your question?"

Tears smarted Laurel's eyes. She was so touched, she couldn't talk.

"Good evening, ladies!" The subject of their conversation breezed into the kitchen, looking smart in his tan suit. He kissed his wife's neck. "What can I do to help?"

"Hey, Mom?" Joey burst in right behind him, carrying the empty ice bucket. He put it on the counter. "There's a car in the driveway. Should I get the door?"

"Why don't we leave that to your Aunt Laurel."

Laurel felt Brent's inquisitive gaze on her as she dabbed at her eyes. Later she'd thank him for being the best brother-in-law on earth.

"Come on." She reached for Joey's hand. "We'll greet our guests together." They passed Mike on his way back to the kitchen for the rest of the salads.

Joey was so eager he ran ahead and opened the door on two surprised men who hadn't rung the bell yet.

Her nephew stared up at Nate in awe. "I know who *you* are."

Nate grinned. "You must be Joey."

"Yup. And you're Uncle Scotty's best friend, Hawk!"

"That's right."

"His real name is Nate, Joey. And please say hello to his brother, Rick."

"Hi, Rick."

"Hi, yourself." The handsome man in the stone-gray suit was grinning, too.

"Come on in," Joey piped up. "We've been waiting for you all day."

The innocent remark reminded Laurel that she was standing there mesmerized by the sight of them, just like her nephew. The blood rose to her cheeks before she had the wits to invite them inside.

"This is for your mother." Rick produced a bottle of wine, which he handed to Joey.

"Thanks. But I heard Dad say she can't have any alcohol because she's going to have a baby, too!"

"That's all right, Joey," Laurel interjected. "She'll appreciate it, anyway. Why don't you take it to her."

"Okay. I'll be right back!"

"Out of the mouths of babes. I warned you," an embarrassed Laurel said as she eyed Nate.

His understanding smile sent a current of warmth through her body. "So you did." From behind his back he produced a beautifully wrapped baby gift. There was a yellow rattle tied up in the ribbon. "This is for you."

"You shouldn't have, but I'll admit I'm excited you did. Come into the living room and make yourselves comfortable while I open it."

The two men followed her into the other room. They waited until she'd found a chair before they sat on the sofa facing her.

Laurel read the little card first, then looked over at Nate. "You obviously went to a lot of trouble to find such a perfect sentiment," she said. With hands that trembled, she undid the wrapping.

"Oh, how darling!" she said, lifting the sleeper outfit from the tissue. Beneath it was a chenille baby blanket in a soft yellow. She spread it over her knees. "I love it!"

She raised her head. "Thank you, Nate. What beautiful gifts! You've *really* got me excited now."

His eyes smiled back. "I'm glad."

At this point, the rest of the family had joined them. Everyone rose while Laurel made formal introductions. But the second Brent started shaking hands with Rick, he had a strange look on his face.

"Wait a minute... With a suit on I didn't recognize you! Honey," he called to Julie, who'd wandered over to admire the baby gifts. "This is Lucky Hawkins! You *are* Lucky, aren't you?"

Rick's lips curved into a broad smile. "Guilty as charged."

"I'm sorry," Julie murmured, eyeing her husband helplessly. Laurel was equally confused.

"Mom, he's that Formula 1 race car driver on TV. He's won a ton of races. Dad and I always watch them."

"You're right, Mike!" his father chimed in, looking as full of wonder as his son. "He's Colorado's own famous driver. I saw you interviewed in England a few weeks ago, after that win. You drove a spectacular race."

"Thank you. It was a tough one."

"You're so cool!" Mike cried. "That's what I want to be when I grow up! How did you learn to drive cars like that?"

Apparently golf was out. A new hero had entered the scene.

"Why don't we have dinner first, then maybe he'll answer some of your questions," Julie admonished in a gentle tone.

"Can I sit beside Nate?"

Good for Joey, who wasn't swayed by a glamorous sports star. At that instant, Nate met Laurel's smile with a private one of his own, as if he could read her mind.

"I'll tell you what," their mother said. "We'll seat you between Nate and Laurel. Mike can sit next to Rick."

With Brent at one end and Julie and Laurel at the other, the men could converse to their heart's content.

An hour later all five males were still deep in conversation and had finished up a second helping of gelato. Laurel and her sister disappeared into the kitchen to load the dishwasher.

"You'd think the topic of race cars and F-16s might've been exhausted by now," Julie muttered.

"Are you kidding?" Laurel shook her head. "You haven't been around this kind of thing before. *I* have. Mike and Joey are having the time of their lives."

"So's my husband."

"Try living with it twenty-four hours a day," she said while she washed the china by hand.

For once her sister didn't smile. "That would be too hard for me on a regular basis."

"It *was* too hard at times," Laurel confessed. "Whatever you do, point your boys toward careers that don't have to do with speed. One day their wives will thank you. And Julie? Thanks for putting on this dinner for me."

"It was a team effort."

"I know, but it's your home. I love you."

"I love you, too. Besides, it was a lot of fun." She dried the last of the crystal. "They're both extraordinary guys."

"Not your run-of-the-mill variety, that's for sure," Laurel agreed.

"No. It's refreshing to meet men who aren't full of themselves. Some of Brent's golf buddies from work are insufferable."

Laurel frowned. "You know, the more I'm around Nate, the more I sense that Scott wasn't as confident as the Hawkins brothers. That's probably why he always had to beat everyone else. I'm not criticizing my husband. It's more an observation than anything. You do wonder what instills confidence, why one person has it and another doesn't."

Her sister let out a deep sigh. "If we had the answer to that question... We've tried to raise Mike and Joey the same way, yet Joey's the one who doesn't worry what anyone else thinks. Mike's already having a harder time."

Laurel cleaned the sink. "The business about the hand that rocks the cradle is downright scary."

"No, it isn't," Julie insisted. "You're just feeling broody."

"Is that what I am?"

She didn't hear her sister's reply because Nate had entered the kitchen. He was alone.

"I knew I'd find the two of you in here with the dishes done. Forgive us."

Julie shook her head. "With two celebrities in the house, I wouldn't have expected anything else."

"Your sons are delightful. So was dinner. Whether you believe me or not, that was the best meal Rick and I've had in years."

"We're glad you enjoyed it. Now, if you and Laurel will excuse me, I'm going to rescue your brother.

My boys have school tomorrow and they need to get ready for bed.''

Laurel tried to be unobtrusive about putting her shoes back on, but it was a lost cause.

"Please don't bother on my account," he said behind her.

"Caught in the act." She chuckled as she turned around. "Despite current opinion, pregnancy is not an unalloyed joy."

She saw the concern in his eyes. "You've overdone things today. You should lie down."

"I will."

"But not until we leave, so I'm going to say goodbye now."

"Please don't go," she blurted before she realized how desperate that sounded. "What I mean is, with the children around we didn't get a private moment to talk."

His gaze played over her upturned features. "I'm going to be in Denver tomorrow on business. I could stop by."

"That would be wonderful. Other than my weekly doctor's appointment at eleven, I'm free."

"How are you getting there?"

"My sister. She doesn't work on Tuesdays or Thursdays."

"Why don't I drive you instead?"

"I—I couldn't let you do that," she stammered.

"I'd like to." He seemed to mean it. "Afterward, we could bring some Mexican food back to the house. That way you could rest."

He was one of the most considerate men she'd ever met. "What about your business?"

"It can be accomplished before I come for you. How far is your doctor from here?"

"Ten minutes."

"Then I'll come by about quarter to eleven."

"All right. Thank you. I'll be ready."

With a slight groan she bent over to pick up her shoes. If he heard her, he was gentleman enough not to comment. Instead he held the door for her.

Brent and Rick had moved to the living room with Julie. When Laurel saw them from the foyer, they were locked in more conversation. Rick must have seen his brother because he got to his feet, and soon everyone had congregated at the front door.

Brent shook Rick's hand. "Thanks for the most exciting evening we've had around here in years. We also appreciated the wine. After our baby arrives, my wife and I will enjoy it."

"That's the idea." Rick grinned. "I'm already looking forward to our golf date. According to the weatherman, there's no more snow forecast in the foresecable future."

"Let's hope he's right for once. It's been a long winter."

"Tell us about it," Nate muttered. He reached out to shake Brent's hand. "I want to thank you for not knocking me through the lodge's plate-glass window the other night."

Her brother-in-law's embarrassed laughter made Laurel smile.

"Was I that obvious?"

"You had every right. I'm afraid my behavior was reprehensible," Nate admitted.

"It's forgotten."

"It is," Laurel assured Nate, looking up at him. "You made Joey's night. Thanks again for the beautiful baby gifts. I'll see you tomorrow."

He nodded before opening the front door. Rick filed out after him, and Laurel watched them walk quickly to the Blazer. When she realized too much cold air had come in, she hurriedly shut the door.

Her sister followed her into the living room, where she'd gone to gather up Nate's gifts and the wrapping paper.

"What was that about tomorrow?"

"When Nate said he was going to leave, I tried to detain him so I could find out why he didn't come to Scott's funeral. I have a feeling he resigned his commission in the Air Force for the same reason.

"He said he already had business in Denver in the morning and could stop by. When I told him I had an appointment at the doctor's, he volunteered to drive me."

"That's going beyond the call of duty."

"I know. He's trying to make up for what happened in Breckenridge."

"I think it's more a case of wanting to talk to you alone. With the boys around tonight, no one could get a word in edgewise."

"True. It *was* a fun evening, wasn't it?"

"Fun doesn't cover it. Brent's eyes almost fell out of his head when he met *the* Lucky Hawkins in the flesh! Imagine two such gorgeous men belonging to one family."

"Now that I think about it, Scott once mentioned that Nate had a brother who was involved in racing, but I never gave it any thought."

"Why would you when your worlds were so far removed?" She flipped off the lights. "Let's get to bed."

"Nate said the same thing when he saw me trying to put my shoes back on."

"Perceptive man."

They climbed the stairs. "Can you believe what lovely presents he got me?"

"They'll be perfect to take the baby home from the hospital."

"That's what I was thinking." They reached Laurel's bedroom door. "You did so much for me tonight, Julie. After my baby arrives, I plan to be here for you whenever you need it."

"That's a deal. Good night. Sleep well."

"You, too."

Laurel entered the bedroom, dropped her shoes on the floor and walked straight to the crib. She shook the little rattle a couple of times, then placed it in the corner next to Winnie-the-Pooh.

Without conscious thought, she put the sleeper outfit on the mattress. Taking the blanket, she spread it over the bottom portion, trying to imagine a real live baby lying there.

Tomorrow she'd find out just how close she was to having her baby. She hoped it happened before Nate figured out his plans and left Colorado. It would be nice if he could see the baby dressed in the things he'd given her. If not, she'd take a picture and have copies made to send out with the birth announcements.

Though it was past time to get into bed, she read Nate's card one more time. *God keep you both in His care.* Moved by the words, she felt her eyes moisten before she took some tape from the drawer and fastened the card inside her new baby book. Her first gift.

NATE WALKED in the back door ahead of Rick. The red light on the kitchen phone was blinking. Maybe it was Laurel calling to tell him there'd been a change in plans and her sister would be driving her to the doctor after all.

His brows drew together at the thought. He picked up the phone to listen to the message.

"Boys? It's your dad. I would've called on your cell phones, but I misplaced your numbers. I hope all is well with you. Pam and I will be home on Saturday afternoon, a day earlier than planned. Don't worry about picking us up from the airport. We'll take the shuttle bus to the Copper Mountain Inn. I'll call you when we've checked in. If you two don't have plans, we'd like to have dinner with you that evening. See you soon."

After that, there were no other messages.

"Anything important?" Rick murmured.

Nate handed him the phone. "I'll let you be the judge."

When his brother hung up, his grave expression echoed Nate's state of mind. "So now he feels he can't come home?"

"How can he when Mom's things are still in their bedroom…"

"Oh, hell…" Rick rubbed the side of his neck, an unconscious gesture on his brother's part. He was as distraught as Nate.

"One thing's certain. He doesn't sound like the father we used to know. I couldn't tell if he was holding back because he realizes he's made a horrendous mistake, in which case Pam will be the one to suffer. Or—"

"Or he doesn't want the honeymoon to end and doesn't dare let us know," Rick finished the sentence for him. "Pick your poison."

"No, thanks," Nate muttered. "If the answer is the latter, then this business of tiptoeing around us is going to have to stop."

Rick nodded. "One thing we can do before he gets home is pack up Mother's personal things and store them. That way he can go through them when he's ready."

"Good idea," Nate agreed. "After I return from Denver tomorrow, we'll get busy."

"I'll round up some boxes from the back of the store. It shouldn't take too long. At least they'll be able to use the room."

"There's no way we're going to let our father check into some hotel whenever he and his wife are in Copper Mountain because he's trying to spare our feelings."

Rick eyed him solemnly. "On the other hand, maybe Dad's decided he'd rather live here, with or without Pam, and isn't quite sure how to tell us he's changed his mind about selling the business."

"It's a good thing we haven't said anything to Jim about future plans. I think I'll hold off on that meeting at the bank tomorrow."

"Maybe you'd better. It could be a wasted trip."

"What are you going to do while I'm with Laurel?"

"I thought I'd take a run over to the raceway in Mom's car. Say hello to some of the guys."

"Sounds good. I'll probably be back from Denver by three."

"Don't hurry on my account," Rick murmured. "Want to finish our chess game before we hit the sack?"

"Why not? Let me change first."

"Those two little guys were something else," Rick said as they bounded up the stairs. "Reminded me of the time the folks invited those Olympic downhillers from Austria to the house for the weekend."

"I remember." Nate chuckled as they entered his bedroom. "We were about the same age as Brent's boys."

"They gave us private ski lessons so we could learn their technique. I thought I was the greatest thing going and bragged about it at school until nobody would talk to me."

"That's because you *were* the greatest thing going—on skis, bikes, go-carts, you name it. The other kids were envious. If you want to know the truth, so was I," Nate told him.

Rick scoffed.

"Why else do you think I picked a career that took me off the ground?"

"You're putting me on."

"Not completely." He hung up his uniform and slipped into his sweats. "You were a natural at whatever you tried, just like Mom and Dad."

He shook his head. "That's what I always thought

about you. Nobody was better than my big brother at everything, including grades. I spent my life playing catch-up.''

Nate's hands went to his hips. ''Look at us now.''

''You mean out of work and washed-up?''

''That's about it.'' He followed him to his room. ''Rick, I need an answer to a question. It's important. Whatever you do, don't spare me.''

His brother swung around, giving Nate his full attention.

''If Dad moves to Texas with Pam, is there a part of you that would like to build Mom and Dad's ski business into something really big, provided I was your partner?''

''No,'' Rick said without hesitation before removing his jacket and tie.

''I didn't think so, but I had to be sure.''

''You don't want that, either.''

''No.'' Nate shook his head. ''It was their dream, not mine.''

They stared at each other for a moment. Then Rick donned a similar pair of sweats. One of the gifts from their mom the Christmas before last, when they'd had a reunion here at the house. She'd tended to treat them like twins. The memory was bittersweet.

''Now Dad's dream is smashed.''

''Yup.''

''So is Laurel's....''

Rick threw him a brief glance. ''When she opened your gift, she acted as thrilled as any expectant mother I've seen. During dinner I don't recall her talking about the past. If I didn't know the history, I couldn't have guessed she'd lost her husband.''

"She's a great actress. However, you weren't in the kitchen when I told her goodbye. She didn't want me to leave. I knew why…" He drew in a deep breath. "Laurel's desperate to talk about Spade."

"How do you know that?"

"She associates everything about me with him. She's hungry for what she's lost and needs me for one last trip down memory lane."

"That's the reason you're driving her to the doctor's appointment?" Rick said.

Nate nodded. "Since I couldn't be at Spade's funeral, I figured this would be a way of paying my final respects."

"I'm sure it'll mean a lot to her."

"I doubt it. Nothing's going to bring Spade back. Rehashing the past might even make it worse for her. She's having his baby. I don't know how she's coping. I don't know how Dad's coping."

"Let's not talk about that right now." He started out the door. "Come on downstairs. We'll forget chess and watch the news on TV."

"I've got a better idea. Let's have a few drinks. How long has it been since we did that together?"

His brother's head whipped around. "Years, but it's the best idea you've had since we came home last week. Just one problem. You might not be in the best shape when you pick up Laurel tomorrow. I'll tell you what—"

Rick checked his watch. "It's only ten after ten. She's probably still awake. While I hunt for the Jack Daniels, why don't you get her on the phone? Explain that something unavoidable has come up and you can't take her to the doctor, after all. It doesn't sound like you were looking forward to it, anyway. In the end, it'll save both of you a lot of unnecessary pain."

By this time his brother had reached the foyer, but Nate couldn't seem to make it the rest of the way down the stairs.

Rick stood at the bottom waiting for him. "What's wrong now?"

"For a minute I could've sworn you were serious."

CHAPTER SEVEN

THE PHYSICIANS' OFFICE building formed part of the complex with Aurora Regional Hospital. One reason Laurel liked it was the fact that there was always plenty of parking.

"You don't need to come with me," she told Nate after he'd pulled to a stop near the main entrance. "My doctor is amazingly punctual for an OB, so I shouldn't be long."

He ignored her comment and got out of the Blazer. Opening her door, he said, "When I told you I'd drive you to the doctor's office, I assumed you understood that I was going inside and waiting for you."

"But you'll have to sit in a roomful of pregnant women with their youngsters running around. Most men hate it!"

"I've faced scarier situations."

"I don't know...."

His mouth lifted in a half smile. "Let me worry about it. Come on."

In her tailored navy maternity pants outfit she felt less self-conscious swinging her legs around in front of him. He grasped her arm to help her down.

Nate was even more solicitous of her needs than

Brent. But when her feet touched the ground, all thoughts of her brother-in-law fled.

Maybe it was the smell of spring in the air, or a sudden awareness of the man standing next to her. Whatever the reason, she experienced a moment of exhilaration.

It had come right out of the blue.

The sensation was so foreign to her, she felt almost giddy and had to cling to Nate for support.

"I can't believe how fast the snow's melted after the last storm," she blurted to hide her reaction. Six months ago she couldn't have imagined feeling this alive again.

"It's supposed to reach sixty-five degrees today. That's Denver weather for you." He kept a hand on her arm as he ushered her inside the building.

The euphoric feeling was still with her when they entered the reception room two doors down from the front entrance. Dr. Steel shared a practice with several other OBs.

"It's so crowded!" Laurel observed, realizing they wouldn't be able to sit together. "Grab that chair by the window quick while I check in."

"All right." He gave her arm a gentle squeeze before letting her go.

While she waited behind another expectant mother at the reception desk, she watched Nate walk over to the table for a magazine. In his dark-brown leather jacket and tan chinos he drew the eye of every female in the room.

"Mrs. Pierce?"

"Oh!" Laurel turned around. "Hi. I'm here for my eleven o'clock appointment with Dr. Steel."

"He's running about five minutes behind. Have a seat and his nurse will call you."

"Thanks."

As she went to find herself a place, an older pregnant woman seated next to Nate got up and approached her. "Go ahead and sit with your hubby."

Before Laurel could correct her, the woman moved to another part of the room to find a chair. She probably didn't hear Laurel's murmured thank-you.

Nate was smiling by the time she sat down. "That was accommodating of her."

"Husbands are a rarity in here."

The second she said the word, she wished she hadn't. She didn't know exactly why. However, it was evident that Nate felt comfortable with the situation or he wouldn't have offered to come inside.

"That's too bad," he said in a low voice. "A man could learn a lot by observing what his wife has to go through while they're waiting for their baby."

Curious, she asked, "What have you deduced so far?"

"Something I've always suspected." His gaze traveled the room. "Women are strong in ways a man could never be. There's a dignity in their patience that's humbling."

Dignity in patience? She'd never thought of it that way before.

"Don't forget men bring certain strengths a woman needs. If a couple pulls together, they can have a strong marriage."

His face darkened. "So how does a single expectant mo—"

Laurel knew what he was asking, but she never

got to answer him because Dr. Steel's nurse called her name.

"Excuse me, Nate. I'll be back in a few minutes."

"Take all the time you need. I'm not going anywhere."

Not yet anyway... The thought of Nate's leaving Colorado brought the only cloud to an otherwise perfect morning.

She got up from the chair feeling like an old woman and waddled her way around the front counter to the examining rooms, aware that a pair of intensely blue eyes was following her progress.

"Who's the fabulous-looking guy sitting out there with you?" Merline asked while she waited for Laurel to take off her shoes and get on the scales. Merline knew about Scott.

"A close friend of my husband's. They were pilots together."

"Whew."

"You sound like my sister Julie. What is it with all you happily married women?"

Merline winked. "If you need an explanation, then I'll tell Dr. Steel to refer you to the eye doctor down the hall."

Laurel chuckled, but her amusement soon subsided. "Oh, no—I've gained two more pounds this week."

"It's a sign you're about ready to deliver. Okay. Where's my present?"

Laurel opened her purse and handed her the small sack containing a urine sample.

"Need help getting up on the table? Or shall I call

in the troops?'' Merline's eyes twinkled. She obviously meant Nate.

Warmth crept over Laurel's body. She was still feeling the effects of his touch when he'd assisted her from the Blazer.

''I think I can manage.''

No sooner had she situated herself than Dr. Steel breezed into the room with a broad smile on his face. ''How are you doing, Laurel?''

''I'm fine.''

''That's what I like to hear.''

Her OB was a grandfatherly type who'd delivered thousands of babies, including Joey after Brent and Julie had moved to Denver. Laurel had the greatest confidence in him. He took her blood pressure, then began the exam. It was over within minutes.

''The baby's head has dropped since your last appointment. Have you had any backache?''

''Some. Especially last night after I went to bed. We had a dinner party and I'm afraid I overdid it.''

He nodded. ''This baby might come sooner than we expected. Keep your feet up. Cut out all salt. No more walking around the mall.''

At least he hadn't ordered her to bed.

''I'll be careful.''

''Did you arrange for a pediatrician?''

''Yes. I'm using the one my sister goes to. His name is Dr. Duffy.''

''He's an excellent choice. All right. Tell the receptionist to mark you down for a week from today. We'll see if you make it.'' He smiled again.

''Do you think my due date was off?''

"No. Your baby's just a little more eager than some to make an appearance."

"My mother-in-law told me Scott came ten days early."

"Every mother's different, every pregnancy's unique. Don't worry. Whatever happens, you're in great shape. If you have questions, call me anytime, no matter the reason."

"I will. Thank you, Dr. Steel."

In a minute Laurel had made herself presentable and left the room, eager to rejoin Nate. Merline was in the hall weighing in another pregnant woman. She grinned at Laurel.

"I never saw a woman at your stage of pregnancy move so fast." Her brows lifted in query. "Where's the fire?"

It was no idle question. A blush crept over Laurel's face. She walked even faster, shocked to think she'd sent such obvious signals to Merline.

If the reason for her joy was that transparent to Dr. Steel's nurse, had Nate picked up on it? She hoped not.

THE SECOND NATE SAW Laurel, he shot to his feet in alarm. Her heightened color led him to believe she'd been crying. Whether it was over Spade's absence at such a crucial time or bad news about her pregnancy, or both, Nate couldn't tell, but he was going to find out. He tossed the unread magazine on the table.

"Hi! I hope you didn't die of boredom while I was back there. Shall we go?"

She sounded too cheerful and her eyes seemed to avoid his. She started out of the office ahead of him.

He caught up with her at the door and held her arm all the way out to the Blazer.

Once they were both inside, he turned in the seat to face her. She wasn't the same woman she'd been half an hour earlier.

"Laurel? Are you all right?"

She fastened her seat belt. "Of course."

He could feel her tension. "Don't insult my intelligence by putting on a brave front. Tell me what's wrong."

"Not a thing. Honestly."

"You wouldn't say that if I were Spade."

A smile appeared. "If you were Scott, you wouldn't have come to a routine doctor's appointment with me."

Her reply stunned him. "Why do you say that?"

"Because he always hated the idea of going to the doctor, whether it was for him or me. That's one of the reasons I had the implant done while he was away. To spare him."

Nate shook his head. How many other things didn't he know about Spade?

"Then use me for a shoulder to cry on."

"You're very kind, but I don't need one. Thank you anyway."

"Laurel?" He swallowed hard. "Did the doctor say something to worry you?"

"Not at all, but I am retaining fluid. He wants me to keep my feet up. I'm afraid any food we eat out will have too much salt. Maybe it would be better if you just dropped me off at home. Then you'll have the rest of the day to make other plans."

Whatever she was trying to hide, he wasn't about

to let her get away with it. "I thought we were going to talk."

She turned to him at last, but she had a guarded look in her eyes. "We've been doing that since you picked me up at the house. It allowed us to make up for the other night, when Joey and Mike took over the conversation.

"Nate—" Her voice caught. "You have no idea how much I appreciate your taking me to the doctor. I'll never forget your kindness...or your bravery," she added, obviously trying to lighten the atmosphere. But Nate had the impression she was telling him goodbye.

He sat back in his seat, his emotions in chaos. Almost in slow motion he fastened his seat belt, then started the car.

Halfway to her sister's house she said, "There *is* one question I've wanted to ask. You don't have to answer if you don't want to, of course. Maybe you can't talk about it. If that's true, then I'll understand."

By now she'd done a good job of twisting his insides. "What is it?"

"Having met you, spent time with you, I know you would've been at Scott's funeral if you'd been able to come."

"If you're asking why I didn't, it was because my mother had just been killed."

"Oh, Nate! Your mom?" she cried with heartfelt compassion.

In the next instant she reached out to cover his hand, which rested on the gearshift. He cast her a veiled glance and discovered her eyes filled with tears.

"Tell me what happened."

Unable to hold back, Nate found himself relating the agonizing details. It was the first time he'd talked to anyone about it, outside of Rick.

"Her two best friends were killed with her. It rocked the whole community."

"I'm so sorry," she whispered.

"So am I. She and Spade died within days of each other. While you were burying him, my family was holding a funeral service for her. I got word about Spade too late to do anything more than phone you and write a letter."

She shook her head. "I don't know how you managed to function, let alone try to contact me." Her hand remained on his although he didn't think she was aware of it. "How old was she?"

"Fifty-three."

"She was still so young! That's tragic."

"No more tragic than Spade being taken in the prime of life," he muttered before he could catch himself.

Suddenly the warmth of her touch was missing. It was as if the mention of her husband's name had caused her to remove her hand.

"How has your father taken it?"

Her husky tone told him he never should have said anything. When she reached the house, she would go inside and cry her heart out over Spade.

"At first he was so devastated, I didn't think he'd ever come out of his depression. Then a couple of months ago he met a woman. Now they're married."

After a long silence, she said, "I'm glad he found happiness again, but it couldn't have been easy for you and Rick."

"No." That was an understatement.

The fact that she saw nothing strange in his father's remarrying so soon after his mother's death surprised Nate. He struggled to hide his reaction.

"When you spoke to me at the lodge restaurant," he said, "I was dancing with the second Mrs. Hawkins. We'd just come from the chapel where they were married."

"So *that* was the wedding party you'd referred to... I thought the woman in your arms might be your new bride. When you walked away from me, I was doubly horrified to think I'd upset you while you were enjoying the beginning of your life as a married man."

Nate couldn't believe what he was hearing. Talk about appearances being deceptive. "That's a night I'd like to blot from my memory."

"So would I." Her voice trembled as she spoke.

When he realized what he'd just said, he reached for her hand. In case she tried to pull away, he tightened his grip.

"I didn't mean that the way it sounded. I was already feeling depressed *before* I saw you on the elevator with Brent. Later when I was so unconscionably rude to you, I knew I'd reached rock bottom.

"I despised myself for it, but I couldn't seem to control my thoughts or emotions at the time. That's what I meant about wanting to forget that night."

She stared at him. "Why were you in such low

spirits?'' Her persistence held an underlying earnestness he couldn't ignore.

''It's a long story.'' He had to let go of her hand to turn into the Marsdens' driveway. The Cavalier wasn't there. ''You don't really want to know.''

''That's where you're wrong. If you don't mind a roast-beef sandwich for lunch, come into the house and I'll make us both one while you tell me.''

He'd thought she wanted to be alone to mourn her loss. *What was going on with her?*

''I have a better idea. If you'll let me fix the food while you rest on the couch, then I'll stay for a little while.''

''Good.''

Within ten minutes they'd settled in the den to eat. To his surprise, she'd allowed him to do everything for her, even rummage around in her sister's kitchen.

He found he was starving. After she'd eaten, she lounged on the couch with her feet propped up, watching him wolf down a second sandwich. He finished it off with a cold lemonade. Her eyes smiled as if she found his appetite amusing.

''I've been patient long enough,'' she began when she saw him put down the empty can. ''Why don't you start by telling me why you resigned your commission.''

He sat forward with his hands clasped between his knees. ''After Mom's funeral, Dad went downhill fast. Rick and I assumed there would come a point where he'd snap out of it, but he never rallied. We learned from Dad's assistant at the ski shop that he wasn't taking an active interest in the business anymore.

"When I heard that, it became impossible for me to concentrate on my career. My brother had a similar problem. After many phone conversations, we came to the same conclusion. Dad needed us here."

"So Rick gave up his racing career, too?"

"Yes. But when we got home, hoping to bring some happiness back to our father's life, he shocked us by announcing he'd met a woman and was getting married."

She sat up straight. "Your father must be a remarkable man for you and your brother to have sacrificed your careers for him. But it also explains why you were so depressed at the lodge. I know how much you love to fly. Your brother must feel the same way about racing. Now I understand what you meant on the phone about your decision to leave the Air Force being premature.

"Surely with your dad remarried, the two of you can explain your situations to those in charge and get right back to doing what you love."

Nate stared at her in bewilderment. She didn't understand. She didn't have a clue that his pain was coming from a completely different source. That was because she was still in too much pain herself.

"I can reapply." He said the words, but felt no accompanying sense of excitement. At this particular moment, he didn't know *what* the hell he wanted.

She blinked. "You mean you'd have to go through the whole process all over again?"

"That's the way it works."

"But you're a hotshot! How long have you been retired?"

"Two and half weeks."

"Then the paperwork on you won't even have been processed! All you have to do is make a phone call to your commanding officer. I'm sure he'll pull strings for the legendary Hawk!"

He pursed his lips. "A phone call right now could also be premature."

"Why?"

It was time to change the subject.

"What aren't you telling me?" Her eyes implored him, as if what he had to say really mattered.

"Dad's marriage might not last. Then Rick and I will be back at square one."

"Did his new wife say or do something that's alarmed you and your brother?"

Unable to stay seated during this kind of inquisition, Nate got up to gather their plates and his soda can. To his chagrin, Laurel followed him into the kitchen in her stockinged feet.

"I can tell you're upset." She put a hand on his arm. "Nate, are you afraid to talk about it for fear of being disloyal to your dad?"

He wished she wasn't standing so close to him. He didn't want her to touch him again.

"Let's just say I have my reservations about things working out for them."

"I see." Her hand fell away. "I'm sorry if it sounded like I was prying. It's none of my business. Chalk it up to my concern that the Air Force may have lost another of its best." She left the kitchen.

Damn. He'd hurt her when that was the last thing he'd wanted to do. After he'd cleaned up the lunch mess, he walked back to the study, where he found her resting on the couch.

Their eyes met.

"I appreciate your concern, Laurel."

"But you can't talk about it," she murmured. "I've been there before. I should've known better."

I know you've been there.

She was still missing Spade so badly she hadn't opened up to Nate about him yet. He'd thought sharing happy memories of her husband was what this day was supposed to be about. It hadn't been, not even close.

A haunting smile broke the corners of her mouth. "Forgive me?"

"You know better than to ask me that," he said thickly. "I'd better go so you can follow your doctor's advice."

She didn't try to stop him. That told him all he needed to know.

"Thank you for everything today," she called to him as he left the den.

He turned to look at her one more time. "It was my pleasure. Are you still figuring on the same due date?"

"Yes, but the doctor says it could be sooner."

"I'll keep that in mind. Is there anything I can do for you before I leave?"

"I'm perfect, thanks. Julie ought to be home soon."

You're lying. Covering up. You can't wait for me to get out of here so you can break down.

"Say hi to her for me."

"I will. Drive safely."

"You must be confusing me with Rick."

"No. Top guns are notorious for maneuvering

their vehicles ten feet off the ground if they can get away with it.''

Is that what Spade did?

Hollowness welled up inside him.

"Take care, Laurel.''

She held back her tears until she heard the Blazer door shut. Then she started to cry: convulsively and uncontrollably.

Ten minutes later she felt an arm go around her. "Laurel, what's the matter? I heard your sobs the second I walked in the front door. Where's Nate? I expected him still to be here.''

Laurel lifted her head from the cushion. "I guess he had other things to do.'' She eased herself to her other side so she could see Julie, who'd knelt down by the couch. Her sister looked anxious.

"Is something wrong with the baby?''

She shook her head. "The baby's fine. It's me. There's something horribly wrong with me.''

"Then why didn't Dr. Steel put you in the hospital?''

"I'm sorry,'' Laurel cried. "I didn't mean physically. I think maybe I'm losing my mind.''

"Why do you say that?''

"I don't know. I'm just a jumbled mass of feelings and contradictions. Maybe I need a psychiatrist.''

"If you're worried about having the baby, remember Brent and I will be there for you all the way.''

Laurel's eyes filled with fresh tears. "I know that, Julie. You're both wonderful. But that's not what this is about.''

"Did Nate say something that disturbed you?''

"Not exactly.'' Laurel sat up with a sniff. "If anything, I'm upset about what he *wouldn't* tell me. I wanted him to confide in me, but he left too soon." She grasped Julie's arm and took a shuddering breath.

"It shouldn't have mattered to me if he wanted to go," she went on. "After all, he was Scott's friend, not mine. That's the whole point! That's what's wrong!" she cried out, struggling to her feet. "I know I should be thinking about Scott. This is his baby, but—"

"But Nate Hawkins has arrived on the scene."

"Why should that make any difference?"

Her sister stood up. "What happened while you were with Nate today?"

She averted her eyes. "Nothing. He took me to the doctor's, then brought me back and made our lunch. After he did the dishes, he left."

"Laurel, this is your sister talking. I know you. Something went on while you were with him. No matter how guilty you feel, tell me."

"Why do you say that?" she snapped. She knew she was reacting defensively because her sister had just put her finger on the problem.

"Guilt is the only emotion that makes you evasive," Julie said frankly. "If I'm wrong, then look at me."

With the greatest reluctance she obeyed her sister. "You're not wrong," she admitted in a shaky whisper.

"Go on."

"When he left a little while ago, I didn't want him to leave."

"What's so terrible about that? He's a terrific guy."

"I know."

"And he's probably one of the best-looking men you or I will ever meet."

Laurel moaned. "I agree."

"So what great sin have you committed?"

Once again Laurel's cheeks felt hot. "I—I'm attracted to him."

"Who isn't?"

"You know what I mean, Julie."

"I'm not sure I do."

"Stop teasing! How could I feel like this when I'm about to have Scott's baby?"

"Feel like what?" she prodded.

"Like everything's exciting again. This morning while he was helping me out of the Blazer...I hoped he'd put his arms around me."

"That's because life goes on and you've met a real man," Julie said. "One who's worthy of you. My dear sister, you don't need a psychiatrist to tell you *that*."

"No," she confessed. "But he was only being kind to me because I pushed to see him after our dinner party. When he left the house just now, he didn't tell me he'd call again, or come by."

"Nate must have said *something*."

"He asked how soon the baby was due. When I told him, he said he'd keep it in mind. Then he was out the door."

"Cheer up. As long as he didn't say, 'Goodbye, I'm going overseas,' I don't know what you're worried about."

Laurel stared into space. "I hope you're right, Julie. The thought of never seeing him again—"

The phone rang in the background.

"I'll get it!" Laurel cried, hurrying past Julie to the kitchen. What if it was Nate and he hung up before she answered?

"Hello?" Ooh—she shouldn't have moved that fast. Now she had a painful stitch in her side.

"Laurel, dear—"

She closed her eyes tightly. "Reba?"

"I'm glad it's you. Ever since our last conversation I've wanted to apologize. Of course you couldn't have flown out to Philadelphia at this stage of your pregnancy. So Dad and I decided to surprise you."

Her mind reeled. "Surprise me?"

Julie had just entered the kitchen, looking alert.

"Yes. We're in Denver with everyone's showers gifts. Dad booked us a room at the Turquoise Inn here in Aurora."

Laurel felt as if she might faint from shock. "When did you arrive?"

"We reached the motel about ten minutes ago."

What? Julie mouthed the word.

Just a minute, Laurel mouthed the words back.

"Don't worry. We have a rental car to get around. The last thing we want to do is inconvenience you or Julie. Your mother tells me your sister is pregnant, too. Isn't that amazing?"

"Yes." Laurel could barely talk.

"How soon can we see you, dear? Would this afternoon be all right?"

She bit her lip so hard she could taste blood.

"Later in the day would be fine." Her eyes swerved to Julie's for confirmation. Her sister nodded.

"We can't wait to see you!"

Laurel cleared her throat. "It'll be wonderful to see you too, Reba."

"Shall we say four?"

"Four will be fine."

"Can you give us instructions on how to get there? I'll write them down for Dad."

"Let me find Julie. She knows Aurora much better than I do. Just a minute."

She grabbed her sister's arm and pulled her into the dining room. "I can't believe it," she whispered. "My in-laws are here!"

"You're kidding! For how long?"

"I don't know. All she told me was that they're staying at the Turquoise Inn and need directions to get to your house. I'm sorry, Julie. She should've given me warning."

"If she'd done that, you would have put her off. She's determined to see you." Julie sighed. "Sounds like she's running true to form."

"They've brought shower gifts from the family."

"I guess a party's in order. I'll get dinner started."

"No, you won't! After I open presents, I'll go out to a restaurant with them."

"The doctor wants you off salt."

"I can order a vegetable salad."

"Then go to the Mesquite Steak and Grill. It's right by Fordham's."

"Good idea. It's not too far for Wendell to drive, and neither of us will have to slave in the kitchen."

They both returned to the kitchen. Laurel picked up the phone. "Reba? Here's Julie. See you at four."

"We're counting the minutes, Lori Lou." Her father-in-law's pet name for her.

"Wendell?"

"How's the little mother-to-be doing?"

"I'm fine. How are you?"

"I'll be a lot better when I see you. We've missed you. It isn't the same without you and Scotty."

Laurel's guilt intensified. "I've missed everyone, too. It'll be marvelous to see you again. Hang on, Wendell. Julie's going to tell you how to get here from the motel."

Dazed by her conflicting emotions, she thrust the phone at her sister.

Oh, dear God. Help me.

CHAPTER EIGHT

"I THOUGHT we were going to do this project together."

Nate put the last of his mother's sweaters in the box before glancing at his brother, who'd just entered their parents' bedroom.

"I got back early. When I saw you'd already brought the boxes over from the store, I decided to get a head start."

Rick grabbed an empty one and started packing their mom's dresses and robes from the closet. Years of loving memories flashed through Nate's mind as he watched her clothes being removed from hangers only to disappear.

Their dad's suits and shirts remained. Her half of the closet stood empty. His eyes stung.

"How's everything at the track? Any of your old friends around?"

"Chip was there. We chatted for a while. He's in the middle of a messy divorce, and his wife is fighting to deprive him of his visitation rights. She's moved to Denver. Doesn't want their children to grow up with a racetrack for a backyard."

"Isn't that marriage number two?" Nate started packing their mother's shoes and handbags. One of them had a wallet with some old snaps of the family. He removed the pictures and put them in his pocket.

Rick nodded. "Dad predicted it wouldn't last."

"Did you ever notice how he's always been right about people and relationships?"

"Notice!" He laughed almost angrily. "Why do you think I'm terrified to settle down? Dad warned me a race car driver's chances of establishing a solid marriage were shaky at best."

"I got the same warning," Nate muttered.

He didn't have to look at Rick to know they were both thinking the same thing. Their father was a man who'd seemed to have such a clear and decisive understanding of life. How could he have done something that went against the kind of wise counsel he'd given them since they were little boys?

"Did things go okay with Laurel?"

Just hearing her name had the power to knock the wind out of him.

"I took her to the doctor, then fixed us lunch because she's on a salt-free diet. We talked for a little while and then I took off."

He'd packed his mom's jewelry box and begun to empty the dresser drawers. All they needed to do was go through the end tables at either side of the king-size bed, discard her toiletries from the bathroom and their bittersweet task would be finished.

Pretty soon there'd be no evidence of their mother's thirty-year life in this house. Not in the bedroom anyway.

"Are you going to see Laurel again?"

"No. All debts are paid. The book is officially closed on Spade's widow."

"It's strange how you always refer to her like that. Why don't you just use her name?"

"Because that's how I think of her. She's still in love with her husband and always will be."

"Did she tell you that outright?"

"She didn't have to. In any case, none of it matters."

"If that's true, how come you're looking so angry?"

Nate's head jerked around. "What are you talking about?"

"The last time I saw you this wound up, she'd had the audacity to approach you on the dance floor. You wouldn't by any chance be blaming her for something else she isn't aware of...."

He didn't know how Rick did it, but his brother had better instincts than a hunting dog bearing down on its prey.

"She asked me why I didn't attend Spade's funeral. I explained, and one thing led to another. I thought if I told her about the events leading up to the night of Dad's wedding dinner, she'd understand why my mood was so savage."

"But she didn't?"

"The fact that Dad remarried after six months washed right over her. She interpreted everything I told her to mean I was upset because flying was my life and I'd given it up."

Rick cocked his head. "There's more than a kernel of truth in that. Admit it."

"That might've been the case once. Now I'm not so sure."

"But she doesn't know that, *and* she was married

to a pilot," he continued. "Not just any pilot. According to you, Spade was the best of the best."

"He was. That's why he'll always be bigger than life to her. And once she has his baby, those feelings will never change."

"If you're saying you think Laurel Pierce is going to go through the rest of her life without a man, then you need a physical to find out what's wrong with you. How old is she?"

"Spade said she was two years younger than he was. I guess she'd be twenty-eight."

"She's still a young woman. Once her baby's born and her life gets back to normal, the men will be camped outside her door."

He suddenly remembered the guys flocking around her photographs in the barracks. And the male diners staring at her as she walked into Fordham's Pancake House.

"I'm putting you on notice now...."

Nate turned to his brother. "What's that supposed to mean?"

He'd loaded his arms with boxes. "I plan on asking her out. I hope that's okay with you. If it isn't, tell me after I come back from the basement."

"Even if you were serious, I'd have no problem with it," Nate muttered.

"Thanks. That's all I needed to hear."

Without wasting any time, Nate scooped up the rest of the boxes and followed Rick down two flights of stairs to the storage room. They worked in silence, arranging places on shelves for the boxes.

Rick dusted his hands. "I guess that's it. All we

have to do now is give the bedroom and bathroom a good cleaning.''

''The whole house could use one.''

''We'll tackle it in the morning. Hey, look what Chip gave me. He said these were payback for a favor I did him last year.'' Rick produced two tickets. ''The Nuggets are playing the Jazz tonight. What do you say we drive to Denver for a steak dinner, then head over to the basketball game?''

Now that they'd removed all of their mom's things from the master bedroom, Nate had the feeling Rick was as anxious to leave the house as he was.

''Those tickets couldn't have come at a better time. Let's get ready and go.''

They started up the stairs.

''Before I shower, give me Laurel's phone number. I'd like to make plans with her for Monday night.''

Rick was starting to get on his nerves.

''I don't know what I did with her letter. You'll have to look it up.''

''Okay. Brent said he was in the phone book.''

When they reached the foyer, Nate watched Rick head for the den while he continued upstairs. From the doorway of his room he saw his brother disappear into his own bedroom carrying the directory. He closed the door behind him.

Rick could badger you to death when he wanted to get you to give in on something, but he wasn't the type to play practical jokes. Nate sensed that his brother was serious about this.

When he thought about it, he remembered how Rick had engaged Laurel in conversation at dinner.

Before that, they'd talked on the phone out of Nate's hearing.

Suddenly the adrenaline surged through his veins, propelling him into his brother's room unannounced.

"Put your phone away."

Rick's head swung around. "What?"

"You can't call Laurel."

"A little while ago you said you were okay with it."

"I'm not anymore. She's off-limits."

"To you maybe. Not to me. She's a beautiful, charming woman I'd like to know better."

"Spade was my friend, Rick."

"Why would that preclude *me* from having a relationship with Laurel if she decides she'd like to go out with me?"

"It's a question of honor!" he blurted.

"Whose?" His brother's searching question demanded an answer.

"I know things about Laurel. Intimate things Spade shared with me over the years. You're my brother. The thought of you with her…"

Rick studied him for a moment. "I had no idea your feelings for her went so deep."

"Did I say that?"

"You didn't have to."

Lord.

"Thanks for stopping me before I did something that could've hurt you. Here." He got up from the side of the bed and handed Nate the tickets.

"What are you doing?"

"I'm not the one in the family who enjoys basketball."

Nate gave him a puzzled look. "But we had plans."

"By now it should be obvious to you that I'm in the mood for female companionship. I might get lucky and meet a snow bunny night-skiing in Breckenridge. Of course, I couldn't say that to Chip and hurt his feelings."

Before Nate could make much sense of anything, Rick tossed him his cell phone.

"While I get cleaned up, why don't you call Brent Marsden and ask him to go to the game with you tonight? I learned he's a big Nuggets fan. It'll be a nice way to repay their family for dinner. He might even forget you ever gave Laurel a bad time on the dance floor."

It wasn't until Nate dialed the number he'd memorized that he realized his brother had just pulled off the one and only con of their lives. Nate hadn't seen it coming, but it was too late to do anything about it now.

A woman had picked up on the other end and already said hello. Just hearing that slightly breathless quality held him spellbound.

"Laurel? It's Nate."

There was a brief pause and then she said, "I'm so glad you called, Nate. When you left today, I had the impression I'd offended you. It was the last thing I wanted to do. If I did, please accept my apology."

"You didn't do anything of the kind." He rubbed the back of his neck. "I figured if I left, you'd be able to get your proper rest."

"That was very thoughtful of you, but you don't

have to worry about me. All I do is lie around the house."

"It's all you *should* be doing until the baby's born." He glanced at his watch. Ten to four. "I'm calling to see if I can patch things up with your brother-in-law."

Silence. Then she said, "Brent's not upset with you."

"Maybe not. But to be on the safe side, I was hoping he'd let me take him to the Nuggets game tonight. That is, if he's free and it's all right with Julie. I happen to have two tickets front row, center."

"He'd *kill* for seats like that. Even if he has other plans, he'll change them. I'll tell Julie and she'll get hold of him at work."

"Sounds good. If he can go, he doesn't need to call me back. Tell him we'll grab some dinner on the way to the game."

"This is going to make his day."

"I hope so."

"Nate, did he say something to you I don't know about?"

"No. But let's agree my behavior at the lodge was reprehensible. I'd like to replace that image if I can."

"You already have, but if it'll make you feel better…"

"It will. Trust me."

"Then I'll hurry and get off the phone so Julie can call him."

"Thanks, Laurel. Talk to you soon."

CHURNING WITH CONFLICTING emotions, Laurel hung up the phone. She didn't have time to analyze her feelings. There were voices coming from the foyer. That meant Julie had returned from picking up the boys at school.

Before Laurel's in-laws arrived, she needed to tell her sister about Nate's phone call. Dressed in the purple and black outfit she'd worn to the pancake house, minus the sweater coat, she left her bedroom. The boys were just coming upstairs.

"Hi, you guys!"

"Hi!"

"How was school?"

"It was okay," Mike muttered before rushing past her.

Joey slowed down. "Good."

Laurel could always count on a positive response from Julie's youngest.

"Did your mom tell you we're going to have company in a few minutes?"

He nodded. "Uncle Scott's parents. Was his dad a pilot, too?"

"No."

"How come?"

"Bad eyes."

"Hawk told me you can't be a pilot if you wear glasses." Those bright hazel eyes shone up at her. "Mine won't go bad!"

He was so cute she reached out to hug him. "Of course they won't." She let him go and continued down the stairs. "Julie?"

"In the living room!"

Laurel found her straightening cushions on the love seat. "I'm glad you're back. I just got off the phone with Nate."

That piece of news brought Julie's head up. She sent Laurel a knowing smile, then glanced at her watch. "It's only been three hours since he left. And you were so worried," she teased.

"It's not what you think." *I don't know what to make of it.* "He called to invite Brent to the NBA game tonight."

Julie's eyes widened. "You're kidding! It's the Nuggets' first playoff game. Brent tried to get tickets, but it was sold out. He's going to be ecstatic!"

That went without saying. "You're supposed to call him and tell him Nate will pick him up at six. They'll stop for a bite to eat on the way to the game."

"Mom?" Mike interrupted them. "Uncle Scott's family just drove up. What are Joey and I supposed to do again?"

"Go outside and see if they need help bringing things into the house."

"Where shall we put their stuff?"

"In here."

"Okay."

"Call Brent," Laurel urged her sister before turning to her nephew. "Come on, you guys," she said as Joey dashed up to him. "Let's go say hello to my in-laws. Do you remember them?"

Mike nodded. "She cried all the way through Uncle Scott's funeral."

"Dad told us she couldn't help it because Uncle Scott was her baby."

Laurel nodded wordlessly and squeezed Joey's shoulders.

When they walked outside, Wendell was just

opening the trunk. Scott had resembled his father in build, a wiry man of medium height now losing his brown hair. Reba, blond and slender, had bequeathed her vivacious brown eyes and attractive facial features to her last-born.

The sight of them was at once dear and familiar, bringing a pang to Laurel's heart. There couldn't be two nicer people in the world. They looked wonderful. However, Laurel knew that in their case, appearances were deceiving. Scott's parents weren't even close to conquering their grief. At times, Laurel wasn't sure they even wanted to try—especially Reba.

As the boys approached them, Reba glanced up. "Oh, Laurel—" she cried and hurried toward her. The next few minutes passed in a blur of tears, prolonged hugs and kisses.

Wendell would have pulled her into a crushing embrace if it hadn't been for the baby. "Lori Lou, you don't know how good it is to see you." Scott's parents stood there staring at her protruding belly, tears running down their cheeks.

"I feel the same way," Laurel assured them.

In all honesty, it was a relief to see them and not fall apart. Since the funeral she'd dreaded a reunion for fear the pain would start all over again. But that hadn't happened. Not at all...

She couldn't pinpoint the exact moment, but somewhere along the way she'd said goodbye to Scott. He'd gone to a special place in her heart where he would always dwell. If anything, seeing his parents now brought a blessing of peace to her soul.

They would be grandparents to her baby. It was

Play the Romance Crossword Game

and get... 2 FREE BOOKS

and a

FREE GIFT...

YOURS to KEEP!

Scratch Here!

to reveal the hidden words.
Look below to see what you get.

DETACH AND MAIL CARD TODAY!

Yes!

I have scratched off the gold areas. Please send me my **2 FREE BOOKS** and **FREE GIFT** for which I qualify. I understand that I am under no obligation to purchase any books as explained on the back of this card.

336 HDL DRTX   **135 HDL DRUF**

FIRST NAME

LAST NAME

ADDRESS

APT.#

CITY

Visit us online at
www.eHarlequin.com

STATE/PROV.

ZIP/POSTAL CODE

ROMANCE	MYSTERY	NOVEL	GIFT
You get **2 FREE BOOKS** PLUS a **FREE GIFT!**	You get **2 FREE BOOKS!**	You get **1 FREE BOOK!**	You get **a FREE MYSTERY GIFT!**

The Harlequin Reader Service® — Here's how it works:

Accepting your 2 free books and mystery gift places you under no obligation to buy anything. You may keep the books and gift and return the shipping statement marked "cancel." If you do not cancel, about a month later we'll send you 6 additional books and bill you just $4.47 each in the U.S., or $4.99 each in Canada, plus 25¢ shipping & handling per book and applicable taxes if any.* That's the complete price and — compared to cover prices of $5.25 each in the U.S. and $6.25 each in Canada — it's quite a bargain! You may cancel at any time, but if you choose to continue, every month we'll send you 6 more books, which you may either purchase at the discount price or return to us and cancel your subscription.

*Terms and prices subject to change without notice. Sales tax applicable in N.Y. Canadian residents will be charged applicable provincial taxes and GST. Credit or Debit balances in a customer's account(s) may be offset by any other outstanding balance owed by or to the customer the natural progression of things, and she knew her child would adore them.

No longer afraid, she put her arms around both of them. "Come into the house with me. The boys will bring everything in."

Julie greeted them lovingly at the door. While she ushered them into the living room, her expressive eyes sent Laurel a private message that said Brent had been informed. Laurel felt a fluttery sensation in her chest. In less than two hours Nate would be coming by the house.

Scott's parents insisted Laurel open her gifts right away. They'd brought presents from both sides of the family. By the time she'd finished, not only had she caught up on all the latest news from back home, she'd acquired enough adorable outfits, booties and receiving blankets to outfit Julie's baby, too.

"Everyone's been so generous I can't believe it. Thank you for coming and bringing all these beautiful gifts. I wish the baby was here right now to enjoy them."

Wendell nodded. "So do we. Another little Scotty."

"It might be a girl," Joey inserted.

Laurel couldn't help smiling as she recalled a certain conversation....

"It isn't fair that he didn't live to see their first child," her mother-in-law said in a tearful voice. From that point on, conversation focused on Scott. Laurel understood their need to talk about him and joined in as they reminisced.

"Going through this pregnancy alone must be so hard on you, dear."

"She hasn't been alone," Mike spoke up. "We're with her every day."

"That's the truth. I'm the luckiest person in the world." Laurel got to her feet and hugged him. "Let's take everything upstairs, shall we?"

"Where are you putting my grandson?" Wendell wanted to know.

"Come with us and you'll see."

Soon they'd all congregated in Laurel's bedroom, the room that had once been Joey's nursery and had become a partial nursery again. The boys helped Laurel put all her new things in the drawers.

"Oh, good! You have a baby book." Reba reached for it. "I was going to buy you one if you hadn't thought of it."

Joey lifted his head. "Mike and I gave it to Aunt Laurel for her birthday last month."

"What a wonderful present. Every baby should have a book. You should see Scotty's."

"Mom made baby books for me and Mike, too."

"Did she?" But Reba's voice sounded far away. Laurel noticed she'd opened it to see what was inside.

Other than a family tree showing pictures of Scott and Laurel and both sides of their families going back to the baby's great-grandparents, nothing else had been done yet. She was waiting for her baby. Then it would start to fill.

Laurel watched Reba glance at the empty pages, then stop. She pulled a tiny card out of its envelope and turned toward Laurel. "Nate? As in Nate Hawkins?"

A strange little tremor passed through Laurel's body. She'd forgotten about putting his card inside.

"Yes," Joey answered before Laurel could. "Hawk was Uncle Scott's best friend in the Air Force."

"I know. When they were stationed in Nevada, Scotty sent us pictures of the two of them. In fact we have videos of them talking and laughing together."

"He brought Aunt Laurel some presents the other night. His brother gave Mom a bottle of wine, but she can't drink it until after her baby's born."

"The major was here at the house?" Reba asked. Laurel doubted her mother-in-law heard the rest of Joey's running commentary.

"Yes. He's from Colorado and came home to attend a family wedding."

"We all had dinner together," Mike informed her. "His brother's a Formula I race car driver. Have you ever heard of Lucky Hawkins? He's so cool you can't believe it!"

"Do you want to see what Hawk gave the baby?" Joey opened the drawer and lifted out the sleeper and blanket.

At that moment Brent appeared in the doorway. "I might've known I'd find all of you in here." He sounded and looked more exuberant than usual as he hugged Scott's parents. They chatted for a few minutes.

Wendell cleared his throat. "We hear you had Scotty's old friend over for dinner the other night."

"That's right. He and his brother, Rick."

"If he's still in town, we'd like a chance to meet

him. Of all Scott's friends, he was the one we most looked forward to seeing at the funeral, but he didn't make it."

"His mother died around the same time as your son, Wendell," Julie explained. "That's why he didn't know about it until later. Brent is going to an NBA game with him tonight." She turned to her husband. "You'll tell him Scott's parents are here, won't you, honey? Find out what his plans are?"

"Of course." Brent clapped a hand on Wendell's shoulder. "I wish *I'd* known you were coming to Denver. But Nate has front-row seats. I'm afraid I'd offend him if I canceled this late."

"No, no," Wendell said. "You go with him. Maybe we'll be able to see him tomorrow."

"How long are you and Reba going to be here?" Brent asked.

"We're flying back on Sunday."

"Then we'll get together tomorrow."

"That'll be fine."

"See you in the morning. Come on, boys. Let's allow your Aunt Laurel some time alone with Scott's parents." Brent ushered his family out and shut the door behind him.

The clock on the dresser said five fifty-seven. Laurel had a hunch Nate would be right on time, and the whole issue could be avoided, at least for today.

Reba studied her a moment. "You've cut your hair. I've never seen it short before. You look so different this way."

"Since I've been pregnant, I always seem to be hot. It felt good to cut it."

"She looks beautiful. Radiant," her father-in-law declared.

"Thanks, Wendell."

"I didn't mean you don't look lovely this way, Laurel."

"I know. And, after wearing my hair long, it's a big change for me, too."

"I can remember Scotty making you promise you'd never cut it."

Any change was difficult for Reba.

"As you would know after five children, having a baby transforms your life. I also remember promising him I'd never get fat. But as you can see…"

Laurel had hoped to bring a smile to their faces, but didn't succeed. She decided to introduce a different subject.

"Are you two hungry, or would you like to eat later?"

"I could use a bite," Wendell said. "How about you, Reba?"

Her mother-in-law shrugged her shoulders. "What do you want to do, Laurel? We're here for you."

"I know, and it's wonderful." She hugged both of them again. "I thought it would be nice to drive over to the Mesquite Steak and Grill. It's not far from here. Since I've been living with Julie and Brent, I've become addicted to Mexican food. Fajitas are the Mesquite's specialty. I know you'll love them."

She would order a green salad and a yogurt.

"That sounds fine."

"Sit down for a minute while I phone. I don't think we need a reservation this early, but I'd better make sure.'' She reached for the directory on the shelf of her nightstand to find the number.

The window above it overlooked the street. Nate's Blazer was just backing out of the driveway. She felt a surge of guilt as she reflected that Scott's parents had flown to Colorado to talk about their son with her, yet all she could think about was the next time she'd see Nate again.

What's wrong with me?

BRENT MARSDEN WAS a terrific guy. Nate couldn't remember when he'd enjoyed anyone's company more. If he'd experienced a certain dissatisfaction during the game, it had nothing to do with the man seated next to him.

The truth was, he'd expected to see Laurel when he went to the door to pick up Brent. Instead he'd found her brother-in-law locking his car, which he'd parked in front of the house. Another car, a rental stood in the driveway; apparently they had out-of-town visitors. Nate would never know if it was simply perfect timing, or if Laurel had something to do with the reason Brent had been outside waiting.

As Nate slowed down and pulled into the driveway, the car he'd seen behind the Cavalier earlier was no longer there. It was twenty after ten. By now Laurel would be in bed. Tomorrow Nate's father would be returning from his honeymoon.

An emptiness stole through him because he didn't know when another opportunity would arise to see her again. With the tickets Rick had given him, he'd run out of his last legitimate excuse to hang around the Marsden family.

Brent turned to him. "Are you in a hurry to get home?"

Nate's heart began pumping the way it did in the cockpit at takeoff. "No."

"Then let's go inside and give the girls a bad time. They're huge 76er fans. Little do they know that the NBA championship is going to come out of the Western Conference. After the Nuggets' close win tonight, I'm in the mood to celebrate."

Nate grinned. "Aren't you from Philadelphia, too?"

"Yes, but I've converted since my transfer to Denver."

"What happens when you're sent someplace else?"

"I won't go. Julie and I love Colorado. We plan never to leave."

That pleased Nate in ways he couldn't take the time to examine right now. "I've lived and traveled all over the world. Each time I come home, I realize how fortunate I was to have been born here."

"That's how we feel about living in this state. Fortunate."

They both unfastened their seat belts and got out of the car.

CHAPTER NINE

"THEY'RE BACK! I heard a car door slam."

Since her return from the restaurant two hours earlier, Laurel had been in an agitated state, and she realized it was because she'd missed seeing Nate when he'd come for Brent.

Julie had turned on the TV in the den so they could watch the game, but it had only served as background noise while they discussed Reba and Wendell's depressed state.

"Is Brent coming into the house alone?"

"Hold on." Her sister got to her feet and peered through the shutters. "I see two figures walking toward the porch."

Laurel was so excited she sat up too fast. A cry of pain escaped her lips.

Julie went into the foyer to greet her husband, who'd entered the house with Nate. Laurel followed at a slower pace. Her muscles still hurt from her abrupt movement off the couch.

"No gloating!" Laurel heard her sister warn Brent.

"Did I say anything?" he asked before both men broke into laughter.

Nate was still smiling as Laurel appeared in the

hallway. His gaze found hers. "I thought you were supposed to be in bed," he said in a quiet voice.

"I've been lying down all evening. Now I'm wide awake."

"Come on into the kitchen, everybody," Julie urged. "We figured you guys would want dessert, so I made brownies. There's ice cream to go with them."

While Julie served them at the kitchen table, Laurel made herself a fresh lemonade. As Nate devoured his third brownie, he darted her a guilty smile.

"My time will come," she said, reading his mind. "Then I'm going to buy myself a big bag of salty potato chips and some clam dip."

"It probably won't be long before I'm taken off salt, too," Julie murmured. "Men don't have a clue what it's like to be pregnant."

"The best part for us is getting our wives in that condition. Of course I haven't told the boys that yet."

"Brent!" Julie cried in protest.

Laurel smothered her laughter. Nate smiled, but something else must have been on his mind because his gaze unexpectedly switched to Julie.

"Dessert was delicious. Your husband's a lucky man. Now I think I'd better leave so you two pregnant ladies can get to bed."

That sounded final.

Laurel's spirits plummeted. Struggling not to react, she got up from the chair. "I'll see you out."

Brent rose to his feet and shook Nate's hand. "I can't thank you enough for the great evening. If you don't have other plans, how about getting together for a game of golf tomorrow? I meant to tell you that Scott's parents are here visiting Laurel. They'll be flying back east on Sunday. They're very anxious to meet you. Wendell loves golf, so we could make it a threesome.''

''I'd like that,'' Nate said, ''but I'm afraid tomorrow's out. My father's returning from his honeymoon. He's planning to discuss the future of the business with us—we have a lot of things to settle. Please tell Scott's parents how sorry I am.''

Laurel had the strong impression she wouldn't be seeing Nate again. With a heavy heart she walked through the dining room to the foyer. He caught up to her.

''I'm sorry our outing has kept you up this late. I noticed you're limping tonight. You need to take care of yourself, Laurel.''

That was it? That was all he had to say? She couldn't bear it.

''I pulled a muscle getting off the couch. It's nothing.'' Looking up at him, she said, ''You made my brother-in-law a happy man tonight.''

''We had a great evening.''

''Any fears that he'd still like to toss you through a plate-glass window?'' she teased.

Nate shook his dark-blond head. ''Laurel, I've got to run now.''

This was goodbye. She could feel it in her bones.

''Don't let me keep you, then.''

She opened the door for him. He made a swift exit. After she'd locked it, she hurried up to her bedroom, straining all the way. By the time she reached the window, his Blazer had already disappeared.

Nate...

She crept to her bed. As she lay down on her side, the sobs started. They were relentless.

"The last time I saw you in this condition, Nate was responsible for your tears, too."

It was her brother-in-law. He sat down at the end of the bed.

"He's gone, Brent. I'm never going to see him again."

"I'd like to be able to tell you otherwise."

His words confirmed her worst fears.

"It's evident that he cares about you," Brent continued. "You're the widow of a man who was his best friend in the Air Force. Even if he'd like to, he probably can't separate you from Scott in his mind. A best friend doesn't move in on his buddy's territory. Nate has proven he's an honorable man."

She lifted a tear-ravaged face to him. "So you think any feelings he might have for me are platonic?"

"I can't answer that question."

"But you're a man. Have you picked up on anything while you've been around him?"

After a slight hesitation, he murmured, "There is one thing."

Her heart leaped. "What?" she cried. At this point she was desperate for any crumb he could throw her way. Brent was nothing if not honest.

"He never talks about Scott. Never brings him up in conversation unless someone else mentions him first. I find that strange when they were so close."

"I've noticed that, too. I decided it was because

he wanted to spare me more grief. What other reason could there be?''

''Perhaps to spare himself grief.''

''You mean because he still misses Scott.''

''No, although I'm sure he feels sadness his friend is gone. He could be trying his damnedest to forget that Scott was once your husband. An impossible task, considering you're carrying his child.''

''Brent, what can I do? Because I know I have feelings for him that aren't connected to Scott....''

''I've tried putting myself in his shoes. If Nate's attracted to you, then he has to overcome some pretty deep feelings of betrayal. It would take a very strong man. I feel for the poor guy if that's his problem.''

''But I *want* him to be attracted!''

''You sound like Joey. When he knows what he wants, he's fearless. Everything seems crystal clear.''

''I'm a mess, aren't I?''

''Not at all. You've come back to life. That's healthy. But because it's Nate who's responsible for this rebirth, it's also complicated.''

She wiped her eyes. ''If I don't hear from him again, do you think he'd be repulsed if I made a small overture to let him know I'm interested? That probably sounds like a ridiculous question to you, but I've had almost no experience with men. Scott was my first and only boyfriend.''

''You want my honest opinion?''

''If you have to ask me that, then I already know the answer,'' she lamented.

''I think that if he can't come to terms with the situation on his own, you're both better off going your separate ways.''

"I'm glad we had this talk," she said bleakly. "I know you're right, but...."

"Maybe it's just as well that Nate couldn't see the Pierces this weekend." Brent made a noise in his throat. "If his emotions *are* involved, then meeting Scott's parents at this early stage would probably overwhelm him with guilt and kill any chance for the two of you to explore your feelings."

"I can see that now." But Laurel would give anything to know if Nate had used his father's homecoming as an excuse, so he wouldn't have to meet Wendell and Reba.

"As we told the boys in the car when they said they didn't want a sister, some things have to be left to a higher power. I think this is one of those things. I'm sorry, Laurel. You know I'm on your side."

"I do. Thanks for your honesty, Brent."

"Try to get some sleep."

"I will. Good night."

When he left the room, she knew it was going to be a long, agonizing night. She needed some task to fill the hours.

Writing thank-you letters for all the beautiful gifts might not be what she wanted to do right now. However it would keep her occupied until she was ready to deal with the real possibility that she'd seen the last of Nate Hawkins.

RICK FINISHED VACUUMING, then glanced around the living room. "I think we've got this place looking pretty clean. You're a better window-washer than anyone I know."

"Thank the Air Force. A long time ago, our

squadron had to keep the barracks windows clean for daily inspection.''

Nate had been up since dawn washing all the windows in the house, inside and out. After a sleepless night in which Laurel's image haunted him until he couldn't lie in bed any longer, no job was too big to tackle today.

''We're done, and it's only ten after one. I thought it would take us longer. Ready for lunch?''

The thought of food nauseated him, but he didn't let on as they walked to the kitchen. They'd just put everything away in the utility closet when Nate heard a noise.

He wheeled around at the same time as Rick. Their father stood in the kitchen, looking fit and tanned as only a person could who'd just returned from the Hawaiian islands.

''Dad!'' they blurted in stunned surprise.

He broke into the half smile that was his trademark. ''Hello, boys. You're a sight for sore eyes.''

Meeting them halfway, he enfolded them in his familiar bear hug.

For a moment it was as if they'd been transported to the past. Nate expected to see their mom appear in the doorway any second now.

''We thought you were going to phone us from the inn after you arrived. Where's Pam?'' Rick asked before Nate could.

''It's a long story. Come on into the den and we'll talk. I've got something for you.''

The den had been the place for hundreds if not thousands of talks with their father. Nate exchanged a private glance with his brother as they followed Clint through the house.

If he and Pam were having marital problems already, he was covering it well. In truth, he seemed to be in better shape than either Nate or Rick.

"Pam wanted to be here to give you these in traditional fashion. She had them specially made for you." There were two boxes sitting on the coffee table, and he handed them each one. Again, Nate caught that trace of pleading in his eyes.

He concentrated on taking off the lid. In an instant the fragrance from a fresh lavender-blue Hawaiian lei filled the room. The hue of the flowers reminded him of a pair of heavenly eyes.

Rick's lei was made of creamy white and yellow flowers whose perfume brought the scent of the islands with it.

"They're beautiful," Nate murmured. He raised his head. "But why isn't she here to do the honors?"

"Sit down and I'll tell you."

The three of them assembled around the coffee table.

"When I left the message that we'd be coming home today instead of tomorrow, it was because Pam had just learned that her cousin Audra Jarrett's been injured in a car accident in Austin. At the time, she wasn't given details, but the two of them are very close, more like sisters.

"We talked it over and decided to cut our trip a day short in case Pam was needed. Later she found out that her cousin might lose her leg, so she flew to Austin from Los Angeles this morning to be there for her. I plan to join her in a few days."

"Jeez," Rick muttered.

Nate groaned. "That's rough. Why didn't you go with her?"

Their father looked at them for a long moment. "Because I'm needed here."

"What do you mean?" Rick asked, frowning. "We're taking care of things. Jim and Nina are dealing with the business just fine."

"But you two aren't fine."

"Sure we are, Dad," Nate protested.

Their father shook his head. "I had no idea you were both so worried about my state of mind that you'd actually walk away from your careers to come to my aid. No greater love could be shown a father than that...."

His eyes glistened with tears, and Nate's throat swelled at Clint's openly emotional words.

"You boys have always been the light of my life and your mom's. You always will be. I've always known how remarkable you are.

"But when you accepted Pam without question because you were trying to honor me, you proved what outstanding men you've become. I'm proud to be your father," he whispered. "I love both of you more than you could know."

"We feel the same way." Rick's voice quavered as he spoke.

Nate wiped the moisture from his eyes. "Your happiness means everything to us, Dad."

Their father cleared his throat. "I'm happy, but I know my boys aren't. Let me finish," he said when they started to protest again.

"Years ago, it became clear to your mother and

me that neither of you would be interested in running our family ski business one day. Because Anja and I were lucky enough to make our dreams a reality, we decided early on that you two should be allowed the same privilege. We wanted you to follow your heart's desire, whatever it might be, wherever it took you.

"When I told you I was leaving the ski shop to you, I only said it so you wouldn't feel like you'd been hurled from a pinnacle with no safety net."

That was exactly how it had felt. Nate exchanged another private glance with his brother.

"You two arrived without advance warning at a very precarious moment for Pam and me. She was terrified of you long before you came home."

Somehow that wasn't news to Nate.

"I had to act quickly or lose her." His admission wasn't something Nate had expected to hear. The frown on Rick's face revealed his surprise, too.

"I hoped against hope that you'd hang around the shop until I returned from Hawaii. When I walked in here a little while ago and saw that the spring house-cleaning had been done, I realized that once again my boys had pulled through for me."

"Did you go upstairs?"

"Yes." He stared hard at Rick, then Nate. "Thank you. I could never bring myself to deal with your mother's things. Trust my wonderful sons to know what to do."

Nate was relieved their father felt all right about it. "We put her belongings in the storage room. Pam's your wife now."

"*This* is your home, Dad. Not the Copper Mountain Inn!" Rick declared with emotion.

"This will always be *our* family home," their father amended. "As for the business, I'm planning to sell it to Jim." He rested his hands on his thighs. "The only question of real importance is: where are my sons' homes at this point in time? We have to talk, boys!"

All of a sudden he was sounding much more like his old self.

"Isn't that what we're doing?"

"So far everything's been about me, Nate. Because of me, you two have put your futures at great risk. I'm not budging from Colorado until I can feel assured that your lives are back on track."

Back on track?

How the hell was that supposed to happen when Nate couldn't see one step in front of the other right now?

"Tell me about Natalie."

Rick got up from his chair. "We're not seeing each other anymore."

"Am I the reason?" Clint's voice was pained.

"Of course not. To be blunt, I couldn't imagine being married to her for the rest of my life. It was best to break things off before she got hurt."

"I see. What about you, Nate? I know you were involved with someone before you left Holland."

"It wasn't anything serious."

Their dad sat back against the couch. "When I used to tell you boys how careful you needed to be in choosing the right woman, I must've done *too* good a job. You're both starting to scare me. Haven't you two ever met someone who shook the very foundations out from under you?''

Visions of Laurel overwhelmed Nate. He closed his eyes tightly.

''I've felt tremors here and there,'' Rick teased their dad. ''But I'm still waiting to be knocked flat.''

''That's somewhat encouraging,'' came the dry retort. ''What about you, Nate?''

Taking a deep breath, he turned to his father. ''Sometimes the wrong woman rocks your foundation.''

''That sounds cryptic. Who is she?''

''Spade's widow.''

His father studied him in that direct way of his. ''Do you rock her world, too?''

''I have no idea. She's expecting Spade's baby in the next three weeks.''

''How long have you been feeling this way?''

Might as well get it all said now and be done with it. ''Since your wedding dinner. We...bumped into each other on the dance floor.''

''I thought your friend was from the East Coast.''

''He was. Pennsylvania. She's living in Denver with her sister and brother-in-law at the moment.''

''They had us over for a fabulous dinner the other night,'' Rick added. ''Laurel comes from a very nice family. Their two boys reminded me of Nate and me when we were their age.''

Nate could have done without his brother's embellishments.

''I hope you're going to return the favor, son. How many times did we talk about getting Spade and his wife to come and visit our family? Somehow it never happened.''

There were reasons....

"He's gone now, Dad."

"So? Invite her to the house."

"I don't think so."

His dad stood up. "Have you made arrangements to get recommissioned?"

"Not yet."

"What's holding you back?"

When Clint got started on an interrogation, he was as bad as Rick.

"I'm considering my options."

"That'll be a first for my son who planned to be a hotshot until retirement." His gaze was unrelenting. "I have an idea. Since I need to join Pam in a few days, why don't you get on the phone and invite Laurel and her family for dinner tomorrow night?"

Before Nate could reject his offer, he barrelled on. "Last month Pam spent some time in the kitchen teaching me how to cook authentic Tex-Mex. I'm pretty good at it now. You two can help."

"I've got an even better idea," Rick interjected. "I want to talk to Dad about getting another sponsor to back me. Brent made a suggestion at dinner that might have possibilities. Why don't you leave now and deliver your invitation in person? Take these leis with you while they're still fresh. Laurel and Julie will love them and I'm sure Pam won't mind."

"She'd be thrilled," their father affirmed.

Rick placed the boxes in Nate's arms and virtually pushed him out the door.

LAUREL'S MOTHER-IN-LAW had brought one of the Pierce family scrapbooks so the two of them could reminisce over dozens of family pictures that included Scott both before and after their marriage.

Little did she realize that her daughter-in-law had pored over similar scrapbooks with many of the same photos in the weeks following the funeral. But for Reba's sake, Laurel tried to concentrate.

It was impossible.

After her talk with Brent last night, Laurel had been forced to give up hope of seeing Nate again. *What if she never got him out of her system?*

This was a different kind of pain than she'd known before—because Nate was alive. And Copper Mountain wasn't that far away....

Thank goodness for Joey. While he waited for a friend to come over, he showed great interest in all the pictures having to do with his favorite uncle.

It seemed the rest of the family had deserted them. Julie was downstairs in the kitchen making dinner. Mike had gone with Brent and Wendell to play nine holes of golf.

"That's Kyle," Joey said when the doorbell rang. "See ya later."

After he ran out of the bedroom, Reba expelled a heavy sigh. "Laurel? I've wracked my brain wondering why Scotty would choose to do anything as dangerous as flying jets."

"You're not alone, Reba." Men like Nate and Scott were a rare breed. "My friend Carma, the one who lived next door to me on the base in England, used to cope by saying 'Someone has to do it.' I'm afraid I found little consolation in those words."

"It's so strange," her mother-in-law mused mournfully. "Neither Gary nor Tom showed the kind of interest Scotty did in—"

"Laurel?"

She looked up to see her sister in the doorway. "Excuse me for interrupting," Julie said. "Could I talk to you for a minute?"

"Of course." Laurel patted her mother-in-law's arm. "I'll be right back. Take a look at the baby clothes Julie's handed down to me. They're in the rest of the drawers and the closet," she said, getting up to leave the bedroom.

Once in the hallway, her sister caught her around the shoulders. "Nate's downstairs with Joey," she whispered as they descended the staircase.

The words she'd never expected to hear created such a burst of excitement, Laurel almost lost her footing. If it hadn't been for the railing she would have fallen.

"He knows Brent's out golfing with Wendell, but he didn't ask about Reba. To be honest, I don't think he wants to meet her right now."

"Then let's not force it. If she comes down and sees him, we'll let him handle it."

"Good plan. Now don't rush," Julie cautioned. "Joy goeth before the fall."

Joy was the word. Pure joy when she walked into the living room to find Nate standing there in a navy T-shirt and jeans. He looked so good....

"Hello, Laurel."

"Guess what he brought you and Mom?" Joey said before she could respond.

Dazed, she could only stare at Nate. "I have no idea."

"Neither do I," Julie murmured.

He nodded to Joey. "Go ahead."

Her nephew walked over to the coffee table, where there were two large boxes. He lifted the lid off the first one and drew out the most gorgeous yellow-and-white lei Laurel had ever seen. Both she and Julie gasped.

"That one's for your mother. You know what to do."

"Yup." He was concentrating hard. "Okay, Mom. Bend down." Julie did. "Aloha from Hawaii." He said the words perfectly.

"Aloha, honey." She rubbed her nose against her son's. He sprang away embarrassed.

Nate chuckled. "Okay. The other one's for your aunt Laurel."

Out came a second lei in beautiful shades of blue and lavender. The flowers were still so fresh, perfume filled the whole room.

Her nephew studied her for a moment, then looked back at Nate. "I don't think she can bend low enough."

"Joey!" his mother cried.

Laurel burst into laughter.

"You may be right. Give me the lei."

There was a gleam in Nate's eyes as he moved toward her. His sensuality reached out to her like a living thing, and her heart began to pound with almost sickening intensity.

When he lowered the lei over her head, she felt his taut stomach against her belly. The unexpected contact set off a tremor that shook them both. It wasn't something she'd imagined.

"You have to say aloha!"

"You're right, Joey." Nate's breathing sounded ragged. "Aloha, Laurel."

"Aloha," she answered in a husky whisper. It was pure torture to be this close to him when she couldn't do anything about it. She fought to suppress a moan as he eased away from her.

"This morning my father returned from his honeymoon in Hawaii." Nate seemed fully recovered, but she was sure she'd never be the same again. "As you can see, he arrived bearing gifts. Rick and I felt two lovely women like you would do them more justice."

"They're absolutely incredible," Julie exclaimed.

"They are." Laurel buried her nose in the blossoms. "Thank you so much."

"You're welcome. Dad might not have met Spade, but he always wanted to. In a few days he'll be leaving for Texas to join his wife. When he found out you were living in Denver, he asked me to invite all of you for dinner tomorrow night. I know it's short notice."

"We'd love to come." Laurel tried to keep her voice steady. Her thoughts were already leaping ahead. Reba and Wendell would be leaving at eleven in the morning. That would give her time to rest before the drive to Copper Mountain.

Julie gave him an enthusiastic nod.

"Good." His eyes sought Laurel's once more. "Out of deference to you, we thought five o'clock so you won't have to be up too late."

"That's very thoughtful. Please thank your father for the invitation and the gifts."

"I will. See you tomorrow evening. I'll let myself out."

The minute the front door closed, Joey asked, "Can I go find Kyle? He was supposed to come over."

"We're having dinner in half an hour, so don't be long."

"I won't."

Laurel hurriedly removed the lei and put it back in the box. Julie did the same. She shot Laurel a quick glance.

"While I put these on the back porch, you go upstairs and tell Reba I needed your help with the dinner menu."

"I hate lying to her, but in this case—"

"It's for the best," Julie broke in. "Believe me."

Laurel nodded, then started for the foyer. If Reba had come down, Laurel would've been forced to introduce her to Nate.

Thank heaven it didn't happen!

Laurel hadn't forgotten what Brent had told her last night.

If Nate's emotions are involved, then meeting Scott's parents at this early stage would probably overwhelm him with guilt and kill any chance for the two of you to explore your feelings.

Knowing she'd be seeing Nate the following evening made her so happy, she was able to enjoy her in-laws' visit to the fullest. She even forgot the ache in her lower back while she devoted the rest of her time to them.

Because she couldn't go inside the terminal on Sunday morning to see them off, she got up at seven and drove to the motel in Julie's car. She wanted to spend this last hour with them alone before they left to drop off their rental car and check in.

To her surprise she still had her backache. She must have wrenched it after her near-fall the day before, when Julie had told her Nate was downstairs.

Reba shut her cosmetic case, then glanced at Laurel. "Your mother says she'll be flying out when your baby comes."

"Yes. Julie and I are looking forward to that."

"Promise you'll phone us as soon as you have the baby?" Her voice trembled.

"Oh, Reba…" Laurel gave her a tight hug. "Do you even have to ask? You'll be the first people I call. Don't forget, we'll be seeing each other as soon as the doctor says I can travel with the baby."

"We'll have Scotty's room waiting for you, Lori Lou." Wendell sounded as emotional as Reba. He'd been weepy all morning. "Just think. Before long we'll have another little Scotty."

Laurel bit her lip. She knew Scott's wishes when it came to names, but she couldn't think about that right now. Unfortunately, his parents couldn't imagine her giving birth to anything but a son.

"Maybe it'll be a girl," she said carefully.

"I wish you'd been more curious, Laurel."

"This is one time I want to be surprised. With my next baby, I'll probably want to know."

The comment slipped out before she realized what she'd said. The shock on their faces would've seemed comical if she hadn't been so aware of their suffering.

Wendell reached for her. "It's a damn shame Scotty's not alive to give you another child. Take care of yourself, Lori Lou."

"I will." She lifted her head from his shoulder. "Thank you for coming and bringing the gifts. I love you both so much," she murmured.

They left the motel room and walked out to their cars. "Have a safe flight. Call me to let me know you got home safely."

"Will do." Wendell blew her a kiss.

She hugged them once more, then watched as they got into their rental car and drove off. After one last wave, she eased herself into Julie's car. Tears welled up in her eyes as she started the engine.

Her burgeoning feelings for Nate were absolute proof that she'd put the past behind her. The tears she was shedding now were for Scott's parents.

Please God. Help them find a way to move on, too.

CHAPTER TEN

NATE'S FATHER WALKED into the kitchen, followed by Rick. Nate was already there, finishing some last-minute preparations. Laurel would be arriving in another few minutes, the endless hours of waiting were almost over.

"What's in the oven?"

"Everyone will love your dinner, but Laurel's on a salt-free diet. I put some chicken and vegetables in a roasting bag for her, the way Mom used to do it."

"Your mother's doctor took her off salt with both her pregnancies, too. It still didn't help that much at the end."

"What do you mean?" Rick stole a nacho from the hors d'oeuvre plate.

Their father smiled. "Right before you were born, Anja asked me to help get her foot into one of her ski boots, just to see if she could still do it."

"And?" Rick prompted.

"She couldn't. Not by a mile."

All three of them broke into laughter.

"Laurel couldn't get her shoes on the other night, either." She'd looked so flustered to realize Nate had witnessed it. She'd looked vulnerable and, heaven help him, desirable....

"There's the phone," their father said. "It's probably Pam with an update. I'll take it in the den."

"What do you make of Dad's marriage at this point?" Rick asked after their father left the kitchen.

"Same as you. It's still too early to tell much of anything."

No sooner had Nate spoken than his father reappeared.

"Nate? Phone's for you. It's Brent Marsden."

He jerked around. "They should be here by now. I wonder what's wrong."

He hurried through the house to the den and grabbed the receiver. "Brent?"

"Hi, Nate. I hate to do this to you and your family, but it can't be helped. We were just outside Silverthorn when Laurel's water broke. She's in labor. This baby could come fast. I've turned around. We're headed for Aurora Regional Hospital. She'd like you to be there."

Perspiration beaded his forehead. "I'm on my way."

"Just a minute. Don't hang up. Laurel wants to talk to you."

Talk? How could she even *think* at a moment like this?

He had to rein in emotions that were struggling for release.

"Nate?"

"I'm here, Laurel."

"Forgive me. I'm so sorry this happened when you and your family went to all the trouble of making dinner for us. Please—" She paused for a moment, no doubt because she was in pain.

"Please thank your father. We'll have to get together when the baby's born. I—" She couldn't finish what she was trying to say.

"Forget the dinner. Don't try to talk anymore. I'll see you at the hospital."

Nate dropped the receiver on the hook. His wallet and car keys were in his room. He dashed after them. When he returned downstairs, his father and Rick were waiting for him.

"She's in labor!"

His dad stood there with his hands on his hips. "So I gather."

"I've got to go."

"Call us later, Nate."

"I will."

Silverthorn was only twelve miles from Copper Mountain. If he drove fast, he'd catch up to them on the highway.

Rick accompanied him to the Blazer. "Try to stay on the ground." His comment reminded him of something Laurel had said.

Top guns are notorious for maneuvering their vehicles ten feet off the ground if they can get away with it.

He revved the motor. "I'm not promising anything."

"Message received." He grinned. "It's lucky I filled the gas tank on my way to the store this morning. Take a moment to count backward from ten. She's going to be fine, Nate."

She's got to be.

Nate backed out of the driveway and took off. The damn Sunday traffic turned out to be a nightmare and he had to concentrate on his driving. Yet after traveling for an hour over the speed limit, Nate couldn't see Brent's car anywhere. Laurel's brother-in-law had to be moving at a pretty fast clip.

Forty-five minutes later, he pulled into the hospital parking lot. He took off for the E.R. on a run only to find out he'd come to the wrong place. Labor and Delivery were on the fourth floor.

Not bothering with the elevator, he found the door to the stairway and raced up the steps three at a time. An orderly gave him directions to the west wing.

He put his palms against the edge of the nursing station counter. "Where can I find Laurel Pierce?"

A nurse working on charts looked up at him. "She's down the hall on the right. W412."

Thank God she'd arrived safely. "Thank you."

When he tapped on her door, Brent answered. He flashed Nate a broad smile. "What took you so long?"

"Is that Nate?" Laurel called out. "Tell him to come in."

"Is she all right?" he whispered.

"What can I say? She's in labor. Julie and I will be in the lounge."

As Nate entered the room, two things struck him at once. The sound of the baby's heartbeat from the fetal monitor and the scent of flowers. Somehow the lei had made it inside the room. When he saw it hanging over the closet door handle, a lump rose in his throat.

Like a heat-seeking missile, his gaze sought hers. She held out the hand that wasn't hooked up to an IV. "I was hoping you'd get here in time."

"Laurel..."

He crossed the distance between them and grasped it between both of his. As he kissed her fingers, a nurse came in, followed by a doctor.

He nodded to Nate. "There's a lounge around the corner. If you'll please step outside, I'm going to administer her epidural."

"Thank heaven," he heard Laurel mutter between groans of pain. "Please don't leave the hospital, Nate."

"Nothing could drag me away now." He relinquished her hand, although it was the last thing he wanted to do.

THANK GOD for epidurals, Laurel thought. The pain was just so intense. In fact, she'd never known pain like that in her life. Why hadn't her mother told her what labor was really like?

Just then Dr. Steel entered the room. He walked over to Laurel, a concerned expression on his face. "Looks like you're ready to have this baby. How are you doing?"

"Fine, now that I can't feel the contractions."

"That's the idea."

She couldn't believe this was finally happening; it had been such a long time in coming.

"Okay, Laurel. Let's do it," he said a few minutes later. "Give me a good push."

She strained with all her might. It was odd to feel pressure but no pain.

After twenty minutes the doctor said, "The head's out."

"Oh..." She half laughed and cried at the same time.

More medical personnel had appeared in the room.

"I want you to bear down as hard as you can now, Laurel."

Once again she was calling on every muscle in her body. The passage of time meant nothing to her. All she knew was that the doctor eventually murmured, "Here it comes."

She heard a gurgling sound—and in the next instant, a newborn's cry.

"You've got a girl!"

"A girl?" she squealed. "Oh—my baby girl!" Laurel's voice rang out in pure joy.

The doctor placed the baby on her stomach. The newborn might still be covered in amniotic fluid, but she was wailing at the top of her lungs.

Laurel lifted her head a little. "Is she all right? Is my baby all right?" Her voice shook with fear and excitement.

"She looks good."

The doctor cut the cord. One of the nurses started wiping off the wriggling baby, then wrapped her up and placed her in Laurel's arms.

"Oh, you're beautiful!" She began to weep happy tears. "You're perfect. She's perfect! Oh, Dr. Steel, I'm so happy!"

"I'm happy for you, Laurel."

The nurse smiled. "Congratulations. As soon as Dr. Duffy's examined her, we'll bring her right back."

Not long afterward, the doctor declared his job

was done. "I'll look in on you in the morning. Good night, Laurel."

Another nurse made her comfortable, then left the room, too. For the moment, Laurel was alone with her thoughts. Her eyelids fluttered closed.

Our little girl is here, Scott. I promise she'll always love you in her heart.

Laurel had no idea how long she slept, but when she was aware of her surroundings again, Nate was standing by her bed.

"Nate—I have a little girl!"

His smile warmed her clear through. "I know."

"I want you to meet her. Don't leave."

"I have no intention of going anywhere." Compelled by a force he couldn't resist, he lowered his head to kiss her moist eyelids, then her mouth. "Congratulations on your new daughter."

"We second that."

"Julie!" Laurel cried excitedly.

To Nate's consternation, he'd forgotten anyone else existed. With a sudden feeling of guilt he swung away from the bed to make room for them as they crowded around.

"I have a little girl!"

Brent leaned over to kiss her forehead. "We've already seen—and heard—her. There's nothing wrong with her lungs."

Julie bent to hug her sister. "No matter how many times I tried to assure the boys, they were convinced we wouldn't get you here in time, but it all turned out fine."

"Except for Nate's family," Laurel lamented. "I

should've realized I was in labor before we left for Copper Mountain.''

Nate shook his head. ''Don't give it a thought, Laurel. Dad and Rick have probably finished most of the food by now.''

''I hope they'll forgive me. I thought I'd strained my back.''

''That's where labor often starts,'' Julie said. ''I've called Mom. She's thrilled with the news, and knowing her, she's probably phoned the rest of the family by now.

''Dad's away on a business trip, but I'm sure he'll be calling you soon. Unfortunately, Mom's got a bad cold so she can't fly out yet. She sends all her love and can't wait to see her latest grandchild.''

''Here you go, mommy.''

Nate turned to see the nurse come in with a bundle in her arms.

''She's all cleaned up.'' The nurse put the baby in the crook of Laurel's arm. ''She weighed in at seven pounds, one ounce, and measures nineteen inches. Dr. Duffy says she's strong and healthy.''

''Oh, my baby...''

The next few minutes were a revelation to Nate as Laurel kissed and examined her daughter over and over again. ''I think she looks like Dad, don't you, Julie?''

''A little through the chin. That's a Nana Hayes chin. Her mouth resembles Mom's.''

''I think so, too, but the shape of her head reminds me of Wendell's.''

''Her eyes are a muddy color.''

''They'll probably go brown like Scott's.''

"She's got Scott's brown hair—what little there is of it."

"This could go on for hours," Brent whispered in Nate's ear. "How are you feeling?"

"Like *I've* had the baby," he confessed.

"I know what you mean. My turn will be coming up again in about seven months' time."

"Nate? Would you like to hold her?"

Brent flashed Nate an amused smile. "We'd both like the privilege, Laurel. We've been waiting patiently." He nodded to him. "Sit down, Nate, and I'll hand her to you."

Laurel's brother-in-law obviously understood. This was a whole new experience for Nate, who was still feeling a little weak, a little overwhelmed—and terrified of hurting the baby. But after Brent had placed her in his arms, it felt so right he was astounded.

One look into her adorable face and his heart melted.

"Who do *you* think she looks like?"

All he could see through the mist was Laurel. "You."

"I agree," Brent murmured. "She's going to be a knockout, just like her mom."

As if in response to the comment, the baby yawned, and both men chuckled. Nate studied her tiny fingers. She was tiny, yet complete. Perfect.

"I hate to break in on all this happiness, but it's time for everyone to leave so we can help the new mom start to nurse. You can come back in a couple of hours."

Nate didn't want to go, but he had no choice. After

kissing the baby's soft cheek, he stood up and reluctantly handed her to the nurse.

"Please come back," Laurel whispered to him.

Maybe Nate just imagined the ache in her voice.

"He's going home with us," Brent declared. "After we've eaten, we'll return with the boys so they can see their new cousin. One look at her and they won't mind that she's a girl. By the time you come home from the hospital, they'll be fighting over who gets to hold her."

If Nate had anything to say about it, he'd be part of that fight.

Brent's comments produced laughter from both women.

LAUREL WATCHED Nate's retreating figure, then she turned toward the nurse who was cuddling the baby.

"Before I do anything else, I have to call my in-laws. My husband was killed seven months ago. This grandchild is going to mean the world to them."

Laurel knew Julie would've told their mother not to say anything to the Pierces until Laurel had called them herself.

Was it only this morning she'd kissed them goodbye?

"I'll be back in ten minutes."

The second the nurse departed, Laurel reached for the phone. She dialed nine for an outside number, then placed a credit card call.

After three rings, someone picked up. "Pierces'."

"Wendell?"

"Lori Lou! We phoned you as soon as we got

home, but there was no answer.'' She heard him call out to her mother-in-law.

''Hi, Laurel,'' Reba joined in on another extension. ''We got here safe and sound.''

''That's good to hear. The reason you couldn't reach me was that I went into labor. I'm in the hospital.'' She heard gasps. ''You have a beautiful little granddaughter, seven pounds, one ounce, and nineteen inches long. She's got Scott's eyes. I've decided to name her Rebecca, after you.''

Long ago, that was one of the names she and Scott had discussed if ever they were lucky enough to conceive a daughter.

For the next minute all she heard on the other end of the phone was tears and sniffles. ''I'm so delighted, I don't know what to say, dear.''

Just be happy, Reba. Please be happy.

''If only we'd flown home tomorrow instead of this morning.''

''I know, Wendell. The timing is terrible, but I've found out babies don't worry about things like that. Just remember I'll be flying out to Philadelphia three weeks sooner than expected.''

I don't know how I'm going to stand leaving Nate. If he's still in Colorado by then...

''Send us pictures.''

''Brent's coming back with the family in a little while.'' She closed her eyes tightly, praying Nate would be with him. ''I'm sure he'll bring the camera. I'll ask him to scan some pictures and e-mail them to both families.''

''We can't wait to see her.''

"Neither can I. They'll be bringing her from the nursery in a minute so I can start to nurse her."

"You sound wonderful, dear."

"I *feel* wonderful."

"Scott should've been there."

"I'd like to believe he was," Laurel whispered. She heard the door open.

"I've got to hang up now. Talk to you soon."

"Take care, dear. We'll call you tomorrow."

IT WAS ONE in the morning when Nate returned to the house. Not wanting to wake anyone, he climbed the stairs as quietly as he could. Once in his room he stripped, then stepped into the shower.

Hitching a towel around his hips, he decided he was too exhausted to shave. After brushing his teeth, he went back to the room. Before he climbed into bed, he reached for the shirt he'd draped over the chair. In the pocket was a picture of Laurel and the baby. He studied it.

Mike and his dad had brought cameras to the hospital. Mike's was a Polaroid. He'd used up two packets of film.

Mike had been kind enough to offer Nate a photograph—the one of Laurel wearing the lei. She'd wanted it preserved on film before it wilted.

"What have you got there, son?"

Surprised his father was still up, he turned to Clint, who stood in the doorway, wearing his old striped bathrobe.

"Laurel had a seven-pound girl today. I saw her in labor, and then a few hours later, there she was holding this perfect little baby. It was the most incredible experience of my life.''

''Better than your first solo flight in an F-16?'' Rick had just wandered into the room wearing the bottom half of his sweats.

''Nothing could compare to the birth of a baby,'' he said in a serious voice. ''Nothing...''

''Is that my hotshot brother talking?'' Rick asked as he walked over to look at the picture.

''He's right, Rick. Every man should be so lucky as to have that experience.'' His father drew closer to take a peek. ''The daughter resembles her mother. They're both beautiful. Pam will have to see this picture.''

''Laurel wants you to know she feels terrible about ruining dinner. I tried to assure her it didn't matter, but she made me promise to convey her apologies.''

''Tell her we'll try it again when she's up and around.''

''I already did.''

His father gave him a thorough scrutiny. ''You look more exhausted than the woman in this picture. Better go to bed before you topple over. See you in the morning.''

''Good night, Dad.''

When he left the room, Nate turned to his brother. ''Has he heard from Pam yet?''

''No, and the longer he has to wait, the more I'm thinking it's bad news about her cousin. I know more than one driver who's faced similar injuries. It's hell on earth to lose a leg.''

''Maybe you ought to be thankful it hasn't happened to you yet.''

"If that's your unsubtle way of telling me to find something else to do with my life, the line forms behind Dad."

He stared his brother down. "Can you blame him after losing Mom?"

Rick looked shocked. "I thought you were in my corner."

"I am. But a baby was born today." He paused to swallow. "Because of Scott's career, he was killed. He never got a chance to see his wife give birth or hold his child." Nate shook his head. "What you and I do for a living can wipe a man out in seconds."

Judging by his frown, Rick didn't want to hear it.

"You had to be there. When I saw Laurel's joy as she held her daughter in her arms, I knew what Mom and Dad felt when we were born. Since that moment I've asked myself how our parents were able to accept our careers without suffering a nervous breakdown."

"Don't forget they placed themselves in danger every time they ran a race."

"True. But in comparison, you have to admit that strapping ourselves into a race car or the cockpit of a jet increases the danger by quantum leaps. Besides, they were in their early twenties when they gave up competing and settled down. I'm beginning to wonder if Dad didn't get married again to provide an emotional buffer, especially as he gets older."

Rick blinked. "You think he's been suffering anxiety about us all these years and never let on?"

"I don't know. Without Mom, maybe he just couldn't handle it. Let's face it. You and I haven't exactly hung around Copper Mountain for the last ten years giving them grandchildren.''

''Well, if they were truly bothered, they never said a word,'' his brother challenged.

''Sorry, Rick. I didn't mean to put you on the defensive. Today was…an incredible experience for me.''

''That's because you're in love with Laurel.''

Nate's head reared back. The blood pounded in his ears.

''I think you've been in love with her for a long time.''

''Shut up, Rick.''

''No way. Mom and Dad used to ask me why I thought your relationships with women never went anywhere. I had a hunch but I never told them because I didn't have actual proof.''

''What the hell are you talking about?'' Nate lashed out.

''Nine years ago, Spade introduced you to his wife. The three of you spent a day together. Do you want to know why I remember an insignificant piece of information like that?''

Nate's face started to prickle with heat.

''You came home that next weekend in a foul mood. I'd just won my first important race. I felt like celebrating and talked you into going to the Cowboy Bar in Vale for a few beers.

''But you didn't order beer. You ordered whiskey. That's when I knew something was really wrong. You drank enough to make even my tough older brother break down.

''By the time I'd hustled you out of there and into

the car, you were sobbing. You kept saying you'd done the worst thing a guy could do to his closest friend.'' Rick shook his head. ''You scared me when you said that. I asked what it was and you finally said, 'I've fallen for Spade's wife, Rick. I can't ever be around her again. What in God's name am I going to do?'''

Nate groaned. That night had always been a blur to him.

''I assumed your feelings for her would pass. Over the years I thought they had. You never talked about her again. But now that I look back, you always did have an excuse when the folks suggested you invite the Pierces for a holiday. When any of us visited you overseas, you always made sure it didn't include Spade or his wife.

''You couldn't even bring yourself to fly to Philadelphia after Mom's funeral to pay your final respects.

''It's all fitting together now. Your anger at seeing her in Breckenridge with Brent, discovering she was pregnant.

''You weren't just upset for Spade because you thought she'd betrayed him. The truth is, *you* felt betrayed—because you've been in love with her all these years.

''God knows you did everything in your power not to act on your feelings. Now it seems He's seen fit to reward you by placing Laurel in your path.''

''Her being in Colorado at the same time as me is strictly coincidental!''

''Maybe,'' Rick murmured. ''But since the night

she saw you on the dance floor, she's come after you three times of her own free will. Is that coincidence too?

"Sweet dreams, Nate."

CHAPTER ELEVEN

AFTER THE 11:00 a.m. class for nursing mothers on Monday morning, Laurel asked the nurse who'd wheeled her back to her room to wait ten minutes before bringing in the baby. She had a vital call to make first.

As soon as the nurse disappeared out the door, Laurel reached for the receiver to phone her sister.

Last night Nate had gone home while she was asleep. The next time she'd awakened, it was three in the morning and the nurse had brought her a hungry, fussy baby to nurse.

Julie had warned her that, at first, the nursing experience could be frustrating for both mother and baby, but with a little patience it would become both natural and easy. The class instructor had said the same thing to the group of exhausted women who'd just given birth.

She'd also driven home the fact that nursing was a time of bonding, when the mother's whole being was intent on her child, as it should be. The nurse's comment had made Laurel feel guilty, since Nate was never out of her mind, not for one single second.

What if all the attention he'd lavished on her since the encounter in Breckenridge had been his way of being there for her because Scott couldn't?

Would a man go that far for his friend?

Looking back now, she felt as if she'd practically forced Nate to be there with her. The poor man had been placed in a position where it would have been impossible to say no.

The chaste kiss he'd given her yesterday had felt like a benediction. Laurel had wanted it to be more, to mean more. It'd been an effort to hold back certain words she hadn't dared say unless she knew he wanted to hear them.

What if he didn't?

Was it another woman's words he craved? A woman from his past who'd hurt him? Was that the reason he hadn't married yet?

If all this attention to Laurel was prompted by some kind of last-rites favor to his best friend's widow, then Laurel needed to put a stop to it. She'd lived through one agony of loss. She'd never survive it a second time.

"Julie!" She burst into tears as her sister walked into the room. "I was just phoning you. I'm so glad you're here!" She hung up the receiver and reached out her arms.

"What's wrong? Don't worry, your baby's not going to starve to death. I promise she won't."

Laurel sat back against the pillow and wiped her eyes on the sleeve of her nightgown. "The nursing's coming along okay. That's not why I'm upset."

"Then it's Nate." Her sister pulled up a chair next to the bed. "Has he said something about leaving Colorado?"

"No. I have no idea what his plans are. I have no idea about anything."

"What do you mean?"

"Oh, Julie—I'm in love with him."

"I knew it!" she whispered.

"If he doesn't feel the same way about me, then I can't ever see him again. Brent told me I should wait for him to make all the moves, but what if they're motivated by his loyalty to Scott and nothing else? What if he's just being kind to me?

"You have no idea what it's like to see him walk out the door without knowing if he'll be back or not. I can't take any more." She stared at her sister. "I've been so happy since the moment we cleared up the misunderstanding. He's such an exceptional man, Julie. What am I going to do?"

Her sister's expression sobered, and she put a hand to her sister's forehead. "All this emotion isn't good for you. You're running a temperature."

"I know. The nurse gave me something for it."

"Good." After a pause, she said, "Laurel, when Brent told you to let Nate do the running, he meant you should wait for him to make the next move. Since that talk Nate has made several. He was still here when we left last night."

"But if it's because he feels he has to be Scott's substitute through—"

"Then it's time you found out the truth," Julie muttered. "If he was any other man than Scott's best friend, I'd encourage you to be patient and see what happens."

Laurel nodded.

"But this situation is unique. I've discovered for myself that he's honorable yet complicated. If you hadn't been the aggressive one, you would never have resolved that awful misunderstanding. I don't believe I've ever met anyone who keeps things hidden that deep."

"You don't know the half of it. Talking to him is like walking through a minefield. One wrong step and he closes up, or suddenly has to leave."

"He had an abiding friendship with your husband," Julie said. "If he *is* in love with you, I'm not sure he'll admit it. Unless you confront him, he'll go back to his career without ever telling you the truth."

"That's my fear. Right now I'm afraid I won't see him today, afraid he won't call. I can't live this way any longer."

"Not if you don't want to upset the baby."

"That's the last thing I want to do." Tears streamed down her flushed cheeks. "The hospital isn't the place to talk to him. I'll have to wait until I go home tomorrow, where we can be alone."

Whatever Julie would have said was drowned out by hungry infant cries. "Here we are. Time for baby's lunch."

Laurel accepted her baby from the nurse, anxious to try out the tips she'd learned in class. With a few more suggestions from Julie, things went smoothly, and twenty minutes later, her baby fell asleep in her arms, content until next time.

"Thanks for your help, Julie."

"Anytime. Did I tell you the boys have nicknamed her Becky?"

"That's what I plan to call her." She sighed. "It'll probably hurt Reba's feelings."

"How could it do that when you're naming the

baby after her? Wait—forget I asked. Oh, there's the phone. I'll take Becky so you can answer it.''

Their eyes met as Laurel reached for the receiver. Her heart was pounding too fast.

"Hello?''

"Hello, honey. How are my daughter and granddaughter doing today?''

"Dad! We're fine. She just ate and now she's sound asleep. Julie's holding her.''

"I'm thankful you two have each other.''

"So am I.''

"Your mom's got bronchitis. Don't worry. It's not a serious case, but she's still too sick to fly. I think we're going to wait until you come out here. How soon does your doctor figure you can travel?''

"I'll ask him when he discharges me tomorrow.''

"Honey?'' His voice had grown quiet. "Is everything all right? If you need me, you know I'll be there as soon as I can.''

She could read between the lines and she realized it was time for complete honesty—with everyone.

"I know. If you mean am I still missing Scott, then the answer is yes, I'll always miss him but I'm ready to move on. I'll always treasure our memories. I have a responsibility to my daughter—and to Scott—to live my life as fully as I can.'' She paused. "My little girl has brought me more joy than you can imagine.''

"You don't know how happy that makes me,'' he said with a tremor in his voice. "The world's an exciting place. Your lives are just beginning.''

"That's exactly how it feels.'' *That's how Nate makes me feel.*

"Living with Julie and Brent was exactly what you needed. Though your mom and I had a hard time letting you go, we had to trust it was for the best."

"It was."

What if she'd never bumped into Nate? She couldn't comprehend his not being in her life now. But she had to find out if he was emotionally involved with her, too. A plan was forming in her mind.

"We can't wait to see you and the baby."

"Becky can't wait to meet her grandparents."

"Becky, is it?"

"Yes. I've decided to name her Rebecca. That was something Scott and I had discussed."

"I like it. Your mother-in-law will be pleased."

"She cried when I told her."

There was a silence. "I'm proud to be your father, Laurel."

"Thanks, Dad." She wiped more tears from her eyes. "Give Mom my love. I'll call both of you tomorrow when I get home from the hospital."

"We'll look forward to it. Put your sister on for a minute. I want to tell my other wonderful daughter how thankful I am for her too."

"Okay. Love you, Dad."

NATE AND RICK FLANKED their father as they left the bank. When all the paperwork was done, Jim Springmeyer would be the new owner of Eagles' Nest Ski and Bike Shop.

Clint appeared to have no regrets. In fact, since Pam's early-morning phone call to let him know the doctors had been able to save her cousin's leg, he'd been almost jubilant.

"I'm taking you boys out to lunch. Any place you'd like to eat here in Denver."

Nate desperately wanted to head over to the hospital in his mother's car. But since their dad was flying to Texas in the morning, Nate had the feeling he wanted to use this time to discuss his future plans as well as theirs.

"You two decide and I'll follow you," Nate said when they'd found their cars in the underground parking area.

Once he'd driven out to the street, he phoned Laurel's hospital room. After four rings she answered. "Hello?"

"Laurel? It's Nate. How are you and the baby doing today?"

"We're fine, but I'd be lying if I didn't admit I'm exhausted."

If that was a hint she didn't want company, then he wouldn't visit. But his excitement in the day had suddenly vanished.

"That doesn't surprise me."

"I've discovered the hospital is no place to get any rest."

She definitely didn't want visitors. She didn't want *him.* Knowing he wouldn't be seeing her today came as such a great disappointment he was stunned by his reaction.

"How soon can you go home?"

"Sometime tomorrow. Julie will come for me when I'm discharged."

"I'm sure you can't wait."

He'd intended to help her when she was released from the hospital. So much for his plans.

"Would you like to drop by tomorrow afternoon around four to see Becky in the outfit you gave her?" she asked unexpectedly.

Was she inviting him out of kindness? Simple courtesy? "I didn't realize you'd already picked out a name."

"Yes. Scott and I made lists several years ago. I believe this is the one we would've ended up choosing for a girl. His mother's name is Rebecca, although everyone knows her as Reba. I thought I'd call my daughter Becky so there won't be any confusion."

He gripped his cell phone tighter. Of course they'd discussed names. They'd wanted children. Becky was Spade's little girl. Spade's parents were her grandparents. Laurel was their daughter-in-law. She would always be an integral part of the Pierce family's tight community.

Desolate, Nate said, "The name suits her. She's a cutie."

"I think so, too, but then I'm her mother. What I'd like to do is use Mike's Polaroid to take some pictures of you holding her. That is, if you have the time."

"I'll make the time."

Laurel, Laurel. You've turned me inside out. What the hell am I going to do about you?

"Good. After we decide which photo we like best, I'll have several dozen made up and send them inserted in announcements to all the guys in the old squadron. Do you think Duce still has everyone's address?''

After what Nate had accused her of, it was no surprise she was anxious to make certain the guys knew about Spade's child.

''I'm sure he does. He's always been the self-appointed liaison.''

Nate could hear the baby fussing in the background. ''Sounds like Becky's hungry again. I'd better let you go. See you tomorrow.''

''Thanks for calling, Nate.''

Thanks for calling, Nate.

Those words might as well have been goodbye.

After what they'd experienced in the delivery room, her whole demeanor over the phone seemed so detached.... Evidently that was because he was the only one who'd felt any kind of emotional revelation yesterday.

He grimaced. Rick had been wrong.

She would always be Spade's widow. Anyone who'd known Spade could see Becky was his look-alike. She would be a constant reminder of the husband Laurel had lost.

After tomorrow, Nate had no intention of seeing her again.

He stared at the peanut butter and plum jam sandwich he'd made for her. It was lying on the seat in a sealed plastic bag. Joey had told him it was her favorite snack. While Nate searched for the Blazer, which didn't appear to be anywhere in sight, he opened it and ate both halves.

Another minute and his cell phone rang. He checked the caller ID and clicked on. ''Rick?''

"You must be lost in thought—not to mention just plain lost!"

"Where have you decided to eat?" he asked, ignoring the comment.

"We're at Chee-Chee's in the downtown mall."

"I know the place. See you there." He hung up before his brother could needle him any further.

By the time Nate joined them, he'd made up his mind to focus on his father, who was ten years away from early retirement. Over a taco salad and coffee he brought up the subject he knew was on Rick's mind, too.

"What are your plans after you move to Texas?"

"Pam owns a little house on a portion of her family's ranch. She's always wanted to build a bed-and-breakfast Texas-style, on her property, but without the capital and someone to help her, it's still a dream.

"She doesn't know it yet, but I'm thinking of using the money from the sale of the ski shop to turn that dream into a reality. Looking at it as a business venture, it'll be the same kind of thing I'm used to doing. Of course, the product will be different, but it's people-oriented. I like that. We'll live there and run it."

"But is that *your* dream?" Rick's concern was as real as Nate's.

"No," came the blunt reply. "I lived my dream with your mother. Now I'm looking forward to helping Pam achieve hers. She has a lot of impressive ideas and excellent business sense."

Rick shook his head. "Texas is as different from Copper Mountain as Hawaii is from the North Pole. You may end up wishing you'd never moved."

"True. If that happens, then Pam and I will discuss it. We can always sell the business and move back here. What's important is being together."

"Couldn't you have talked her into staying at Copper Mountain and helping you run the ski shop?"

"Your mother's death brought me to the end of an era, Nate. Meeting Pam has set me on a different course. However, one thing will never change. Whether I'm in Colorado or Texas, my home will be your home, too. You understand what I'm saying?"

They both nodded before Nate intercepted a glance from Rick. For the time being, their father's decision seemed firm.

"Enough about me." He turned to Rick. "Have you figured out what you're going to do?"

After a pause, Rick said, "I've decided to fly out to New York tomorrow and spend a few days talking to the Trans T & T people. Nate can drive both of us to the airport at the same time."

Nate sat forward. "Isn't that the company Brent works for?"

"Yes. In the past they've sponsored pro golf. Brent believes they'd be willing to sponsor something else. He gave me the name of a contact. I have no idea how it'll turn out, but it's a place to start. There are other companies in the Big Apple I plan to call on, too."

It didn't look as if their brother-to-brother talk had done anything to make Rick consider finding himself a safer career.

"Well, that takes care of you for the time being." He studied Nate, who fidgeted a little under his steady gaze. "Nate? What are your immediate plans?"

"After I drop both of you off, I'm driving to Colorado Springs to find out what I have to do to get recommissioned."

Rick's eyes flared in surprise but he didn't say anything.

Their father continued to gaze shrewdly at Nate as he finished drinking his coffee. When he put down his cup, Clint said, "Is that still your dream?"

Touché, Dad.

He looked away. "It's all I know. It's what I trained for."

"I thought your perspective might have changed while you've been home."

"You mean since I've spent time with Laurel?" His jaw hardened. "I hate to disappoint you, Dad, but her husband's only been dead seven months. She's just had his baby. Her nephew told me she's going home to Philadelphia as soon as she can travel."

"My disappointment doesn't enter into it," his father responded calmly. "It's your pain I'm concerned about."

He lifted his head to meet Clint's eyes. "What pain are you talking about?"

"Nate, I was there to cut the cord when you were born. You think I don't know when my firstborn is hurting? Do you honestly imagine I don't know you've been suffering for years now?"

Rick gave a subtle shake of his head, as if to say he had nothing to do with their father's astute observations.

Nate believed him. Their father's instincts had always been uncanny. Except for his precipitous marriage to Pam, he'd somehow managed to understand everything in their lives—their hidden feelings and secret desires, their reasons for the choices they made. But right now Nate couldn't take the compassion he saw shining from his wise gray eyes.

Needing to do something physical, he picked up the bill the waitress had put on the table. "I'll take care of this and wait for you outside."

"You're not going to the hospital?"

"No. It turns out Laurel's exhausted. I'll see her once more at the Marsdens' tomorrow after I return from the Academy."

His father studied him briefly. "In that case, let's go home and get in some spring skiing for old times' sake."

Nate knew he couldn't. His heart wasn't in it.

Since his conversation with Laurel, he'd gone numb inside. It terrified him because he had a premonition that this was how he'd feel from now on.

LAUREL STOOD next to the crib, trying to quell the frantic beating of her heart. Nate would be here any minute.

She'd just finished nursing the baby and had dressed in a pair of maternity jeans, the ones she'd bought when she first started to show. At seven months, she'd had to put them away in the drawer.

After considerable debate, she'd chosen a flowing dark-green cotton top. It was round-necked and long-sleeved. For an article of clothing that wasn't made for a pregnant woman, it managed to cover a multitude of sins.

To her relief, she'd lost a lot of weight. Though it was still a snug fit, she could slide her feet into her Italian leather sandals again.

Her hair had grown over the past month. The blow dryer brought out its natural curl. After applying a dark pink lipstick, she reached in her jewelry box for the green enamel earrings she'd purchased in Florence to match her top. Each delicate flower was outlined in gold. She loved them.

For a final touch, she fastened the treasured gold watch Scott had bought her in Toledo, Spain, to her wrist, then put on a dash of her favorite lemon spray.

Although she was no longer pregnant, the figure in the mirror still left a lot to be desired. She'd already accepted the fact that she would never look like the nineteen-year-old Nate had met in Las Vegas. However, once she'd completely recovered from the birth, she planned to work out and make herself as attractive as possible.

"Laurel?"

She swung around anxiously. "You think I look all right?" she asked her sister. "Too much? Too little? Change everything? Tell me the truth!"

Julie shook her head. "After having a baby two days ago, it isn't fair you could look as gorgeous as you do. Nate's never been able to take his eyes off you, anyway. He's going to be speechless when he sees you."

"Thanks for the compliment, but you're biased."

"Even if I am, the truth speaks for itself. I came to tell you he just pulled up in front of the house."

She started to tremble. "Oh, Julie... This is it."

"Frankly, I'm glad it's here at last. As soon as I tell Nate to come upstairs, I'll take the boys to do errands. After that we're meeting Brent for hamburgers. You've got the house to yourself. Make the most of it."

"I could be making the biggest mistake of my life."

"No, Laurel. If he's not in love with you, then it'll be a blessing to find out. Even if brings you more pain for a while."

"You're right."

"There's the doorbell. You know I'm wishing you all the luck in the world." She blew her a kiss and disappeared out the door.

Laurel stood by the crib, where she held on for dear life. Voices filtered up from the foyer, then she heard footsteps on the stairs. Her heart seemed to lose a beat when Nate appeared in the doorway.

He'd come dressed in a tan suit and white shirt. The figured tie had some blue in it that matched his beautiful eyes.

A stillness seemed to surround him as his gaze traveled slowly from her hair, to her body and finally to her sandaled feet.

"Hi." It was all she could manage to say because her trembling had grown worse. "T-there's a chair by the window," she stammered after a moment. "I'm still kind of sore, so I've decided not to go downstairs until tomorrow. I hope you don't mind."

"Why would I mind?" He sounded almost angry as he crossed the room to sit down. Something was wrong. His implacable expression gave nothing of his feelings away.

"The baby's still asleep, but it won't be for long. When she starts to wake up, I'll take some pictures."

"Do you need help walking to the bed?"

His question brought more heat to her face. He could tell she was shaking. What he didn't know was why.

"I'm fine. Really."

She reached the side of the queen-size bed and lounged back against the pillows propped next to the headboard. "I'm afraid I can't see you from this angle. Why don't you sit on the end of the bed and face me."

His hesitation was tangible but he did as she asked. The proximity of their bodies sent her temperature soaring.

"That's better. You look very official. Have you been to a meeting of some kind?"

"That's right. Today I've taken steps to be recommissioned."

Laurel struggled not to cry out.

"Does that mean you'll be at the Academy for a while?"

Please God—don't let him leave Colorado yet.

"No. My old commanding officer thinks he can pull a few strings. If that happens, I'll be back in Holland sometime next week."

She lifted questioning eyes to him. "Is that what you really want to do?" she whispered.

His grim expression devastated her. "My father doesn't need me. He's making a new life for himself in Texas. There's no longer any reason for me to stay."

Laurel eased herself forward. It brought her face a little closer to his. Never in her life had she contemplated anything this daring, but she was fighting for her life. As far as she was concerned, that gave her permission.

"What if you had a reason?" she whispered.

"I'm not sure I understand."

Was he evading the issue because he didn't want to hurt her, embarrass her with the answer?

She tried to swallow. "Maybe your father doesn't need you, but *I* do."

Color receded beneath his tanned complexion. "Spade and I go back a long way. You can always count on me to be your friend, Laurel, wherever I am."

"I'm not talking about friendship."

She couldn't call back her words. She didn't want to. For better, for worse, she'd said them. Nate couldn't claim to misconstrue their meaning now.

He got to his feet and stood at the window, as if he felt suffocated by the confining walls of her bedroom.

"You miss Spade," he said in a faraway voice. "The birth of your daughter has made you long for him. When you see me, you see your husband. It's perfectly natural."

Nate was still hiding behind that forbidding veneer. She couldn't lose courage now. "Would you answer a simple question for me?"

A palpable silence settled in the room before he turned to her. His carefully impassive expression told her he was concealing some strong emotion. It gave her the impetus to go on.

"When you look at me, do you see Scott?"

She sensed him retreat although he didn't move a muscle.

"Let me ask it another way. Do I remind you of him?"

"No," he muttered. "But it's not the same thing. Except for that one time years ago, I never saw the two of you together."

"It's equally true that except for the day the three of us spent at Nellis nine years ago, I never saw you with him either. But I'm not confused, Nate."

Driven by overwhelming emotions, she slipped off the bed. "Since we met again in Breckenridge, have you been acting for Scott in everything?"

His throat was working. He couldn't meet her eyes.

"When you kissed me after the delivery, was that for him, too?" Her heart hammered. Surely he could hear it.

"Laurel—" He sounded like a broken man.

She moved closer until she could put her hands on his arms. His powerful body quaked in response.

"Let me make this clear. I couldn't mistake you for anyone else. You're all I've been able to see or think about since the moment I saw you on the dance floor at the lodge. Do you have any idea how hard it was for me not to kiss you back?"

He shook his head. Torment flashed in his eyes. "I shouldn't have taken that liberty. You were lying there helpless."

"Helpless with wanting you! Maybe this will convince you." She started to slide her hands to his face.

"No, Laurel. Don't!" He grasped her wrists in a firm grip. "I can't do this to Spade."

"He's gone to a happier place, Nate. There's only you and me. If you don't hurry and kiss me, I—"

"It wouldn't be right—" he broke in. His breathing had grown shallow.

"I'm *giving* you the right!" she protested.

"For the love of heaven, Laurel—you've just had his baby—" He backed away, relinquishing his hold on her. "I've got to go."

Pain wracked her body. "Then I was wrong, wasn't I?"

Her words stopped him at the door. "What do you mean?"

"I thought you came around because you couldn't help yourself any more than I could. But you've just proved to me that everything you've done has been out of loyalty to Scott, nothing more.

"No one could ever doubt what great buddies you were. Just so there won't be any misunderstanding, I need to explain that I've fallen in love with you. The last thing I want is a buddy."

"You don't know what you're saying." He sounded aghast.

Angry tears sprang to her eyes. "That's right. A man only says that when he doesn't want to hear the truth. I'm sorry if I've repulsed you, but I had to find out what's motivated your visits.

"Now that I know it was all for Scott's sake, I wish to God I'd never forced a confrontation with you. It was my mistake from start to finish."

She darted him a brief smile. "Consider your duty accomplished. Go back to Holland and forget what happened here, Major Hawkins. Now if you don't mind, I'm tired and could use some rest before the baby wakes up. On your way out, will you please push in the night lock?"

Nate, her heart cried in anguish as he disappeared from the doorway. She crumpled on the bed, her sobs reverberating in the room before she could smother them with a pillow.

CHAPTER TWELVE

OUTSIDE HER BEDROOM, Nate lay against the wall listening to the sounds of a woman who sounded utterly grief-stricken.

Just so there won't be any misunderstanding, I need to explain that I've fallen in love with you. The last thing I want is a buddy.

Could it possibly be true?

He wanted to believe it so badly his entire being trembled.

Every sob coming from the bedroom resounded deep in his soul, tearing him apart until he couldn't take anymore. He approached the doorway again.

Her prone body shook the mattress. That beautiful face and body, which had haunted him from the first moment he'd laid eyes on her...

The longing to touch her drove him to the bed. He sank down next to her. She gasped and turned on her side. When she looked up at him, her drenched eyes exploded with light.

"Nate!"

"God forgive me, but I couldn't leave."

"There's nothing for Him to forgive."

She threw her arms around his neck and pulled him toward her. "Kiss me," she begged. "I need you so terribly, you can't imagine."

How little Laurel understood of his desire for her. The fire she'd unknowingly lit inside him years ago had never been extinguished. Now she was going to discover the extent of that long-suppressed hunger.

He stared at the exquisite mouth he'd fought not to look at after Spade had introduced them. Then he covered it with his own.

Her first ardent response produced an ecstasy that came close to making him lose consciousness. Groaning in need, he stretched out to feel every feminine inch of her while he kissed her over and over again with slow deliberation. Long, deep kisses that would never be long enough or deep enough.

His fingers twisted in her glistening black hair. It was like silk to the touch as he knew it would be. Her skin…pure satin. The voluptuousness of her curves…

Nine years of dreaming could never match the reality of holding this woman in his arms. She pulsated with a desire equal to his own. He felt like he'd come home after years of wandering in a strange wilderness.

They kissed with mindless abandon, losing track of time and place in their desperation to communicate.

He traced the natural arch of her dark brows, marveling at every feature, pressing his lips against each one to memorize their feel and shape.

"You're so beautiful I can't find the words," he whispered into her neck.

She kissed his temple. "The first time I saw you with the guys from the squadron, you were outside playing volleyball. None of you had shirts on. When

I jokingly asked Scott who the tall blond god was, he turned to me with a smile and said, 'That's Hawk.'"

She'd thought of him that way? When he lifted his head, her adoring eyes played over his features.

"I've lived with that image of you for years, Nate. When I saw you on the dance floor, your back was toward me, but I knew that body could only belong to one man.

"You really are something," she whispered against his lips, drowning him in sensation. "I knew I was in love with you the morning you drove me to the doctor. When you helped me down from the Blazer, I wanted you to take me in your arms.

"Nate—promise me you won't ever let me go!" she cried urgently before covering his face with moist kisses.

As he was coming to find out, she was a woman who loved with her emotions as well as her body. Her words only added to his euphoria. He rocked her in his arms.

"Can you see that happening now?"

"N-not if you take me to Holland with you." Her voice faltered.

Holland? He'd forgotten about that. He'd forgotten about everything in the heat of her embrace.

"I'm sorry—I shouldn't have said that. I had no right." She tried to ease away from him.

"Come back here." He pulled her against him, then found her mouth once more. "You had every right," he finally whispered.

"No." She shook her head against his shoulder. "Kissing me doesn't constitute a commitment on your part. The one thing I couldn't stand is dishonesty from you. The joy of knowing you feel an attraction to me will have to be enough for now.''

"Attraction— Oh, Laurel—'' He let out a deep sigh. "How little you understand.'' He lay back against the mattress.

She raised herself on one elbow to look at him. Her other hand cradled his jaw. "Then tell me.''

He turned his head to kiss her palm. "I fell in love with you after spending ten minutes in your company back at Nellis.''

An incredulous expression entered her eyes.

"Spade put up pictures of you in the barracks. Every guy in the squadron fantasized over you. I had to listen to your husband go on day and night, talking about your beauty, your grace, your—''

Laurel kissed his lips quiet.

"It's strange how well you can get to know a person without ever having met them. I liked everything he told me about you. If ever a woman made a man happy, you did that for him. The truth is, I envied Spade. Then I met you,'' he whispered in a husky voice.

His eyes closed as memories of that meeting overwhelmed him. "My torture began when Spade interrupted our game to introduce you to everyone. There you were at last. Laurel Pierce in the flesh. The cherished wife of my best buddy. I took one look at you and fell so hard I never recovered.''

"Nate…''

"My parents raised me to honor the Ten Commandments. Until I met you, I never dreamed I'd have trouble with Thou Shalt Not Covet Thy Neighbor's Wife.

"That night, when the three of us said goodbye, you gave me a kiss on the cheek. It burned right through me. I knew then I'd be in serious trouble if I ever spent time with you again. I had to make sure it didn't happen."

"So *that's* the reason we never managed to get together?" He could hear her shock. "I always wondered why."

"As I said, it was vital that I avoid you."

"I had no idea. So many times I wanted to ask Scott about it, but I sensed he wouldn't tell me the truth even if he knew. That was because he liked you too much, respected you too much.

"Over the years I learned to live with it. However, in my heart there's always been this fear that you harbored something against me."

"I'm sorry, Laurel." He reversed his position so he could lean over her. "But I had to shut you out or stop being Scott's friend. I wanted to visit you after his funeral...."

She stared at him. "You're a noble man. No one else I've met even comes close."

"Don't make me out to be a paragon. I was a terrified man, Laurel. So terrified, in fact, that I was cruel to you on the dance floor. Still, I couldn't understand the pain in your eyes when you looked at me. Not until this moment did I realize that my past actions had any effect on you." He shook his head. "I don't know how you forgave me for that night."

She brushed her mouth against his. "Because I'd

met you once before and I knew the man at the lodge was acting out of character for a reason.''

He fingered her earring. ''Now you know all my deep dark secrets. Every one of them had to do with forbidden thoughts of you.''

''You did quite a job of covering up.''

''Only my father and brother have figured it out. They understand that if I haven't settled down yet, you're the one to blame. Twice I came close, but in the end it was your presence lurking in my heart that stopped me.''

''I'm so glad it did!'' she cried, reaching for him with an eagerness that made him wonder how he'd existed all these years without her. After kissing her again, he said, ''Your daughter's hungry.''

Laurel groaned. ''Her timing is terrible.''

''She's the perfect chaperone. At this point I need one.'' He got to his feet. ''She doesn't sound like she can wait for picture-taking. Why don't we put it off until another time?''

''You're not going!'' The alarm in her voice revealed the fragile state of her emotions. His weren't any different.

''You need time with Becky and I have something to do that can't be put off.''

''When will I see you again?''

''When do you want to see me?''

Her eyes were still glazed from the passion they'd shared. ''I never want you to leave.''

She slid off the bed and wound her arms around his neck. All she had to do was raise her mouth to his and all rational thought disappeared.

By now Becky was crying loudly.

With reluctance he wrenched his lips from hers. "How soon will I be welcome in the morning?"

"Six."

If this wasn't Brent's home, Nate would be back to join her in bed, to hold her all night. "Make it ten and we've got a date."

He turned to the baby who needed some serious attention. "Be a good girl for your mommy. Tomorrow we'll get better acquainted." After kissing Laurel on both cheeks, he headed for the hallway without looking back.

"Nate?"

The longing in her voice was going to be his downfall if he didn't get out of there right now.

"I'll call you tonight."

"I'll be waiting."

That quavery sound in her voice melted his bones. It took all the self-control he could summon to leave the house and get in the car.

Nate felt like he'd left the gravitational pull of earth and was hurtling through space toward the stars.

He didn't remember the drive into downtown Denver. Nothing registered until the salesman inside Cramer's Fine Jewelry said, "A natural blue diamond is costly. I can sell you something comparable in a sapphire for two-fifths the price."

"The color's not the same."

"That's true. They're very rare. I only have one to show you. It's pear-shaped."

"May I see it?"

"Of course."

The jeweler drew a small envelope out of a file

drawer. When he returned to the counter he let the stone fall onto the velvet. He used a tool to manipulate it so Nate could see its intense color.

He lifted his head. "How long would it take to mount it on a plain gold band like a solitaire?"

"It can be ready tomorrow after three."

"Good."

"What size are we talking about?"

"I don't know, and I don't want her to suspect anything. Pick an average ring size. If it's not right, she can come in later to have it adjusted."

"I'll need a down payment now, the rest when you pick it up."

Nate reached into his wallet for his credit card.

As soon they'd transacted their business, he left the mall for home. En route he placed a call to Colonel Harker's voice mail at the Academy. Once again, Nate's plans had to be put on hold. He could only hope that when his old commanding officer learned the reason he might be understanding about Nate's apparent indecisiveness....

By the time he'd grabbed a burger and pulled into the driveway, it was nine-thirty. Before he climbed out of the car, he phoned Laurel but got a busy signal.

He felt for his tie lying on the other seat and hurried into the house, deciding the phone in the den would be a better connection anyway.

It felt good to get out of his suit jacket and shirt. He tossed them over the back of the couch. He hadn't even had a chance to grab the phone when his cell rang.

Laurel? His pulse raced as he said hello.

"That was fast."

"Rick…"

"Sorry to disappoint you."

Nate frowned. "Who said anything about being disappointed?"

"Look, Nate. You don't have to pretend with me. I know you're feeling bad right now. With Dad in Texas and me in New York, there's no one at home to talk to, so I thought I'd check in."

"Thanks." Nate cleared his throat. "Have I ever told you how glad I am you're my brother?"

There was an abrupt silence. "Now you've got me scared. You haven't been getting friendly with Jack Daniel's, have you?"

Nate could still feel Laurel's body wrapped around him. Friendly didn't quite cover it. "Let's just say not with Jack."

"Hell—I shouldn't have gone to New York. For several reasons it might've been a mistake."

"What's wrong? No, wait. I've got something I have to do, then I'll call you back."

"That'll give me time to book a flight home in the morning. I'll expect to hear from you in twenty minutes." His brother ended the call.

Anxious to reach Laurel before it was too late to call the Marsden home, he punched in their number. Someone picked up after the first ring.

"Hello?"

"Laurel?"

"I wanted it to be you. Did you try to call earlier?"

"A few minutes ago."

"Joey was on the phone with Kyle and didn't realize I was waiting to hear from you."

Nate still had a hard time believing all that breathless emotion was for him.

"How are you feeling? How's Becky?"

"We're both fine. Did you accomplish whatever it was you needed to do?"

"Yes." *Oh, yes.*

"I wish you were here now."

The taste of her mouth still clung to his. "It's probably better that I'm not." He managed a grin. "Maybe you'd have to be a man to understand."

"Women understand these things, too."

She *was* a woman—in every sense of the word. Her loving response had changed the rhythm of his heart forever.

"Do you think you'll be recovered enough by the weekend for me to drive you and Becky to my house at Copper Mountain? I think Brent and Julie need a break from me and my constant visits."

"I already have a lot of mobility. By Friday I know I'll feel like getting out. There's nothing I'd love more than to see your home."

"Then we'll shoot for Friday and see what happens."

"Does that mean you've changed your mind about coming by tomorrow morning?"

"I'll be there at ten. If you don't know that by now, then you don't know me at all."

"I love you, Nate," she cried. "I need you here so I can show you how much."

After all the pain, Laurel was actually saying those words to *him*. He still couldn't believe it.

"Until tomorrow," he said softly before hanging up.

This was the first time in nine years he was waiting with excitement for tomorrow. Not since before that traumatic day with the Pierces—when he'd been forced to hide his feelings for Spade's wife—had he known true happiness.

RICK WAS IN THE MIDDLE of making a stir-fry when his cell phone rang. He took the frying pan off the burner to answer it.

"Hello?"

"Rick?"

"Hi, Dad."

"You've been on my mind. How are things going in New York?"

"Actually I'm back home. I flew in this afternoon. Nate picked me up at the airport a little while ago. Now we're at the house."

"That was a quick trip. Tell me about your visit with the man at Trans T & T."

"Ira Sharp turned out to be a good contact. He took me to dinner with the CEO and three of the board members. It was all very positive. They said they'd draft a contract and courier it to me in about a week. Of course that'll only be the first step. Their lawyers will have to talk to Mayada's."

"The important thing is you're happy with it, son. As for their company, I never had any doubts they'd pick you up. Lucky Hawkins is one of the hottest properties on the racing circuit and they know it."

Except that Rick was no longer sure of what he wanted to do; he might have approached the Trans

T & T people for nothing. But all he said was, "Thanks for the vote of confidence."

"You've always had it. Now let's get to the real reason you left New York so fast. I know Nate's in bad shape."

For once in our lives you're wrong, Dad.

Nate was walking around in a euphoric daze, but Rick had been sworn to secrecy until his brother decided to tell their father what was going on.

"We talked after he got out of his meeting with Colonel Harker yesterday," his father continued. "It was a one-sided conversation. Nate closed up on me as only he can do. Pam understands the situation. Since she wants to spend time with her cousin who's going to be in the hospital for a while, she's urged me to return home.

"I was calling to let you know my flight will be in tomorrow morning at 11:45. The three of us could fly down to Cabo for a few days, do some deep-sea fishing."

"It sounds like a great plan, Dad, but I think Nate ought to hear this. Just a minute and I'll get him."

Rick put down the phone and dashed out the back door. Nate had already washed their mother's car. Now he was cleaning the inside, getting it ready to bring Laurel and Becky to the house tomorrow.

He'd never seen his brother this happy in his life, not even when he'd received a scholarship to the Air Force Academy his senior year in high school.

"Nate, you're wanted on the phone."

"Laurel?"

Man, he had it bad.

"No. It's Dad. Don't worry. I didn't say a word,

but you're going to have to tell him the good news now."

"Why?"

"Because he's coming home in the morning and wants to take us on a deep-sea fishing trip to Cabo."

"You're kidding!"

He dropped the rag on the front seat of the car. Rick entered the kitchen first and handed him the cell phone. "Do you want privacy?" he muttered.

"No. Keep cooking. I'm starved."

Rick chuckled as he returned to the stove.

Nate grabbed a handful of the cashews his brother was about to add to the stir-fry, then put the phone to his ear.

"Hi, Dad. How's Pam?"

"She's relieved her cousin's going to be all right."

"I'm sure she's a lot happier now that you're there. What's this about a fishing trip?"

"Does the idea appeal to you?"

"Any other time I'd love it, but something's happened that prevents me from going anywhere for the moment."

"When we talked on the phone yesterday, you were on your way to see Laurel. I presume this has to do with her."

You know it does. "Today I bought a ring. Tomorrow evening I'm going to ask her to marry me."

The silence following that statement lasted so long, Nate thought maybe they'd lost the connection. "Dad? Are you there?" His question brought Rick's head around.

"Thank God," his father finally said. "Your

mother and I prayed for this day. Congratulations, son.''

"She hasn't said yes." Tomorrow night couldn't come fast enough.

"Of course she has. Otherwise she wouldn't have wanted you at the hospital for the birth of her baby."

"She's Spade's baby, Dad."

"He gave her life, but make no mistake. Becky's going to be your daughter. You held that child in your arms soon after she was born. That makes you her father—and me her grandfather."

He could hear what his dad was saying, but it still felt like some fantastic dream.

"You can't imagine my delight," his father went on. "When Laurel's wearing your ring and you've come down from the heights long enough to remember you've got a dad, call me and I'll fly home to meet her and Becky."

Nate shifted his weight restlessly. "If she accepts my proposal, we'll phone you."

"I'll be waiting. Now—if Rick's nearby, will you put him on the phone for a moment?"

He turned to his brother. "Dad wants to talk to you again."

Rick nodded. "Check on the rice, will you? Everything else is done." He hurried over to take his phone.

"Hi, Grampa," he said. "Pretty fantastic news, huh?"

"It is as long as Nate doesn't cut and run. I recognize all the signs. He's still terrified to step into Spade's shoes. I'm depending on you to help him."

Nate was watching him with guarded speculation.

Rick hadn't guessed at his brother's extreme vulnerability behind all that happiness. Yet it had only taken a few cogent comments from their father to show him how fragile Nate felt.

He smiled into the phone. "Don't you know that's what uncles are for?"

"That's right, Uncle Rick. You're responsible for making sure your brother doesn't fall apart before tomorrow night. Don't let him be alone. Apply some of those famous Lucky Hawkins strategies you use on the track when you can smell victory but there's still one final obstacle to overcome."

"Okay, I'll do my best." Rick glanced over at Nate. "I can hear Pam's voice in the background. Say hi from both of us. We'll talk again soon." Rick turned off the phone.

"What was that all about?"

"Dad's thrilled at the prospect of being a grandfather. To tell you the truth, I haven't heard him this excited since I won my first junior world slalom championship in Vale twenty years ago."

"Hmm." Nate sounded noncommittal, as if he wasn't really paying attention.

"I've got an idea. Let's get out the videos and watch them while we have dinner. I think they're still in the den. Mom had all the old family ski movies put on cassettes. It's years since I looked at them. Were we oblivious or what?"

"I don't understand."

"I think Dad and Mom hoped one of us would want to train for the U.S. ski team. I'm pretty sure that's why they decided to settle here rather than in

Sweden. Did you have any idea they cared about it that much?''

"No."

"Let's take everything into the other room. I imagine there's at least three hours of footage to get through."

Nate helped him carry their plates and a couple of sodas into the den.

''Not that it would have made any difference if we *had* known their true desires,'' Rick went on. ''It wouldn't have changed anything. I suppose we should be thankful they didn't tell us. Otherwise we'd have felt guilty…''

He put his plate down to find the videos.

''Ah—here's the first volume.''

He turned on the TV and put the tape in the VCR slot. Within seconds they were looking at Nate shortly after he'd been born.

''Fast forward it to the snow scenes,'' his brother urged.

It took a while to get to the place where their parents had put Nate in his first pair of skis.

''You couldn't be more than two in these scenes. Look at Mom and Dad taking turns working with you.''

Pretty soon came the baby pictures of Rick. Sure enough, around two years of age his parents were doing the same thing with him.

After an hour and a half of nonstop ski scenes, Nate got up and shut off the TV.

''Hey—we're only halfway through.''

Nate turned to him. "I'll look at the rest later. Laurel's expecting me to call."

Rick watched his brother leave the room. *I did my best to keep his mind occupied, Dad.*

CHAPTER THIRTEEN

"I'LL SETTLE Becky in the den, then come back for you. Don't you dare move." After a fleeting kiss that left her desperate for more, Laurel watched Nate unfasten the baby's car seat and carry Becky into his house.

Laurel couldn't take her eyes off him. From the moment he'd picked them up at Julie's, he'd done everything in his power to ensure their protection and comfort. Anyone seeing them would think he was her doting husband...and the loving father of her child.

She had to admit she'd visualized him as her husband. At the hospital he'd become Becky's father in her heart. Not in a way that displaced Scott, not at all. Nate could make Becky's father real to her, could share things about Scott that no one else even knew.

If she hadn't forced him to acknowledge that he had feelings for her, she would have lost him forever. Until the other day in her bedroom, she couldn't possibly have known how deep those feelings were, how long he'd hidden them to preserve the integrity of his relationship with Scott.

She wasn't fooling herself. The enormous leap from the place they were now to the place she wanted to be might never happen.

An honorable man didn't move in on a buddy's territory, didn't get involved with another man's wife. That was what Brent had said.

Prophetic words. Nate had held his silence for nine years. Even when there was no further obstacle, he'd still tried to respect Scott's memory and been ready to walk away with his secret.

Laurel might have removed the first hurdle, but she knew she couldn't force anything else. As a wise brother-in-law had told her, if Nate couldn't learn to forgive himself on his own, then they were better off apart. She believed that, although she hated to admit it.

She also believed something else. He might resume his career as a pilot, and if he did, she couldn't live with it.

Death came in many forms and ways. It was a fact of life everyone on earth had to accept. But answering the door to another commanding officer telling her that her husband had been killed in the line of duty would destroy her.

If those issues couldn't be surmounted, then spending any more time together would bring nothing but heartache.

Almost ill with a combination of anxiety and her uncontrollable desire to belong to him, she decided she would tell him it was too soon to be out, after all. She'd ask him to please drive her back to Julie's.

But the words refused to come when she saw him striding toward her with that look in his eyes. The look that said he couldn't wait for them to be alone…

Nate's arm went around her waist, pressing her

against him as they walked into the house. He paced his steps to match hers.

The moment the front door closed behind them, he wrapped possessive arms around her. Emotion turned his eyes a darker blue. "Until a few days ago, I never allowed myself to dream what it would be like to have you all to myself under this roof. Laurel—"

His cry of longing seemed to come straight from his heart. He bent to touch her mouth with his. For the last few days she'd sensed that he was curbing his passion out of consideration for her condition, out of respect for Brent and Julie's hospitality.

This kiss was different.

It was the kiss he would have given her if there'd been no Scott, no baby. It was a man's kiss, hot with desire. A kiss that said he wanted her, wanted every part of her body and soul, that anything less wouldn't do.

A voluptuous warmth spread throughout her system.

"Nate." She gasped at the exquisite pleasure of his hands roving over her body, molding her to his powerful frame. This time there was no baby between them.

"I love you," she cried against his mouth. "I know I keep saying that, but I can't help it," she murmured feverishly.

She felt a tremor pass through his body before he wrenched his mouth from hers. He put her gently away from him, his glazed eyes revealing the depth of his rapture.

"I was going to wait until later." He sounded like he'd been running a marathon.

"To kiss me?"

"No." He grasped her hand. "Come with me."

They left the foyer to enter an attractive den with a fireplace and two matching couches. He'd placed the baby in a comfortable-looking easy chair.

On legs that felt weak, Laurel walked over to reassure herself Becky was still asleep.

"All's quiet for the moment," Nate whispered against her neck. He'd come up behind her to slide his arms around her waist.

Compelled by overwhelming desire, she turned to kiss him again. A woman who'd just had a baby was surging with hormones. The wonder of Nate's love sent them flying off the charts.

He cupped her face before his lips traveled over her cheeks and jaw, her eyes, her mouth. "There's something I have to get from the kitchen, but I don't know if I can let you go long enough to do it."

"Then take me with you."

"No." He kissed her throat. "You're supposed to be resting."

"You think I could rest after the way you've made me feel?"

Nate smoothed the hair from her temples. "No," came his impassioned whisper. "But I need you to humor me." He backed her carefully to the couch so she'd sit down. "Don't go away."

"I'm counting the seconds."

"So am I." He made a swift exit through another door, leaving her a trembling mass of emotion.

Here she was in his home. She'd been so excited

at the thought of learning everything she could about him, but right now she found it impossible to concentrate. All her energy was focused on the door as she waited for him to return.

An instant later, he reappeared and sat down on the couch beside her.

"Do you see this?"

She tore her gaze from his to look down. She gasped when she saw a gold engagement ring lying in his palm. The blue pear-shaped stone dazzled her eyes.

"You know what it means. I love you more than I thought I could ever love a woman. I want you for my wife, Laurel. I realize it's too soon, but after nine years..."

Unless he can come to terms with the situation on his own...

Joy beyond description welled up inside her.

"Marriage to you is all I've been able to think about since the day you took me to the doctor," she admitted. "If you'd proposed to me in the Blazer, I would've said yes. That's how much I want you as my husband.

"But before you put that ring on my finger, we have to talk about something that's been keeping me awake nights.

"It's not what you think!" she cried when his face darkened. "It's not about Scott."

"Go on."

"There's no easy way to tell you."

He sprang to his feet. "Just say it," he demanded. Already that forbidding wall was in place. His whole body had gone taut.

She was terrified of losing him, yet if she wasn't honest now...

"I *have* to say this, for your sake as well as mine. I know flying is your life and someone has to do it, but I'm selfish enough at this point to want my husband to come home to me at night. Every night. I need to know he's on the ground, where his chances of surviving are better than in the air flying combat missions.

"I crave a normal life, Nate. I should never have asked you to take me to Holland with you. I said it in a moment of weakness because I couldn't bear to be apart from you. But the truth is, the thought of you being in a war or out on deployment for weeks or months at a time—"

She buried her face in her hands, unable to go on.

"That's it?" He sounded incredulous. "*That's* the thing that's been keeping you awake nights?"

"Yes." She tried to smother her sobs. "I know it's too much to ask."

The next moment, he was crouching in front of her. "Look at me, Laurel."

She lifted a tear-ravaged face. His eyes shone with a new light.

"I went about this proposal all wrong. My plan was to spend the whole day with you before I asked you to marry me. But as you found out, once I got you inside the door I couldn't wait even five minutes.

"Laurel." He reached for her left hand and kissed the palm. "My flying days are over."

She shook her head. "No, Nate. This is exactly what I was afraid of. You say it now, but tomorrow you'll be climbing the walls. You'll want to be back with your buddies talking the talk, one-upping each other, bragging about some dive you pulled out of at the last second."

When he started to speak, she stopped him with a raised hand. "If you weren't so totally hooked, you couldn't do what you do. Believe me, Nate, I'm the last person who'd ask you to give it up. You'd learn to hate me for it. I couldn't bear that."

He pressed her hand to his cheek. "When I was a teenager, I admit the idea of being a fighter pilot became my obsession. The day I got my wings, I thought nothing could surpass that feeling. I thought I'd never want anything else.

"Then I met you," he said in a husky tone. "That's when my real education began. I suddenly realized there was something else in life, something I wanted even more. But I couldn't have you. From that point on, my career became a job. *You* became my obsession."

"Nate—"

"Let me finish. With hindsight, I can see that if it hadn't become just a job to me, I wouldn't have resigned my commission, not even for my father's sake. I could have asked for a leave of absence. Instead, I got out. Are you still listening to me?"

She nodded, scarcely able to believe what she was hearing, yet wanting to believe it with every part of her.

"Before I picked you up today, I talked with Colonel Harker, my old commanding officer. I told him I was getting married—if you'd have me. We've worked everything out. I'm going to be a flight instructor for the Academy."

"In Colorado Springs?"

"There's only one Air Force Academy," he drawled.

"Forever?"

"How about until you and I decide it's time for me to retire."

"You don't ever have to go overseas again?"

"Not unless our president calls every boy and man to arms."

"Oh, darling!" Laughing and crying with happiness, she threw her arms around his neck. They both ended up on the floor in a heap of tangled arms and legs. By now Nate's joyous laughter had joined hers.

Their noise woke Becky, whose frightened cries were growing by decibels.

"Quick. Put the ring on my finger." She held out her left hand.

"I don't know if it'll fit."

His hands trembled, yet she wasn't worried. He never left anything to chance. Just as she'd expected, the ring slid home without a problem.

She gazed up at him with her heart in her eyes. "You've done it now. You're all mine. To have and to hold from this day forth."

He gave her mouth a hard, swift kiss. "As soon as you've fed our little girl, I'm going to make you keep that promise. Let me help you onto the couch." When she was sitting down again, he handed the baby to her.

"Come here, little sweetheart. Did we frighten you?" She rocked her back and forth to quiet her. "I know you're upset and hungry, but your daddy's just made me the happiest woman in the world."

Laurel looked up at him. "You have, you know. The love I feel for you is so intense, it actually hurts."

"I've been in pain for a much longer time."

"I'm going to take it away," she promised him. "All of it."

"Our wedding day can't come soon enough for me," he said softly. "While you feed Becky, I'll get our lunch."

WHEN NATE OPENED the fridge, he saw something that hadn't been there when he'd left for Denver earlier in the day.

He smiled as he pulled out a bottle of non-alcoholic champagne. Rick had taped a note to the label.

"A nursing mom can't drink the hard stuff yet, but who needs it when you're both floating ten feet off the ground? I couldn't be happier for you, Nate. Enjoy!"

Nate felt a surge of gratitude to his brother—and for him. But as he started making sandwiches, he thought about Rick.

His brother was struggling.

Maybe it was the wonder of Laurel's love that had given him second sight. All he knew was that if Lucky Hawkins had done something as drastic as break his contract, there was a reason. A reason beyond their dad's state of mind...

Absorbed in Rick's dilemma, he hadn't realized Laurel had come into the kitchen. The feminine arms that slipped around his waist left him breathless.

"What can I do to help?" she asked.

"If you want to know the truth, I'd like you to sit

down at the table. I can't think, let alone function, while you're touching me.''

She kissed the middle of his back through his shirt. "I'm just the opposite. I can't think or function *unless* I'm touching you. Give me one kiss and then I'll do it.''

He laid the knife on the counter and turned around. "You think one kiss will satisfy me?''

She looked at him adoringly. "I hope not.''

Those lips were an enticement he'd never be able to resist. Not in a thousand tomorrows.

One kiss became another, then another, until there was no beginning, no end. Ten minutes must have passed before he slid his hands to her shoulders. Pressing his forehead against hers, he said, "I want to marry you now. This instant.''

"I feel the same way.''

Nate drew her against him, burying his face in her hair. "I've hungered for you too long. I want it all now. I don't know how to be patient. I haven't even met your family yet. Our engagement's going to shock your parents.''

"A wonderful shock.'' *My in-laws will be another matter.* "I can't wait to tell my whole family. But first let's eat this delicious lunch you've made for us.''

"Lunch. What's that?''

She pulled away from him with a grin. "It's what keeps you alive. And Nate—I want you alive.''

He opened Rick's gift and poured it into champagne flutes before sitting next to her. He raised his glass. "To you. To Becky. And to us.''

She raised her glass, too, gazing directly into his

eyes. "And to Scott." Tears gathered as she whispered, "I think he'd be happy for us."

Nate nodded solemnly.

"I love you, Nate," she said. "I love this sapphire ring. I've never seen anything so breathtaking. The pear shape—it's perfect."

"It's a blue diamond to match your eyes."

"A blue diamond? I've heard of them. They're horribly expensive. Oh, darling, I never expected a ring! You do too much for me." She looked at him through her lashes. "This isn't a dream, is it?"

Emotion made his throat close up. "If it is, we're in it together."

"After we eat, I want to call Mom and tell her our news. Dad'll still be at the office. We can phone him there."

"He's a newspaper columnist, isn't he?"

She finished another bite of her sandwich. "In the beginning. Now he's a managing editor for the *Philadelphia Inquirer*."

"I'm impressed. That newspaper must be one of the top five in the whole country."

She smiled. "He's a hotshot in his own right. Between him and my mother with her Neapolitan heritage, there's never a dull moment."

"Does she speak Italian around the house?"

"Oh, yes. When my grandparents come to visit you should hear them."

Delighted by all he was learning, he asked, "How about you?"

"Growing up, I only understood and spoke a little bit. But as soon as we were stationed in Italy, I went to a local university for two years. I received enough credits in Italian that I only need to do some under-graduate general education courses at a university here to obtain my BA. Once I've done that, I plan to go on to graduate school and eventually teach Italian at the college level.''

Spade had never told him that. There was still so much to learn. Every minute with her was an adventure.

"Of course, my grandmother never fails to inform me I speak with a northern accent.''

Nate broke into laughter. "My mother was from Are, Sweden. She had an accent too.''

"I was in Are with my girlfriend two years ago!'' Laurel blurted. "She lived next door to me on the base in England. In high school she'd been an exchange student to Stockholm and she wanted to go back to visit the family who'd hosted her. We traveled everywhere. That's a fabulous ski area.''

More information Spade hadn't confided. Laurel had spent a lot of time on her own as an Air Force wife.

"You're right. I have a grandmother who still lives there with an aunt. My mom learned English at an early age, but she always retained an accent and my dad teased her about it. Now he's married to a Texan.''

Laurel chuckled. "When we get everyone to-gether, it'll be hilarious. Is your father a native of Colorado?''

"No. He was raised in Stowe, Vermont.''

"Ah… No wonder he became an Olympic skier.'' She nudged him. "What happened to you?''

His lips twitched in response. ''To my parents'

disappointment, Rick and I found other fields to harvest.''

''You certainly did. When you introduce me to your father, I'll tell him how thankful I am he raised such an independent spirit. Otherwise we wouldn't have met.''

Those were Rick's exact words.

The worshipful look in her eyes entranced him. *Laurel, Laurel. Is this really happening to us?*

She drained her glass. ''How did your parents end up in Colorado?''

''They met during the Olympics when they won their medals. Before that, they'd raced in some World Cup events here and they both fell in love with the place. After they got married, they decided to settle in Copper Mountain.

''Both sets of grandparents used to come for long visits until one by one they passed away, except for my mother's mother, of course.''

She reached for his hand and clasped it. ''I want to know everything about you, even down to how much you weighed when you were born. But I can't wait any longer to tell my parents we're engaged. Let's take advantage of the silence before Becky wakes up.''

Nate pulled out his cell phone. ''My father already knows my intentions. He'll be expecting a call, too. What's your parents' number?''

He pushed in the digits as she dictated them. ''It's ringing.''

Laurel took the phone from him and waited for her mother to answer.

After four rings, she heard, ''Hello?''

"Mom?"

"Laurel! Just hearing your voice cheers me up."

"Your bronchitis sounds better than yesterday."

"I'm improving. The doctor told me to keep breathing steam."

"Then you continue to do as he says."

"How's my little Becky?"

"Thriving."

"Pictures are wonderful, but I can't wait to hold her and kiss her."

Laurel laughed. "I do enough of that for three people."

"I haven't heard you this happy in years. Becoming a mother has changed you."

"There's no question about that, but there's another reason as well."

Nate was sitting back in the chair, smiling that half smile that made him utterly desirable.

"I'm in love," she said simply. "We're going to be married."

"Oh, Laurel. This is something you're sure about?"

"Very sure, Mom."

"You've always known your own mind, so I trust your feelings about it." She paused. "Who is he? We want to meet him."

She smiled, nodding to Nate. "He wants to meet you, too. His name will be familiar. It's Nate Hawkins."

A quiet gasp came through the line. "Scott's best friend?"

"Yes. We happened to bump into each other by accident in Breckenridge. He's incredible, Mom. I love him the way you love Dad and I wanted you to be the first person to know.''

"That's a lot of love. Is he on another extension?''

"No. We're at his parents' home. He's sitting right next to me. I'm using his cell phone.''

"I'm glad he can't hear me. Just listen for a moment. You know I'm overjoyed with your news. I'm so glad you're ready to resume your life. Your father will be, too, but don't say a word to anyone else in the family about this yet.''

Laurel knew what was coming.

"While I chat with your fiancé, I want you to be thinking about how you're going to present this to Reba and Wendell.''

"I've already decided. When I fly to Philadelphia with Becky, Nate's coming with me. So are Julie and Brent and the kids. Nate and I will take the baby to their house and tell them our news together.''

"That's probably the best way to deal with it. When I get on the phone with Nate, I'll invite him to stay with us.''

"Thanks, Mom. You're wonderful. Here he is.''

His expression had sobered. "What was that all about?'' he whispered.

She needed to be honest with him, but she didn't dare say too much. Brent's warning still made her anxious.

"Mom realizes I'm in love with you. She doesn't want me to get so carried away I forget to reassure Scott's parents they'll always have access to their granddaughter.''

"That goes without saying. Let me talk to your mother.''

Laurel whispered, "Her name is Silviana Bardelli Hayes. Just call her Sylvia." She bit gently on his earlobe before handing him the phone. "I'll check on Becky."

She left the kitchen without worry. Her mother was not only the soul of discretion, she was also a great conversationalist. Before he got off the phone, she would know more about Nate than Laurel did.

The thought pleased her to no end as she leaned over Becky to kiss her cheeks. Her baby was a good eater and a sound sleeper. It almost seemed as if she was intentionally cooperating.

When Nate walked into the den a few minutes later, he was still talking on the phone. To her surprise, he'd already hung up with her mother and was now chatting with his father.

"Hold on, Dad. She's right here."

Wearing a smile that lit up his eyes, he sat down and placed his arm around her shoulders, pulling her close. "It's your turn," he whispered, nuzzling her neck before he handed her the phone. Everything must have gone fine with her mother.

Ecstatic, she said, "Hello? Mr. Hawkins?"

"At last we speak. You know, Laurel, you've made him a totally happy man."

"I love your son."

Nate squeezed her harder.

"He's a deep one." There was a barely discernible pause. "He needs your love."

His father seemed to be sending Laurel a message, but it wasn't necessary. She knew her husband-to-be was still vulnerable right now.

"If he hadn't proposed, I probably would have. Becky and I can't wait to be with him."

"I can't wait to meet you and my new grand-daughter."

Her child would have three grandfathers. Three wonderful men who'd each bring something different to her life.

"What a lucky little girl she'll be to have a grand-father who was an Olympic champion. Maybe she'll want to become a famous skier like you one day."

His laugh reminded her of Nate's. "I gave up on that dream for Nate the day his mother stuck his first drawing of an F-16 on the door of the refrigerator. However, your words have given me fresh hope.

"As soon as I tell Pam your news, I'll make plans to fly home next weekend and spend a few days with all of you."

"That would be great. Do you want speak to Nate again?"

"If I know my son, he's counting the seconds until you get off the phone and pay attention to him, so I'll say goodbye for now."

"All right. We'll talk to you soon."

Still smiling, she handed him the phone. "I like your father. You and Rick obviously inherited his charm."

He stole a hungry kiss. "Tell me what he said."

"He's planning to fly out next weekend."

"Good. But that's not the part I'm referring to. He said something that made you go quiet."

His father had said a lot in a few words.

"He was letting me know how much your hap-piness means to him." She turned toward him, putting her hands on his chest. "How did it go with my mom?"

His gaze narrowed on her mouth. "She invited me to stay at their home when you're ready to fly out. I made her promise that she'd let me watch all the videos of you."

"You'll die of boredom."

"She said the same thing, but told me it was for my own good. I needed to see what I was in for."

Laurel chuckled, shaking her head. "That sounds like my mom."

"I like her. I like her a lot."

"You'll like my dad, too. Let's call him now."

"She suggested we wait until this evening. He'll want to celebrate and he can't do that while he's working."

Her mother knew exactly what she was doing. At the office, the walls had ears.

"In that case, I want to see all the Hawkins family videos."

"How do you know there are any?"

She held up her left hand. "Are diamonds blue?"

"You'll be sorry. There are at least three hours of them."

"That's good. They'll keep us out of trouble. Becky's not being a very good chaperone right now."

"I noticed, so I think we should get into all the trouble we can until she wakes up."

"Nate." She half moaned his name as he eased her down until she was lying against him. Then his mouth covered hers and there was no more sound except the heavy pounding of their hearts. They didn't surface again until the baby started to whimper.

Laurel's body throbbed from his touch. She ran her tongue over lips that were swollen from his kisses. When she rose to her feet to take care of Becky, she staggered slightly. Nate was there to steady her from behind. His hands caressed her hips and stomach.

"We've got to set a date, Laurel. I can't take much more of this."

"Neither can I."

"Where do you want to be married?"

"Here in Colorado. It's the first place that's ever felt like home to me, other than Philadelphia."

He whirled her around. "How soon will the doctor allow you to travel with the baby?"

"That's really up to me and how I feel. And the baby, of course. After your father comes next weekend, we'll fly out so you can meet my family. We'll spend a week there, then we'll come home and get married. How does that sound?"

His fierce embrace answered her question.

"I'm sorry," he murmured when he finally released her. "You've just had a baby, but the minute I touch you, I forget. When we're alone in this house, you're too much of a temptation. We need to be around people."

"You're serious."

She already knew he had a will of iron. It was in full evidence now, and it was one of the qualities she respected in him most.

"Look at me, Laurel. I'm trembling like a man with palsy. You can watch all the videos you want after we're married. While you feed Becky, I'm going to clean up the kitchen, then we'll drive back to Denver.''

''All right,'' she said in a tremulous voice. ''But you won't leave me?''

''I'll stay until Brent kicks me out. How's that?''

She heaved a sigh of relief. ''That's all I needed to hear because it won't ever happen.''

By now Becky had worked herself into hysterics.

Two and half hours later, they pulled into Brent and Julie's driveway. The timing was perfect, because her brother-in-law was just getting home from work. He drove in right behind them. Joey was on the front lawn with his friend Kyle.

''Home so soon?'' Brent opened the car door for her while Nate dealt with Becky and her car seat.

''Yes. I couldn't wait any longer to show you *this*.''

Brent took one look at the shimmering blue diamond and let out an ear-piercing whistle. Their eyes met. She could read his mind. He was saying ''You did everything right. Now look—you're marrying the man you love.''

He hugged her hard. ''Congratulations. He's my idea of one great brother-in-law. When's the big day?''

Nate came up to them carrying the baby. The two men grinned at each other.

''That's why we came home. We need you guys to help us plan the wedding.''

''Wedding?''

Laurel beamed at Joey. ''Yes. Nate and I are getting married.''

His eyes rounded. "Does Mom know?"

"Not yet."

"I'll tell her. Mom!" he shouted at the top of his lungs, running into the house with Kyle in pursuit.

That was what Laurel felt like doing. Shouting her happiness for the whole world to hear.

CHAPTER FOURTEEN

NATE SAW the Blazer in the driveway. Pleased that Rick was back, he got out of the car and hurried into the house.

"Rick?"

"In the den!"

He found his brother seated at the computer.

"Give me one second to send this e-mail to Wally and I'm all yours."

Wally Sykes had been Rick's crew chief for the last four years. He'd trusted the man with his life, but Mayada owned the team that crewed for him. Even if they hadn't found another race car driver to sponsor yet, they'd make Wally pay big-time to break his contract and go to work under Trans T & T's sponsorship.

The new contract Rick was waiting for would have to make it worthwhile for Wally to defect. He had a wife and family to support, a pension to think of.

"Done!" He shut off the computer and stood up. "I saw the empty bottle in the wastebasket. Looks like the deed is done."

He caught Nate in a bear hug like their father's. "Way to go, man! Like I told you, if you hadn't gotten there first…"

"You really had me going the other day, but the fake champagne made up for it."

Rick grinned. "I'm glad. When's the wedding?"

"We're looking at three weeks from Saturday at the church here in Copper Mountain."

Rick's eyes grew serious. "That's where Mom and Dad always wanted us to get married. She should be here." His voice sounded raw.

"Agreed." Nate cleared his throat. "Will you be my best man?"

"What do you think?"

"You're waiting for that contract. You might have to leave before then."

"I'm not going anywhere until I've heard my brother say *I do.*"

"That means a lot to me. Thanks, Rick."

"You're welcome."

"I mean thanks for everything. You changed my life."

"What are you talking about?"

Nate eyed his brother directly. "You knew me better than I knew myself. I wouldn't be marrying Laurel if it weren't for you."

"One night years ago I saw into your tortured soul. I see a different man standing in front of me now. That's good."

"It feels good. It'll feel even better when the pastor pronounces us husband and wife."

His brother pursed his lips. "What are you worried about?"

"I don't know. It all seems...too perfect."

"She loves you. Hey, did I tell you Dad's coming home next weekend to meet her?"

"You talked to him today?"

"He called me on my cell phone right after he talked to you. I don't think I've ever heard him so happy."

"You know why, don't you? Laurel told him Becky might grow up to be an Olympic champion like her grandfather."

Rick threw back his head and laughed. "Wouldn't that be something?"

"I suppose anything's possible. Colorado Springs isn't that far from Copper Mountain. While we're on the subject, how would you like to drive over there with me in the morning? I need to look at houses for sale and collect some brochures to show Laurel."

"Let's do it."

"We're fitting in a week's trip to Philadelphia right after Dad leaves so I can meet her parents. It doesn't give us a lot of time to find a place to live."

"You'll be able to stay here as long as you want after the wedding. Got any ideas for a honeymoon yet?"

"Laurel's sick of traveling. Frankly, so am I. Julie's offered to keep the baby overnight. Maybe in late August we'll get away to one of the beaches in Southern California."

"You're one lucky guy. All I can say is hang on to your happiness with both hands and never let go. I'll see you in the morning. Are you coming upstairs?"

"Right behind you."

LAUREL REACHED for a clean diaper. "You precious baby. Are you excited about going on a plane trip tomorrow? You've already met Grandad Hawkins who adored you on the spot. Now you're going to meet Nana and Papa Hayes, and Grandma and Grampa Pierce.

"Let's get you fed. Nate's going to be here early in the morning. Then we're all driving to the airport in Uncle Brent's car. We love Nate so much and want to be ready for him."

Twenty minutes later Julie poked her head around the door. Laurel motioned for her to come in. "Becky's asleep now," she said quietly.

"So's the rest of the family. I think we're all packed. We probably shouldn't be taking the kids out of school, but they'll be able to do some homework while we're gone."

"I'm glad everyone's coming. So's Nate."

"Looks like you're ready to go."

"Pretty much."

"Now we can talk."

Both of them were dressed in their nightgowns. Laurel got under the covers and watched her sister stretch out on top of the bed.

"You won't be able to do that much longer."

Julie smiled. "You mean lie on my stomach? I know. Let me see that ring again." Laurel complied. "You're marrying into a wonderful family, you know. I really like Nate's father too. He's so modest about his medals."

"Nate and Rick are just like him in that regard."

"That was a wonderful meal at their house last night. And Brent had the greatest time talking sports with Clint and Rick. It was another exciting evening—even if you and Nate were in your own little world. On the drive home, Brent said you two were so in love it was fun to watch.''

"We can hardly keep our hands off each other.''

"It's no wonder when your wedding's still nine days away. I just got off the phone with the folks. They can't wait for tomorrow.''

"Neither can I, but I'm still nervous about Reba and Wendell. Nate insists we visit them together. He wants them to know he'll do everything in his power to make sure Becky is always part of their life.''

"I'm glad he's going to be there to offer you moral support.''

"I am too, but it'll be a little awkward when they ask why I didn't say anything about Nate while they were out here last week.''

"You'll tell them the truth, of course. Not only hadn't he proposed to you yet, you weren't even certain of seeing him again.''

"That won't matter to them. They'll be hurt that I held anything back about Nate. Let's face it. This will be a huge shock.''

Her stomach tensed. She could picture Reba and Wendell's horrified expressions when they heard she was getting married to their son's best friend less than a year after Scott's death.

"Whether you get married tomorrow or five years from now, be it to Nate or another man, their reaction would be the same. The good thing is, *you* carry the trump card. They'll love their new granddaughter. When they realize you and Nate aren't going to prevent them from having a relationship with her, they'll heal in time.''

"I have to believe that. If they give Nate a chance, they'll find out why Scott liked him so much."

Julie got off the bed. "It's a shame Scott's parents are still in mourning. But don't let their pain cloud the issue here. You're not doing anything wrong in marrying Nate."

"I know, otherwise I wouldn't have accepted his proposal."

"Nevertheless it's a big step for you. I'm aware that Scott's family has had your loyalty since you were a sophomore in high school. You're afraid of doing anything to upset them. I don't blame you. But please promise me you'll keep one thing in mind."

"What's that?"

"Years ago you told me that you and Scott had talked about the possibility of his dying." Laurel nodded. "Do you remember what he said? Because if you don't, I do."

Laurel bowed her head. Now that Julie had reminded her, Laurel recalled the moment as if it were yesterday. At the time, it had washed over her because she couldn't imagine, *refused* to imagine, the reality of his death.

"He said he knew he was the best," she said hoarsely, "but if he crashed and burned, I had his permission to find someone else as long as the guy could halfway measure up."

"That's Scott. Attitude to the end. The point is, he realized his career put him in danger. He didn't want you to suffer forever."

Laurel raised her head. "You're right. Thank you, Julie. You don't know how much you've helped me. I love you."

"I love *you*. I love Nate for not taking you away. When I asked you to come and live with us for a while, I didn't ask just for your sake. I was selfish— I saw an opportunity to keep my best friend with me. What's so nice is that Brent's crazy about Nate too. And Rick.

"Now I'm going to let you get some sleep. Becky's three o'clock feeding will be here before you know it."

When Julie had disappeared, Laurel lay back against the pillows. It was as if the last dark cloud had suddenly lifted and all that remained was glorious blue sky.

NATE HEARD A KNOCK at the guest bedroom door. He finished adjusting his tie, then walked over to open it expecting to see Laurel. Instead her father stood there.

John Hayes was a lean man with broad shoulders, the same height as Nate's father. His brown hair revealed streaks of silver. Though Laurel had inherited her mother's Italian beauty and charm, her blue eyes had been bequeathed by her father, an intelligent and energetic man.

Since their arrival in Philadelphia, they'd spent the afternoon with her parents. They'd finished dinner and were now preparing to visit Scott's parents.

"Laurel sent me to tell you she's ready to leave for the Pierces. Take my car. I put the infant seat in back." He handed Nate the keys as they started down the hallway.

"Thanks, John. Forgive us for leaving so soon. It doesn't seem right to eat and run."

"I'll admit it's a wrench to let you go when you've barely arrived," John murmured. "However, I have to remember that the Pierces are just as anxious to get acquainted with their granddaughter."

"I hope they won't be too disappointed when I tell them I won't be staying the night."

Sylvia gave her daughter a reassuring hug. "Surely they'll understand when you explain that you and Nate are engaged."

"We'll see you both later," Nate said to Laurel's parents.

"We'll be back."

John smiled. "I'm counting on it, Major. I'm looking forward to picking your brain."

Laurel had warned him.

"And I was hoping to learn about the internal workings of one of the nation's great newspapers."

"I can see we're going to need more than a week."

They were both laughing as they descended the curving staircase of the large, gracious old Philadelphia home. Laurel and her mother stood in the foyer. The two women were totally absorbed in the baby.

Nate found himself totally absorbed in his stunning bride-to-be, who was wearing a yellow suit with a snowy white blouse. Her face and figure were nothing short of a miracle, yet she didn't have a vain bone in her body. He felt a tremor of excitement at the thought that she was going to be his wife....

She'd dressed Becky in the little white-and-yellow outfit he'd given her. They both looked springlike.

"You two are going to have to break this up."

At the sound of her father's voice, Laurel's eyes

darted to the stairs. Her gaze met Nate's. The warmth of her smile reached out to him.

Sylvia passed him the baby. "Have a nice time at the Pierces', then hurry back."

"We will, Mom."

Nate kissed the top of Becky's head. She smelled of baby powder. "Come on, little sweetheart. Let's go."

Laurel held his other arm as they walked out to the driveway. As soon as everyone was strapped inside the car, he leaned across the seat to kiss the woman who'd become his whole world. She kissed him back with equal urgency.

He moaned. "You shouldn't have done that. If tonight weren't so important, I'd drive us to a justice of the peace right now."

"All I think about is our wedding day."

"You're not the only one." He started the engine. "Which way?"

"Go down the street two blocks, then turn right. They're three streets over."

Spade and Laurel had gone to the same high school. Their families came from the same neighborhood. When he drove up to the Pierce home, he recognized it from pictures.

He parked the car in the driveway to help Laurel with the baby. She looped an extra receiving blanket over her left hand and arm, hoping the Pierces wouldn't see the engagement ring until it was time to break the news. Once he'd removed the carrier from the back seat, she took Becky to the house. Nate followed.

Before she could ring the bell, the front door

opened. Spade's parents ran out onto the porch to greet her. Nate waited, half-hidden by a lilac bush, to give them time to greet each other. Spade's mother lifted the baby out of her carrier.

"Oh, Wendell—Rebecca's the image of our Scotty!" she cried. "Look at the color of her hair, the shape of her face."

"She's got his eyes, Reba."

"As soon as we go inside, I want to look at Scott's baby pictures again. They look so much alike, it's uncanny."

"We'll see all the pictures and home movies of Laurel and Scotty," Wendell said. "It'll be like old times." He grinned. "We had all the Super 8 film transferred to video."

Nate watched Spade's father hug Laurel, something he must have done many, many times since she was sixteen years old.

"Lori Lou. You don't know how long we've waited for this moment." He wept openly. "Now that you're home where you belong, we're not letting you leave us again."

A band seemed to tighten around Nate's lungs.

"Before we go in, there's someone I want you to meet. He's been anxious to meet you, too. Nate?" Laurel called to him.

"I'm coming. I was just locking up the car." He finished the walk to the porch.

Laurel turned to her surprised in-laws. "You always wanted to know the legendary Hawk. Well, I've brought him with me. He flew out from Colorado with us."

Reba's eyes lit up. "Hawk! We'd hoped to talk to you in Denver."

"I know, but I had family obligations that prevented me from arranging anything."

Wendell clapped him on the shoulder. "We're thrilled you would come over to our house tonight. Laurel explained about your mother passing away at the same time as Scotty. We always hoped for the opportunity to sit down with our son's best friend and have a long talk. Come in."

The first thing Nate saw, on the wall by the staircase, was a row of large portraits of the Pierce brides. There were five of them. Laurel's was at the end. Beneath the veil was the beautiful face and long black hair of the woman Nate remembered from the past.

"Bring Hawk into the family room with us, Wendell."

"We'll be right there. First, I want to show him some pictures in the front room."

"Can it wait?" Laurel interjected in an anxious tone Nate immediately picked up on. "There's something I need to tell you."

"We'll be right there," Wendell said again.

Laurel's eyes flashed Nate a frantic message before she followed her mother-in-law to the other room.

Nate had no choice but to go with Wendell.

Judging by the number of mounted photographs hanging throughout the house, it was evident that the Pierces doted on their children and grandchildren. The mantel in the living room was a virtual shrine to Spade.

Some pictures included Laurel; others included the buddies in their old squadron. There was one of Nate and Spade. They were both grinning like idiots. Scott's F-16 was in the background. You could make out the words *Laurel—My First Love*.

Lord.

"I'm glad we're alone for a minute." Wendell's voice sounded unsteady. "Since the funeral I've wanted to ask you this question. Do you think Scotty knew he was going to his death?"

Spade's grieving father needed comfort. Nate wished to God he could give it to him. Offering platitudes now would be an insult.

"Probably. But when the end came, it was instantaneous, the way he would've wanted it."

The older man put a hand on Nate's arm. "Why did it have to happen to him?"

"I believe we all go out of this world at our appointed time. I know there's no solace in that, but…"

The older man's eyes dimmed. "You never saw two kids more in love in your life. At least we know Lori Lou was able to tell him about the baby. But dammit, Hawk—she'd just found out she was pregnant. When she heard there'd been a crash, she almost miscarried."

At that unexpected piece of information, something unpleasant twisted in Nate's gut.

"We found that out through her girlfriend Carma, who happened to be there with her. She was the one who phoned for an ambulance. If the hospital hadn't have been able to stop early labor, we wouldn't have little Becky with us now. That's why it's been so hard on us with her living clear out in Colorado."

"Wendell?" Reba's voice rang through the house. "Bring Hawk into the family room. You've got to see these pictures! You can't tell Scotty from Rebecca!"

Wendell patted Nate's arm. "Thanks for the chat. Now it's our daughter-in-law who needs attention. She's putting up a brave front, but you know better than anyone how it was between her and Scotty. She'll never get over losing him. You don't recover when the only love of your life is gone."

Nate's legs felt like lead as he followed Wendell to their TV room. Reba held Becky while she made comparisons between the baby in her arms and the photo of Scott soon after he was born.

The moment Laurel saw Nate, she patted the seat on the couch beside her. When he sat down, she reached for his hand and gripped it hard. Reba and Wendell appeared oblivious.

Wendell moved to the TV and put in a video. "We can look at the baby pictures later. Since Hawk's here, I'm sure he'd rather see our movies of Scotty and Lori Lou's wedding."

Seconds later, the screen showed a radiant Laurel and Spade kissing before the camera. Nate averted his eyes, unable to watch.

"These are pictures of the rehearsal dinner the night before their wedding," Wendell explained as he sat down in a recliner.

"I still like your hair better long," Reba murmured.

Nate felt Laurel's tension even before she stood up and walked over to the TV to shut if off.

"I'm sorry," she began. "Another time I'd love

to look at these videos with you. But there are two very special reasons Becky and I came over here tonight with Nate.''

Laurel took a deep breath, then continued. ''Months ago, I promised to bring the baby to see you after she was born. When I made that promise, I had no way of knowing the sun would shine for me again one day. Now that it has, I'm so happy to be back with you and my family. But the circumstances are different from the last time I was here.'' She had to take another breath.

''Something miraculous happened to me when Brent and Julie asked me to live with them. Nate came into my life.''

She smiled at him. ''My whole world has changed. He's asked me to be his wife.'' Laurel extended her hand to show them the ring. ''We're going to be married next Saturday at his family's church in Copper Mountain, Colorado.

''We'd love it if you could be there. Afterward, we'll be living in Colorado Springs, where he's going to be a flight instructor at the Air Force Academy.''

Spade's parents looked like the victims of shell shock. Nate felt bad for them, but he sensed that Laurel needed help. He stood up and put a supportive arm around her shoulders. Her body was trembling from head to toe.

''We want you to fly out whenever you can to see Becky. We'll make frequent visits to Philadelphia with her to see you, as well.''

Tightening his grip, he said, ''You've loved Laurel a lot longer than I have, so you can understand that when I saw her in Breckenridge after so many years, I fell fast and hard. The day she gave birth I was there. Needless to say, I fell in love with Becky, too.

"By the time I left the hospital, I knew my life would never be complete without them. To my great joy, Laurel accepted my proposal. I'm going to spend the rest of my life making her and Becky as happy as they make me."

Reba's gaze fastened on Laurel. "What have you done with Scotty's ring?" she asked in a dull voice.

With that question Nate wondered how much of what he'd said had even penetrated.

Both the Pierces looked dazed. There was a new sadness in Wendell's wet eyes.

Nate understood their pain; it was the same pain he'd experienced when he'd learned that his bereaved father had been kissing a woman other than his mother.

"I've put it in a safe place," Laurel said quietly. "When Becky turns eighteen, I'm going to give it to her. That was the age I was when Scott gave it to me. He'd want her to have it."

Nate kissed Laurel's temple, then walked over to the couch where Reba sat clutching the baby. He sat down next to her. She bristled with hostility.

He could understand that, too.

Anger had been his first reaction when Rick had told him about their father's engagement on the drive home to Copper Mountain. Nate could appreciate their feelings better than they knew.

Spade's parents felt betrayed. They would need time to get over the shock.

"I know how difficult this must be for you," he

began. "My father remarried less than a month ago. It was a big adjustment for me and my brother, as I'm sure this announcement is for you. But I want you to know that Becky will—"

"Her name's Rebecca!" Reba cut him off in mid-sentence. "You call yourself Scotty's best friend?" Her eyes were wild with pain. The violence of her reaction surprised him.

"He loved you like a brother. Laurel's just had his baby! She doesn't love you. She couldn't!"

"Reba!" Laurel cried out, aghast. "You don't know what you're saying."

Yes, she does, Laurel.

Those were the same words Nate had said to Rick about their father and Pam. That seemed a century ago, before Laurel had come back into his life.

"How could you do it, Hawk?" Wendell murmured. "Our Lori Lou's vulnerable to the attentions of any man right now. You above all people must know that.

"Our son confided in you, trusted you. You saw them together and knew how much they loved each other. If Scotty could see what was going on, it would kill him."

"I think you've said enough," Laurel muttered. "You're both overwrought. We'll talk later."

Reba shook her head. "When Wendell and I were in Denver, Brent said you'd come by the house to bring Laurel a gift. I read the little card she put in her baby book. We asked him to tell you we were in town, because we wanted to talk to you about Scotty.

"I thought it was odd that Brent didn't follow through. But now I know why. Obviously you couldn't face us. Imagine our son thinking you were the most honorable man he'd ever known!''

"Don't say any more!" Laurel cried angrily. "We weren't engaged when you came to Denver. In fact, I was petrified that Nate didn't love me. I thought he was leaving for Holland at any minute and I'd never see him again. There was nothing to tell you until I learned his true feelings.''

Nate had to give Laurel full points for trying, but certain home truths had been delivered tonight. He felt as if his insides had turned to stone.

"Scotty was Laurel's first and only boyfriend," Reba informed him. "She's never known another man. Never wanted anyone but him. Did you know that?''

No. Nate didn't know that.

Laurel took the baby from her mother-in-law. "We're leaving, Nate. If you'll bring the carrier…''

Nate got to his feet but he was slow to act.

"Our Lori Lou loved Scotty so much she went through years of agony trying to give him his own baby,'' Wendell said.

"She never gave up," Reba interjected. "That's the kind of love they shared." Her eyelids fluttered for a moment. She looked desperately tired. "To lose a mother is a terrible thing, Major, but it doesn't explain why you didn't want to talk to us in Denver. You avoided us because you felt guilty for betraying our son.''

"I couldn't meet with you because my father was returning from his honeymoon and had already made arrangements to spend the weekend with me and my brother.''

Ignoring Nate's explanation, Wendell said, "One day soon you'll realize you could never measure up to Scotty."

Nate didn't need Wendell to tell him something he already knew.

"Every time Lori Lou looks at Rebecca, she'll be reminded of her husband and everything she's lost. What kind of marriage will you have then?"

"Nate!"

He grabbed the carrier. By the time he'd caught up to Laurel, she'd reached the car. After fastening it to the base in the back seat, he strapped Becky inside. Laurel climbed in the front.

Once he'd reversed the car to the street, she turned to him with a tear-ravaged face.

"I knew Scott's parents were still grieving, but they need professional help. Forget everything they said, darling. When they come to their senses, they'll feel terrible and apologize."

"I don't blame them for anything, Laurel. They were only speaking the truth."

"Whose truth?" she demanded. "Certainly not mine! Wendell and Reba were projecting their own feelings onto me. They treated me as if I wasn't even in the room."

He gripped the steering wheel tighter. "That's because they're convinced you don't know your own feelings. I'm inclined to agree with them."

When Laurel digested what he'd just said, she felt almost incapacitated by the gut-wrenching pain.

"I thought you got past that when you came back to my bedroom," she muttered.

"My desire for you was so fierce it blinded me to certain realities."

"Don't do this, Nate." She shook her head. "Don't ruin what we have."

"You need to know why I was in such a bad way the night I saw you kiss Brent in the elevator. You thought it was because I'd been forced to give up flying." She heard him pause before he said, "Nothing could've been farther from the truth.

"My anger and pain stemmed from the fact that my father could turn to another woman only six months after he'd watched my mother being lowered into the ground. Worse, he'd become engaged and was planning to marry this woman based on one month's courtship."

Nate could have been describing their own situation.

Laurel bowed her head in despair.

It had been hard enough for him to get past his guilt over betraying Scott. But his pain had been compounded by what he viewed as his father's betrayal of his mother, something she hadn't suspected.

Laurel's love might have brought him halfway. Tragically, nothing she could say or do now would bring him full circle. The unintentional scar inflicted by his father went too deep.

What Reba and Wendell had effectively accomplished in their grief was to reopen that wound. Now the scar would be deeper than ever.

How well she understood Mr. Hawkins's message the afternoon she'd talked with him on the phone. Her heart ached for the wonderful man who, after raising two extraordinary sons, had dared to reach out for a new love. Yet in the reaching, he'd hurt his children without meaning to.

All he could hope for was that Laurel's love would heal Nate's wounds. But her love wasn't enough. When Nate made up his mind about something, it was final. That was what he was trying to tell her now.

She wouldn't beg him a second time....

When her tears had dried, she lifted her head. To her surprise, Nate had already pulled the car into her parents' driveway.

Relieved that Becky was still content with her pacifier, Laurel said, "Brent gave me a piece of advice. He told me that if you couldn't come to me heart-whole, of your own free will, then we'd both be better off going our separate ways.

"I chose to ignore his warning by forcing a confrontation with you that day in my bedroom. In doing so, I started a sequence of events that placed you in the dreadful position of having to face Scott's parents. Unfortunately they'll never know what an honorable man you really are.

"My family adores you. They're going to suffer when they find out we're not getting married after all. To make this easier on both of us, let's say goodbye now."

She pulled off his ring and put it on the dashboard.

"It's not too late to call for a taxi. There are so many flights leaving for the West Coast, you shouldn't have any problem being back in Colorado by morning.

"Don't worry about thanking my parents. By now they've gone to bed. Morning will be soon enough for me to break the news. If you'll bring Becky to my bedroom, I won't ask another thing of you.''

It was a struggle to draw breath right now. Those swirling black clouds she'd prayed never to know again were descending on her.

CHAPTER FIFTEEN

"WHAT DID YOU JUST SAY?"

"Laurel and I aren't getting married."

"Why the hell not?"

"Because it can't work, Rick. There's an old saying. *Beware of what you wish for.* You might get it. I wanted her so badly, I forgot it takes two.

"Reba was right. She said Laurel couldn't possibly love me, not after what she and Spade had together. Until tonight, I've been deluding myself, but no longer. Wendell didn't know it, but he was speaking to the converted when he told me I could never fit into Spade's shoes."

"That's bull and you know it! She loves you, man!"

"You mean the way Dad loves Pam?" he scoffed angrily. "Give me a break! That marriage was doomed from the outset. If you don't want to pick me up from the airport, just say so."

"I told you I'd be there."

"After you drive me to Brent's so I can pick up Mom's car, I'll get out of everyone's hair."

The second Rick heard the click, he punched in his father's phone number at the ranch.

"Dad?"

"Rick. What's wrong?"

"I know it's after eleven. I hate to disturb you and Pam, but we have to talk."

"Go ahead."

"All hell's broken loose."

"What do you mean?"

"Nate ended his engagement to Laurel tonight. He wouldn't discuss the details over the phone, but he and Laurel went to Spade's house. Whatever the Pierces said convinced him that Laurel couldn't possibly love him.

"He's headed for the airport to catch a red-eye back to Denver. I'm going to be at the airport at six-twenty in the morning. He wants me to drive him over to the Marsdens' so he can pick up Mom's car. Who knows what he'll do when he's on his own.

"To be honest, he has me scared. Nate's hurting like I've never heard him in my life. It's a long shot, but if anyone can get through to him, you can. Is there any way you could beat him home?"

"Maybe. Pam's uncle has his own plane. If he'll fly me to Odessa, I can get a flight from there. Give me a minute to make a couple of calls and I'll phone you back."

"Thanks, Dad."

Rick hung up in a cold sweat. An earlier conversation with Nate played over and over in his mind.

No pilot or racing pro is a superman, Rick. Every man has his breaking point. We all live in the hope that we'll never have to be tested to that degree.

Had Nate reached his breaking point?

When the phone rang he picked up without checking the caller ID.

"Dad?"

"No. It's Brent."

"How's Laurel?"

"You've heard the news?"

"All I know is, my brother told me the wedding's off and he's on his way home. He's so distraught I didn't even recognize his voice."

"There's more. After Nate left the house, Laurel collapsed. Because she's a new mother, their family doctor had her checked into the hospital for observation."

Rick groaned.

"Their visit to the Pierces ended in a nightmare."

"I know. Ever since Laurel approached Nate in Breckenridge, he's been skating on thin ice. Spade got to Laurel first, and my brother can't get past it."

"How could he after the evening he spent with Reba and Wendell? When Laurel was able to talk, she said enough to her parents for me to understand that the Pierces dumped a mother lode of guilt on him."

"They did, and it's torn Nate apart. Listen, Brent—I've talked to my father. He's going to try to get here ahead of Nate and meet his plane with me. Dad's the only person I know who can make him see reason. In the meantime, when Laurel's capable of listening to you, tell her not to give up."

"I don't know, Rick. It was a replay of his treatment of her on the dance floor. He cut her loose without a life preserver."

"That's my brother. When he decides to close up, it's like trying to penetrate battle armor to get through. Oh—someone's calling me on the other line. That'll be Dad. Keep me posted on Laurel's condition. I'll do the same about Nate."

"Okay." There was a click.

Rick pressed the flash button. "Dad?"

"We're in luck. Pam's uncle has pulled through for me. I'll be arriving in Denver at five-ten on West Skyways Air."

Rick gripped the phone more tightly. "You'll be saving his life. No one else can."

"If he didn't want to be saved, he wouldn't have turned to his brother for help. Everything's going to be all right."

How could his father be so calm? "It has to be. I just found out Laurel collapsed. She's in the hospital for observation."

"I'm sorry to hear that, but it's a piece of information that'll work in our favor." His father sounded so hopeful, Rick couldn't quite grasp it.

"I'll meet you at the curb. We'll have time for breakfast before Nate's flight arrives."

"Sounds good. I'm on my way."

Knowing he wouldn't get any sleep, Rick showered and dressed in a clean pair of jeans and a T-shirt. Once he'd locked up the house, he left for Denver.

There was a sports bar that stayed open all night. He'd shoot a little pool and watch reruns of NASCAR racing so he wouldn't think about the pain his brother was in until he saw him at the airport.

As soon as Nate spotted his suitcase he grabbed it and walked swiftly out of the airline terminal. He didn't see the Blazer at the curb, but then the damn plane had arrived twenty minutes later than scheduled due to headwinds.

Security guards kept traffic moving at the Denver airport. No doubt his brother was making the loop to come back around for him.

His eyes narrowed in disbelief when a few minutes later the Blazer pulled alongside the curb and he saw his dad in the car with Rick.

He was supposed to be in Texas with the second Mrs. Hawkins.

This was one of the rare times in Nate's life when he didn't want to face his father. Damn Rick for taking it upon himself to alert him! Nate resented being treated like a child.

He should never have asked his brother to pick him up.

He sure as hell shouldn't have resigned his commission. That was his first mistake.

Since his return to Colorado, he'd been making one bad decision after another. The only thing he'd done right was to end it with Laurel and pack his bags.

A security guard blew his whistle. Aware he was holding up traffic, Nate opened the back door of the Blazer and shoved his case along the seat before getting in. Rick immediately pulled away from the curb. His father glanced over his shoulder at him.

"You look exhausted. Why don't you try to sleep until we get home."

Nate froze. "That's the last place I want to go."

"Nevertheless it's the only place for the talk we should've had weeks ago."

He raked an unsteady hand through his hair. "What talk would that be?"

"The one I put off to spare your and Rick's feelings. With hindsight, I can see it was the wrong thing to do. I took a calculated risk, never dreaming there would be such far-reaching consequences."

"You're being cryptic."

"That wasn't my intention."

"Sorry, Dad. But I can't do this. It wasn't necessary for you to fly home."

"Probably not any more necessary than it was for you and Rick to leave your careers behind and come to the rescue of your father."

"As it turns out, you didn't need rescuing. Neither do I," he said in a withering tone.

"I'm glad to hear it."

His father's reply caught him on the raw.

"Take the next turnoff for Aurora, Rick," he told his brother.

"There's been a change in plans. You can worry about your mother's car later." His father nodded to Rick. "There's a rest area at the next exit. We'll have our talk there."

Before Nate could say a word, Rick had changed to the right lane. Within minutes they'd left the freeway and pulled past the trucks to the tourist area. He parked some distance from the few other cars already there and shut off the engine.

His father got out first and opened the back door. "Rick bought us some donuts and coffee to enjoy on the drive home. Let's walk over to one of those picnic tables."

Nate couldn't believe what his father was doing.

"This used to work years ago when Rick and I got out of hand, but we're not kids anymore."

"You don't have to be kids for it still to work. The point is, I like to be able to look into your eyes when I have something important to say. It appears I'll have to do it right here."

He put his hands on his hips in that familiar stance. "Neither of you asked me why I married Pam. I haven't told you before now, because I knew you loved your mother, and anything I had to say would hurt you. Unfortunately, my silence has done more damage than I realized.

"You both know your mother was my whole universe from the moment we met until the day she died. Now she lives in my heart and in you boys. What never occurred to me was that my new universe had an unexpected surprise for me.

"One day Pam came into the ski shop and quite simply, we fell in love. It hit fast and hard, just like it did with your mother, just like it did when you met Laurel nine years ago."

Nate blinked.

"The problem is, when you fall in love you have to do something about it.

"I didn't know it could happen again, not after the love Anja and I shared for thirty-one years. It came as a complete and total shock to me, as I'm sure it did to Laurel when she met you again, Nate.

"She went through intense grief after Spade died. I've been through it, too. And now she's discovered what I've discovered. It might be another time and another season, but you can love again with just as much depth and passion.

"If I've learned one thing from this whole experience, it's that life never ceases to unfold new wonders, and the human spirit is more resilient than we know."

Nate just stared at his father, unable to say a word.

"The problem isn't with Laurel, Nate. She's been reborn through your love, just as I was reborn through Pam's. Laurel knows exactly what she wants and exactly how she feels. The problem lies with you.

"By breaking your engagement to her, you've done the worst thing you could do. Don't you understand that her love for you is a miracle?

"You've rejected that love, because in your mind and heart she'll always be another man's wife. You don't see the new woman who's emerged from her grief. What you've done is tell her she must remain in a state of perpetual mourning.

"Laurel has already come out of yesterday, Nate. Today she's ready to embrace life again. If not with you, then with some lucky man who'll come along when the time is right.

"You're the one who's in mourning, not Laurel. My fear is that you'll continue to exist in that unhappy state, just like the Pierces. Now *there's* a tragedy."

He shut the door and climbed back into the front seat of the Blazer. Stunned by his father's delivery, Nate sat there mute as he watched him devour three donuts in a row.

"Those were good." He looked at Rick. "Might as well run by the Marsdens' so Nate can pick up the car before we go home."

"I've changed my mind. Take me back to the airport."

His father glanced at him. "You'd better phone Brent first."

Nate frowned. "Why?"

"To find out if Laurel's up to seeing you. The last we heard, she'd collapsed and was put in the hospital for observation."

Collapsed?

"Why in God's name didn't you tell me sooner?" He pulled his cell phone out of his pocket and started punching buttons.

"Laurel wouldn't have wanted you to feel guilty about that, too, not if you weren't planning on marrying her. I trust the wedding is back on."

Terror seized his heart. "It is if I haven't lost her."

AFTER RETURNING to her parents' home, Laurel had slept, but the anguish was back. The sedative she'd been given at the hospital had worn off. Much as she craved another pill to dull the pain, she knew it wasn't good for the baby.

During the night Julie had brought Becky in to nurse. Now it was morning. In a few minutes it would be time to feed her again.

"Laurel?" To her surprise, her sister had entered the room without the baby. "How are you feeling?"

"Like I want to die, but I know I can't because Becky needs me."

Julie sat down on the side of the bed. "Brent's so protective of you he didn't want me to tell you this, but I have to. Nate's on the phone."

Her heart pounded. *"Nate?"*

"He knows Mom and Dad took you to the hospital last night. Brent says he sounds so broken up you can hardly understand him, but my husband's loyalty is to you. If you'd rather not tal—"

"I love him!" Laurel cried out, sitting up in bed. "Is he on our house phone?"

"No. Brent's cell. I'll get it."

"Please hurry, Julie!"

By the time she'd returned, Laurel had made it to the door. She thanked her sister, then took the phone from her.

"H-hello, Nate?"

"Laurel—don't hang up on me. I know I don't deserve any more chances, but you've got to listen to me."

He was crying. She'd never heard him cry before. His vulnerability melted her heart.

"I had a talk with my father. He told me something I should've known and understood long before now."

Overcome by emotion, she brushed the tears off her cheeks. "What was that?"

"The reason he married Pam was because he was in love with her. Do you hear what I'm saying?"

Sunshine filled her world once more. "Yes, darling."

"I finally get it. You love *me*."

"Yes!" she cried between happy sobs. "Oh, yes!"

"I swear I'll never doubt your love again. We're going to have a marvelous, fantastic life together!"

"We are!" she half laughed, half cried. "Where are you?"

"At the Denver airport waiting for a flight. It's going to be a few hours before I can board."

"Nate—don't get on the plane. Becky and I are coming home to you. As soon as we hang up I'll phone to make a reservation. Someone here will drive us to the airport."

"What about your family? They've hardly had any time with you."

"They're all coming out for the wedding. We'll have a party at your house. But I can't wait any longer to be with you. I need you so desperately."

"Laurel." A minute passed before he could say anything else. "It's what I've wanted for what seems like an eternity. But are you well enough to travel?"

"Your phone call has cured me, Nate."

Another silence ensued. "Forgive me for hurting you last night."

"I already have."

"Brent's ready to deck me again."

"If he is, it's because he wants you so badly for a brother-in-law. When he thought it wasn't going to happen, I swear he was as disappointed for himself as for me."

"It's going to happen, all right."

"Saturday can't come soon enough. I want to hug your father and thank him for the most wonderful wedding present he could have given us."

"No one can drum sense into my head like he can, except for my brother. They're the best." His voice shook. "Once again, Rick's the person responsible for my rescue. He roused Dad out of bed in the dead of night to fly home."

"I love Rick. I love your family. I wish I'd known your mother."

"So do I. You'll have to make do with three hours of videos. She's in most of them."

"I can't wait!"

"Call me the minute you know your flight time."

"I will."

"Don't let anything happen to you and my little girl."

Nate could have no idea what those words meant to her. "I promise."

"I love you, Laurel. We're going to start over. It'll be better than it ever was before."

"It's perfect already."

"Wait till tonight...."

NATE LAY stretched out on Laurel's bed, waiting for her to finish nursing the baby. As he rubbed her back and listened to the little sounds Becky was making, a contentment he'd never known before stole over him.

The day had seemed endless until he'd seen her emerge from the terminal with Becky. By the time he'd helped them into the car, he was in such a fever pitch of excitement, all he could do was crush her in his arms. The words would have to come later.

His heart pounded with frantic abandon when she got up from the bed to put Becky in her crib. Then she turned to him.

Their cries of longing blended into the semidarkness as he gathered her close. "At last," he whispered against her lips. Her avid mouth fastened on his with an eagerness he would remember all his life.

Alone with the woman he'd yearned for, both waking and sleeping, he luxuriated in the taste and feel of her. As their kisses grew more impassioned, he realized where this was leading. The last thing he wanted was to slow them down, but he had to for Laurel's sake, and he had to do it *now*.

"Darling?" he murmured in her hair. "How soon does Dr. Steel say we can make love?"

"All I can tell you is what he told my sister after Joey was born. He'd prefer she wait six weeks."

Nate tried to hide his moan of protest. He failed. Miserably.

Her gentle laughter excited him. "You didn't let me finish."

"Laurel—I don't think I can handle this conversation."

"Julie's never waited longer than three." She smiled up at him with love light in her eyes. "Saturday will make it three weeks and six days."

He kissed her long and hard. "I love your sister."

"So do I. She's helped me keep body and soul together over the years."

Her choice of words alerted Nate that she was trying to tell him something important.

"What are you saying, Laurel?" He kissed her hand. The ring he'd put back on her finger caught the lamplight from the hall.

"I want to tell you about my marriage, then we won't ever have to talk about it again."

For the first time in nine years, the mention of her life with Spade didn't hurt. It didn't hurt at all. That in itself proved how far he'd come.

"Go on," he urged in a quiet tone.

"Scott and I were two kids when we got married. We had no concept of what it meant to take on life-time vows. For Scott every day was an exciting adventure. He lived to fly. He loved me, but I was only one part of his life.

"It was very different for me. I'd come from a large family, where someone was always around, something was always going on. I always had Julie to talk to. With marriage, all of that changed.

"In the beginning, the loneliness, the isolation, were almost unbearable. I had no idea what to do with myself while Scott was gone, sometimes for a couple of weeks at one time.

"All the friends I'd left behind who'd been so envious of my marriage to a hotshot were in college. They thought their lives were boring compared to my glamorous life in the Air Force. What they didn't know was that their letters were filled with the kind of news I hungered for.

"That's when the phone calls started from wherever I was to wherever Julie was. I knew I was behaving like the immature, spoiled little girl I actually was. I *wanted* to be the best wife to him, but I knew I could ruin it if I didn't get a grip on my life.

"When we were first stationed in Okinawa, my sister asked me if we'd decided to start a family yet. I told her we'd been trying since our honeymoon without success. She wanted to know about the friends I'd made. To my embarrassment I couldn't name any one woman.

"When I got off the phone with her, I realized that all I ever did was complain to her about my life. It was humiliating to admit how self-absorbed I was.

At that point, I came to the realization that I didn't like myself, so I'd better do something about it.

"Over the next week, I investigated the possibility of attending a beginning class in Japanese. When I registered, I found out there was another woman from the base, Carol Lowe, also taking the class. We became good friends and ended up adding a flower-arranging class to our schedule."

Laurel smiled. "We rented bicycles and rode everywhere. One day, she told me about this island she wanted to visit by boat. Supposedly it was covered with hundreds of glass balls used as floats for Japanese fishing nets during World War II. She wanted to collect some for souvenirs.

"So we packed our camping gear and took off for three days. We beat the bushes till our hands were raw and bleeding to look for those balls."

"Did you find some?" Nate had been listening in rapt fascination. The picture of the life she'd recounted so far was vastly different from what he'd imagined.

"Dozens and dozens. Our boat almost capsized bringing them home. I bought a whole bunch of little Japanese baskets with lids and put a ball in each one as a gift for all the members of my family and Scott's.

"They were a big hit with my father who devoted an article in the paper to them and their history. Anyway, when I returned from that trip, Scott was waiting for me. I was surprised, because he wasn't supposed to get home until that weekend.

"He was livid. I couldn't understand why. I'd left him a letter explaining everything I'd been doing, where I'd gone, when I'd be back. It didn't matter. We had a terrible fight.

"I finally got to the bottom of the problem, I realized he was just mad because I hadn't been there waiting for him when he walked through the door.

"I was mad, too. Still, I wouldn't have gone anywhere if I'd known he was going to be home. I tried to humor him, but he told me I'd better curtail my activities with Carol from now on. He wasn't kidding.

"For once the shoe was on the other foot. He'd found out what it was like to come home and be alone. Ever since I'd been a sophomore in high school, I'd made him the center of my world. Now I had other interests and demands on my time. He didn't like it.

"Julie called it growing pains on his part. She said I was maturing into an interesting woman, which would make for a better marriage in the long run."

Interesting didn't begin to describe the woman in his arms.

"When we moved to Spain, I took classes in Spanish and lessons in flamenco guitar. My teacher told me I did very well for a beginner and should keep it up."

"Do you still have a guitar?" Nate asked.

"Yes. It's stored with all my things."

"We'll send for them as soon as we find the right house."

She brushed her lips against his. "You won't believe the stuff I've picked up over the years."

"I'm looking forward to helping you unpack."

She stared into his eyes. "I can't wait to live with

you day and night. I guess that's what I've been trying to tell you. I had a wonderful marriage, but it was far from perfect.

"The truth is, I was married to a boy who stayed a boy. That was part of Scott's great charm. It was also his downfall. Instead of coming home to me as soon as he could, he did what the brass wanted him to do first, Scott said it wasn't an order, but…I know he couldn't resist showing off. He climbed in that cockpit to buzz the airfield and give everyone a thrill. You know what happened after that."

She stroked Nate's arms. "Now that I've grown up, I need you. I need your sweetness, your integrity, your manliness. With you I feel cherished and above all, loved.

"Kiss me," she begged. "I'm afraid I'm going to be asking you that for the rest of our lives."

"The way I feel about you, I'll be the one doing the asking. Hold me tight, Laurel. Never let me go."

EPILOGUE

"IF THE CONGREGATION WILL please rise and wait until Major and Mrs. Hawkins exit the church to the garden first."

Laurel was a vision in chiffon the color of her eyes. Nate had already kissed her at the altar, but he found himself doing it again, much to the delight of their families and friends.

"Only a few more hours until we're alone," he murmured against her lips.

"I can make it if you don't leave my side. Did you see that gleam in Rick's eye after we exchanged vows? I have this funny feeling your brother and Brent have something awful planned."

"You can count on it."

"Oh, Nate!"

"Don't worry. I'm ready for anything they try to pull. Come on. I want to show you off."

He slid his arm around her shoulders. Together they started their walk down the aisle as husband and wife.

The first thing he noticed was his father's half smile. He sat in the front pew next to Pam. His moist gray eyes told Nate he believed Anja knew what was happening and approved of their son's choice of bride. Nate nodded in acknowledgment. It was the proudest moment of his life.

For the rest of their walk to the garden, Nate wasn't conscious of anyone but Laurel. She was his wife now. Becky, who'd been a good little girl for her aunt Julie during the ceremony, was now his daughter. He trembled at the thrill of it.

"Nate." She tugged on his arm. "Look who's over there under the trees. They came!"

His first thought was that Reba and Wendell looked lonely standing apart from everyone else.

"Never underestimate the strength of a grandparent's love. That's major progress, darling. Let's make them feel welcome."

She squeezed his hand. "Thank you, Nate. I love you."

When they reached the Pierces, Nate felt an overwhelming wave of pity for them. They'd lost their Scotty, the son who'd once claimed Laurel for his bride. This had to be a difficult moment for them.

"I'm so glad you came!" Laurel darted ahead of Nate to give them each a huge hug. That broke the ice. Soon all three of them were crying. "Julie's somewhere with the baby. I'll go find her and tell her you're anxious to have Becky for a while."

Her eyes sent Nate a private message before she left him alone with Spade's parents. They looked at him with such pained expressions, he said, "Why don't we forget the past and start over."

"Can you do that after the way we talked to you the other night?"

"Of course, Reba."

"We know you're a good man," Wendell murmured. ''Otherwise Scotty wouldn't have loved you. His death has been so hard on us.''

''Of course it has. There was nobody in this world like Spade. He had more energy, more zest for life than anyone I ever knew. It was a privilege to be his friend. He thought the world of you two.''

''He did?'' they said in unison.

''Your pictures were plastered all over the wall of the barracks, along with Laurel's. After being in your house, I can see where he got the idea.''

For the first time since he'd known them, their faces were wreathed in smiles.

''Here we are. Here's your Grandma and Grampa.''

Nate wheeled around to see his wife and child descending on them in a hurry. Pam wasn't far behind Laurel, carrying a baby bottle. After she'd handed it to Reba, Nate put an arm around her shoulder.

Her big brown eyes looked up at him in surprise. Before today, he hadn't been able to view her objectively. Hurt and anger had blinded him, but now he could see her clearly.

In her own way, Pam was very lovely. She had a gentle, soft-spoken quality that had obviously appealed to his father.

''I want to thank you for being so good about letting Dad come and go,'' he told her.

''I'm glad he could help you. He loves you more than anything in the world.''

''I know. I also know he's crazy about you. You've turned his world around. I love you for that.''

Her eyes filled. ''Thank you, Nate. You don't know what that means to me.''

He gave her a hug and she hugged him back warmly.

"How's your cousin?" he asked.

"Much better. She's home from the hospital and doing remarkably well on her crutches."

"You'll have to bring her to Copper Mountain so we can all meet her."

"She'd love it."

"Nate?"

"Excuse me, Pam." He turned to Laurel, who rushed to join him.

"Have you seen Brent or Rick while we've been out here?"

"No."

"I'm getting nervous. There's Joey. Let's pay him to spy for us."

Nate chuckled. "I like the way your mind works, Mrs. Hawkins." He called Brent's son over and whispered in his ear.

Joey's eyes rounded. "I'll be right back."

For the next little while, Nate kept his arm around Laurel while they mingled with her family and good friends Carma and Carol, who'd come for the wedding. As he and Laurel moved from one guest to another, they selected delicious nibbles from the buffet table.

Suddenly Joey reappeared. "They aren't anywhere and Dad's car is gone."

"Thanks, buddy." Nate handed him a five-dollar bill.

"What do you think?" Laurel asked anxiously.

He kissed her quiet. "I think we'll find out when we get to the house. Since we've already spoken to everyone here, we could leave now. Who knows? We might even surprise those two."

"Let's go," Laurel whispered against his lips.

They ducked out of the garden along a pathway that led to the parking lot. Within minutes, they were on their way to the house where they were going to spend their honeymoon.

Rick had been invited to stay with Brent and Julie for a few days. There was no sign of his car or the Blazer when they pulled into the driveway. Everything seemed to be in order.

Nate got out and walked around the other side to open the door for Laurel. As soon as she alighted, he scooped her up in his arms.

"This is the part I've been waiting for."

"Oh, Nate..."

Her mouth sought his before he'd even started for the front porch. He couldn't get her over the threshold and up the stairs to his bedroom fast enough.

That was when he knew something had been done to the house. His door was shut and there was a note fastened to it. Still carrying her in his arms, he walked over to it.

"You read it for us," he murmured. Right now he couldn't concentrate on anything but his bride.

Laurel reached for the paper.

Since you couldn't go to the beach, we've brought it to you. Enjoy.

The Beach Boys

Nate laughed out loud. "Trust my brother to come up with this one. Open the door, Laurel."

She gasped in delight when they reached his room. Rick and Brent had transformed it. She hardly knew where to look first. There were real palm trees on both sides of the bed, and the potted red and pink azaleas were probably a touch provided by Julie.

Mike and Joey's large plastic wading pool from former days rested on the floor at its foot. Filled with water, no less!

Next to it was an air mattress with two wildly colored beach towels. Two beach robes lay across the end of the bed. They said *His* and *Hers*.

There were two pairs of outrageous sunglasses and a tube of suntan cream on one end table. A magnum of champagne on ice and two champagne glasses sat on the other.

She saw all their favorite snacks set out on the dresser, plus magazines, a crossword puzzle and Mike's tape player.

Nate carried her over and put her down so she could turn it on. Immediately the room was filled with the familiar melodic sounds of the Beach Boys.

"Our families are so wonderful." But all her sentimental thoughts vanished when she turned to Nate. He'd already begun undressing and was looking at her with a devilish glint in his eyes.

His hands went to the back of her dress. He began undoing the buttons, kissing her neck each time.

"I think a swim in the ocean first to start things off."

"No!" she giggled. "You wouldn't—"

"The ocean's always a shock to the system when you first plunge in," he said with mock seriousness.

"But don't worry. I'll keep you warm because I'm on fire for you. Stop wriggling, Mrs. Hawkins."

"No, Nate!" She shrieked with laughter. "Please— somebody help me!"

OUTSIDE, IN THE DRIVEWAY of the house, sat two suspicious-looking men in a Blazer.

"Did you hear anything?"

"Yup. Someone's calling for help."

"That's what I thought I heard and it wasn't my brother."

"Nope."

They grinned at each other.

"Mission accomplished. Let's get back to the church."

* * * * *

Watch for Rick's story,
HOME TO COPPER MOUNTAIN,
coming in May 2003.

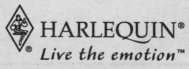

If you enjoyed what you just read,
then we've got an offer you can't resist!

Take 2 bestselling love stories FREE!

Plus get a FREE surprise gift!

Clip this page and mail it to Harlequin Reader Service®

IN U.S.A.	IN CANADA
3010 Walden Ave.	P.O. Box 609
P.O. Box 1867	Fort Erie, Ontario
Buffalo, N.Y. 14240-1867	L2A 5X3

YES! Please send me 2 free Harlequin Superromance® novels and my free surprise gift. After receiving them, if I don't wish to receive anymore, I can return the shipping statement marked cancel. If I don't cancel, I will receive 6 brand-new novels every month, before they're available in stores. In the U.S.A., bill me at the bargain price of $4.47 plus 25¢ shipping and handling per book and applicable sales tax, if any*. In Canada, bill me at the bargain price of $4.99 plus 25¢ shipping and handling per book and applicable taxes**. That's the complete price, and a savings of at least 10% off the cover prices—what a great deal! I understand that accepting the 2 free books and gift places me under no obligation ever to buy any books. I can always return a shipment and cancel at any time. Even if I never buy another book from Harlequin, the 2 free books and gift are mine to keep forever.

135 HDN DNT3
336 HDN DNT4

Name	(PLEASE PRINT)	
Address	Apt.#	
City	State/Prov.	Zip/Postal Code

* Terms and prices subject to change without notice. Sales tax applicable in N.Y.
** Canadian residents will be charged applicable provincial taxes and GST.
All orders subject to approval. Offer limited to one per household and not valid to current Harlequin Superromance® subscribers.
® is a registered trademark of Harlequin Enterprises Limited.

SUP02   ©1998 Harlequin Enterprises Limited

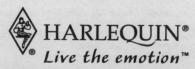